APPARITIONS
TWISTED TALES & YARNS

JIMMY L. CAPPS
LINDA CAPPS FISHER

www.MozarkPress.com

ii

Published by Mozark Press, www.Mozarkpress.com
© 2017 Linda Fisher
PO Box 1746, Sedalia, MO 65302

Cover design and book layout by H. Ream.

ISBN: 978-0-9903270-5-9

CONTENTS

INTRODUCTION

Apparitions is a collection of twenty-six tangled tales and yarns written by the brother/sister team, Jimmy Capps and Linda Capps Fisher. Several stories included in this collection have won prizes in writing contests and have been published in various anthologies.

Storytelling comes naturally to Jimmy and Linda who often listened to their uncles and Grandpa spin tales of strange and mysterious happenings. They grew up in the Ozark hills and that background influences the setting for many of the stories in the book. Jimmy's Navy career lends authenticity to *Fire on Deck* and *Losing Willie*. Linda was inspired to write *The Memory Pillow* after experiencing strange dreams when she used a Memory Foam Pillow.

Dreams, nightmares, life experiences, and family yarns of strange, unexplainable foreshadowing are the inspiration for some stories. Others are woven from the cloth of imagination.

Sit down, prop up your feet, turn on all the lights in your house, and enjoy.

THE LIGHT ON THE CEILING
JIMMY CAPPS

J ake's Story:

Boy, how do I explain this without people thinking I am crazy? I probably can't, but I'll try.

My sister will finish explaining.

It happened in the middle of the night.

My wife was not sleeping with me at the time. No, we were not having problems; it's just that I was snoring so loudly that she couldn't stand it any longer. She moved to the spare bedroom where she could sleep.

Well, as I was saying, I was alone in the bedroom when I saw it. The dog woke me, or I would have been spared. He stood right outside my bedroom window and barked like a banshee. My guess is that he saw it too.

It was the light, literally speaking; I saw the light. Not like Hank Williams, where I got religion, that's not happened yet, thank the Lord. What I saw was the light on the ceiling; actually, it was more on the wall. However, I know what I saw.

I went in and woke my wife to tell her the news. She threw a fit for waking her after snoring her out of the room and all. She said I was a superstitious fool. How do you like that, calling me superstitious, when she's the one who wastes two hours every Sunday at church? That took a lot of nerve, but since she's working and I'm not, I let it go.

Next, I called my brother Benny. Too bad for me, his smart-aleck, college educated wife answered the phone. I asked for Ben, and in the background, I could hear her yapping.

"It's your crazy brother again," she was saying. "I think he's drunk."

You would think a college graduate would have the decency to cover the mouthpiece.

Now for your information, I didn't have a drop. It's just that women always think the worst of a man, especially a brother-in-law.

I tried to explain the sighting to my brother, but he wasn't in the mood.

"Gall-dernit, Jake!" He said, "It's four o'clock in the morning. For heaven's sake, some of us has got to work for a living."

I decided "to heck with him," for throwing that not-working thing in my face. I called my sister. Nearly scared her to death, but she did listen to me. After all, there was a reason I called. I may drink a little, and I did have a couple of minor nervous breakdowns, but by-golly, I did have a purpose for calling.

The point being is that I saw the light. Sure as shootin', somebody in the family was going to die, and due to the fact that our mother was in the hospital, and she was eighty-three years old, I thought someone else ought to know what I saw. I didn't want it on my conscience that she passed over, and I knew it was going to happen, but didn't have the guts to call and share that knowledge.

You know, so they could pay their last respects and all.

Sis asked if I had called the hospital.

"Dern right I did," I told her.

Then I explained how those sorry so-and-so's wouldn't even go in to wake her up. They told me they could monitor her without disturbing her sleep. Besides which, they claimed, she was all better and was going home in the morning anyway.

Sis, she knew exactly what I was talking about when I said I'd seen the "Whittier family light." I guess that's because she's superstitious like me, unlike our idiot brother, Benny.

Sis and me, we are close in age and learned about "the light" at the same time. It was when we were little; I remember it clear as a bell, even though it's now more than fifty years gone.

We were staying the night at Pap and Granny Whittier's. It was cold outside, and a bunch of the old folks had gathered up at Pap's house; they did that back then. We were all sitting around the wood stove as they told stories, each trying to out-lie the other. After "hoop snakes" and "baby stealing panthers" had their run, the subject of the "ghost light" came up.

I remember at the time, I wasn't eager to hear about any ghost light, but what could I do but listen? I couldn't change the channel, and I was too scared to go into another room.

As they explained it, the ghost light showed itself the night before someone in the family was to die. It appeared first on the ceiling, then danced around the room. Granny said one of our long dead great grandmas was a Cherokee, and she passed it down that the light was a spiritual animal, come as a guide to the dead Indian's world.

I remember Uncle Marvin, Pap's youngest, God rest his soul, arguing that the light was a bunch of baloney.

Pap, he set him straight when he said he'd seen it. Marvin didn't dare contradict Pap. 'Cause sure as Ulysses S. Grant was a Yankee, Pap would have boxed his ears.

Now Pap, he swore on a stack of *Farmers Almanacs* that he saw the light when Uncle Cyrus left for glory. He said it was white and shaped like a rabbit.

Great Uncle Mart, Aunt Sadie, and the rest of the old folks jumped right in and vouched for similar events.

After that, and for all the years I was growing up, I thought about the ghost light. As I grew to a man, I became skeptical. I considered all the possibilities. I concluded there probably was a light, Pap wouldn't just make one up, but it was likely that the lights came from passing cars, or reflections from the fire in the wood stove.

And that made sense, because those old timers, back in the day, they didn't have television, so they told stories and improved them as they went. Most of them were superstitious anyway, and of course, they believed in ghosts. It didn't mean they were lying.

Even at that, with my skepticism and all, I still remembered. I made it a habit not to look at the ceiling when I lay in bed, especially late at night. If I got up, I kept my eyes on the floor until I found the light switch. I always tried to sleep with my face down; my wife said I was being ridiculous. I said it was just being careful.

And if that dang dog hadn't been barking up such a fit, I would have been okay; but he did, and I looked, so there you are.

I have to admit, it scared me might near to death as it danced around the room. At first, I thought it was a white rabbit, like in Pap's story long ago, but if I had to describe it, I'd say it was a deer.

So as I talked to Sis, and explained it all, she remembered the old stories but was less than convinced.

"Gall-dernit, Sis," I said, "If you can believe in the Holy Ghost, why in tarn'nation can't you believe in the ghost light?"

"Have you been taking your meds?" Sis asked. I detected a little skepticism as she was referring to my nervous pills.

"Dang right I have. As a matter of fact, I just took a couple extra, right before I called you. And one more thing," I told her, "since them numbskulls down at the hospital won't let me talk to her, I'm going down there myself."

"Jake," she said, "she only went in to get a bone spur removed from her heel. They wouldn't have even kept her, except that her doctor had a late schedule at the hospital, and she's got really good insurance."

"Sis," I tried to explain, "them quacks kill perfectly healthy people every day. Dog-gone-it, an eighty-three-year-old woman ain't got a chance."

I just hung up the phone on her. At that point, I had told Margaret, then I had called Benny, and then I called Sis. Apparently, nobody wanted to hear about it. I decided they could all just kiss my butt. I wasn't going to waste another minute. The talking part was over; it was time to act.

At that, I walked out the door, fired up the Jeep, and headed out as fast as that old Jeep could go.

Sis's Story:

I got a call from Jake this morning, about four o'clock. He was pretty worked up. He rarely calls me, so it rather upset me.

I woke Bradley, who slept through the ringing of the telephone, and we discussed Jake and his latest.

"Why don't you call his wife and see if she knows what's going on," Bradley suggested.

"I just don't know her well enough to call her at this time of the morning," I said.

"I bet she is already awake. What is her name anyway? Shirley, isn't it."

"No dear," I told him, "Shirley was the last one." Then I corrected myself, "Sorry, the last one was Jill…Shirley was the one before Jill… this one is Margaret."

So I called Margaret, she told me Jake had left sometime in the night.

"He just called me a few minutes ago," I said, "so he must have just left."

"Really?" she said. "It seems like hours ago that he came in here from the other room and woke me with some wild story."

"Don't you two sleep in the same room?" I asked.

"That's really none of your business, is it?" she said. I thought that she had gotten just a bit huffy. Then she cut me off.

"Look," she said, "I have to get ready for work." And that was the end of that conversation.

"What should we do?" I asked Brad.

Bradley and I got dressed and drove to the hospital to see Mom. Just in case.

When we arrived, there in the waiting room was my oldest brother Benny. He said the hospital was on his way to work.

He explained that Jake had called him early in the morning, and that Jake's call had worked on his mind until he became worried. He figured that since he was going by anyway, he would just stop. You know, just in case.

"I already talked to the head nurse on the ward," Benny said. "They will bring her down to the front in about half an hour. She's doing good."

"Well," I said. "She's doing well."

"What?" Benny said.

Realizing that I had only confused him, I made some excuses until he went on to explain that she would be in a wheelchair until her foot healed, but there was nothing wrong with her.

"Look," I said to Benny, as I pointed across the parking lot, "here comes Buster and his wife, and it looks like one of his boys is with him."

"Well," Benny said, "you had to figure he would be here, being Mom's favorite and all."

Thirty minutes later, Mom rolled out of the elevator and into the main reception area. By then, my other two brothers had arrived. I had lost track of the grandchildren. All of Billy and Merle's girls were there, and Mom's great grandchildren as well. Four or five little Willmeyer boys were running around in the lobby.

The ladies in the reception area were astounded. Never had they seen so many people arrive to welcome a family member "out of" the hospital.

I heard Mrs. Watson, the head volunteer, say to her co-worker, "My goodness, this must be some kind of record. I've never seen this many people for one person, ever."

They both shook their head in disbelief and pushed their glasses back up on their noses.

"Do you think I should call Channel Six news?" she said. "They're always doing those feel-good stories. Think of the good publicity this would do for the hospital."

"Yes indeed, I say call them," the other lady agreed.

The morning janitor came in and asked if there was some sort of riot going on.

"Not at all," I said.

"Then, where did all these people come from?" he asked. He stood in awe, as more people came marching through the door.

"Damn!" he said. "They're tracking mud all over my floor!"

I walked away so as not to put up with his foul mood.

Mom was deeply moved by the turnout, but somewhat mystified.

"Why are you all here? All I needed was Buster, here," Mom said, as she patted her youngest son's hand.

We were at a loss for words. None of us wanted to say we came because we thought she might croak. Benny and I made lame excuses until Mom caught on.

"Now, cut the crap," she demanded, "and tell me, what's going on?"

"It's Jake's fault," Benny volunteered.

"Yes it is," I said. "He probably called everyone in the family."

"Jake didn't call me," Buster corrected. "You did, Sis."

"Well yes," I admitted, "I did call a few people."

"So did I," Benny confessed.

"And just where is Jake?" Mom asked.

"Probably hiding," said Benny.

As Mom signed her release papers, she asked, "Just what did he do, to get you all here anyway?"

So, I explained. "Jake called me this morning, about four, and said he had a revelation. He was certain that you were a goner."

"That's silly," Mom said. "I'm as healthy as a horse."

Benny, who had walked over to the window overlooking the parking lot interrupted. "Well, look at who's coming."

"Is it Jake?" I asked.

"Yes it is," he said, then added, "Wait a minute. No, I don't see him. I thought it was him, at first, but he must already be here, because here comes what's-her-name."

"Margaret," I said.

Benny headed for the door. "Boy she's in a hurry," he said. "I'll go head her off; she's going the wrong way."

Mom finished signing out. "Roll me out of here, Buster," she said to her favorite son.

I walked beside Mom as we made our way through the grandchildren.

"Just what kind of revelation did Jake have?"

"Well," I said, "you remember those old stories Grandma and Pap used to tell about the ghost light?"

"Who could forget those great old stories?"

"Jake said he saw the ghost light." I went on to explain to Mom how Jake had seen the light on his ceiling.

"Ain't no such thing as a ghost light," Mom said. "Those were just stories, made up to scare the kids, pure entertainment."

"They sure scared me when I was a child," I said.

"Besides," Mom said, "it's stupid anyway, the ghost light wouldn't appear on Jake's ceiling, if I was about to die. It would appear on mine."

"There's Benny," I said to Mom, "I'll see if he's found Jake. We know he's here somewhere, his wife's here."

"What is her name?" Mom asked. "I've forgotten."

"Margaret."

Benny walked straight to us. He didn't look happy. Benny took Mom's hand.

"Did you find Jake?" we both asked.

"Mother," Benny said to Mom, "Jake's downstairs, in the morgue."

"What's he doing there?" I started to ask, then caught myself.

"Mom," Benny said, "Jake hit a deer with his Jeep early this morning. I guess he was coming here. It was a big buck and it came through the windshield. Jake died."

Mom cried. The other kids gathered around, Benny told them the news. Later, Benny motioned me aside, and we walked to the window.

"Sis," Benny said, "it's weird. The cops said he hit an albino deer."

A Man Called Rabbit
Linda Capps Fisher

Folks around here never knew his real name, so they called him Rabbit. His unkempt hair and beard were the color of a Missouri cottontail in summer, and his prominent front teeth gave him a rabbit-like smile. Heck, Rabbit's favorite food was carrots.

How Rabbit came to live in Palmer was a mystery. Speculation was he'd hopped a Rock Island railcar and attempted to become the town's only resident hobo. His welcome wore thin in town, and Rabbit hitchhiked south on Highway 135 toward the Lake of the Ozarks, a sparsely populated area in those days.

Rabbit tramped through an opening in a split-rail fence up the stone walkway crowded with overgrown grass and wildflowers. He raised his fist to pound on a wooden screen door but stopped mid-knock. The owner hulked in the doorway clutching a shotgun as if he would shoot Rabbit with the same disregard given to a cur dog.

"I'm lookin' for work." Rabbit's voice quaked as he stared into the double barrels.

Seth Driscoll propped the gun next to the door, hitched up a strap on his Big Smith overalls and said, "I kin use some help now that all my boys are grown." They reached a handshake agreement that Rabbit would work for room and board.

"You kin live in that shed," Seth told him. "Ain't much, but has a bed and a dresser. Used to call it my dog house, a'fore the ole lady left me."

Rabbit surveyed the sparse building, and admitted, "I've lived in worse."

He noticed Seth staring at the gaping scar that slashed through his right eyebrow. Rabbit touched the mark with his short stubby forefinger. "A hunter's stray bullet 'bout killed me."

At daybreak the next morning, Rabbit tackled his new job. He slopped huge white hogs, repaired fences, tended the truck garden, and completed other chores Seth laid out for him.

Over time, Rabbit became Seth's best buddy. "There's a poker game at Clem's house Friday." Seth said, "We'll be partners."

"Never heard of such," Rabbit replied as he munched on a carrot.

Every evening that week Rabbit and Seth worked on signals and connived a means of making a profit from the illegal neighborhood poker game. By Friday night, their method netted $20, which was a fair gain for 1960.

They pocketed their winnings and as they made their way across the cluttered room to the door, Clem boomed in his loud braggart voice, "Two rich guys from Kansas City 'ill be at next week's game. Y'all plan on bein' here. Should be interestin'."

As they climbed into the truck, Seth spit out tobacco juice and said, "That game will have bigger stakes. Me and you can make some real dough."

On game day, Seth and Rabbit spruced themselves up with new clothes from Kipper's Department Store and haircuts at Bob's Barber Shop. They didn't want to look like hillbillies who didn't know beans from apple butter. Men who look like greenhorns have a hard time bluffing city slickers.

After dark that night, they walked up the worn wooden steps onto a broken-down porch with a steep slant that threatened to throw them backwards. In a low voice, Seth issued a last minute warning to his gambling partner. "We gotta be careful tonight. These guys are dangerous."

The two entered the smoky room where the game was in progress. A pile of chips lay in the middle of the round oak kitchen table. Rabbit's nose began to twitch. Sensing his friend's nervousness, Seth whispered, "What's wrong?"

"I know that guy," Rabbit nodded toward a burly man with a two-day beard and a cigar clinched between long yellow teeth.

Clem yelled out, "Hey, fellas, come join the game."

Chairs scraped the wooden floor as the players made room for the newcomers. The burly man, whose name was Bill, barely glanced at Rabbit and went back to studying his cards.

The game progressed at a faster than normal pace, and it didn't take long for Rabbit and Seth's paltry chips to dwindle away to nothing. The two quit the game at one o'clock in the morning. They grumbled about their losses as they climbed into Seth's dented Ford pickup.

"Are we going to let them get away with cleaning us out like that?" Rabbit asked.

"Ain't much we can do about it," grumbled Seth.

Rabbit twisted his head around and stared at the rifle on the gun rack. "We could rob 'em with this deer rifle."

"They'd know us," Seth said, but chuckled like he thought it was a good idea.

All the way home, they cussed the men who had ripped them off at the game. They plotted, grumbled, and plotted some more. At home, Rabbit wound a rag around his forehead to conceal his scar. He donned a red flannel shirt, a hunting cap with earflaps, and covered his lower face with a handkerchief bandana.

They drove toward Clem's house and stopped just out of sight. Seth backed the truck into the brush. "Wait here," Rabbit said, tucking the rifle under his arm.

Rabbit kicked the door open and pointed the gun at the men sitting at the table. "This is a stick up. Take off your shoes and britches. Lay face down on the floor." Rabbit mimicked John Wayne to disguise his voice and lend authority to his words.

Their slowness irritated him, so he prodded them with threats. "I don't want to kill nobody, but I will if I haff to. You!" he yelled at a young man with fiery red hair, "Put the money in this gunny sack."

Rabbit barked more orders, and the boy gathered up pants and shoes tossing them off the porch and into the ravine below.

Rabbit shoved the barrel squarely between Bill's broad shoulders. His finger flexed on the trigger. Sweat popped out on the big man.

"You probably ain't worth the cost of a bullet," Rabbit said, and kicked him hard on his Fruit of the Looms. "Stay put for thirty minutes or you'll be shot. Two more fellas are hidin' in the woods."

Rabbit sprinted down the road and jumped in the pickup. Seth spun out, throwing brush and gravel everywhere. Rabbit said, "They won't be along anytime soon 'cause I slashed their tires."

At Seth's house, Rabbit told his friend to hide the money. "I'll leave your truck by the trail tree. Tell them I stole your rig after you went to sleep."

"Take your cut of the money," Seth said.

"Where I'm headed, I won't need it." Rabbit revved up the motor and roared into the night.

Sheriff J.T. found Seth's truck parked near the Indian pointer tree. The folks at the poker game knew Rabbit was the thief, but Seth claimed, "I ain't seen hide nor 'hare' of him since."

Life was easier for Seth after the robbery, which due to the illegal status of the game, was not reported. Every Saturday, he chose the freshest carrots at Cooper's Grocery Store. At the Indian trail tree, he always left an abundant supply for the rabbit with a scar above his eye.

A Song for Betty
Jimmy Capps

I can't recall the first time I heard the song, but it's such an old song that I'd probably heard it hundreds of times as a kid.

I *do* remember when I started playing it. I was in college and went to see the movie *Cool Hand Luke*. An actor named Harry Dean Stanton sang the song. I liked it so well that I learned it and played it for a year or two.

Then, I put it away for forty years, which brings me to how I started singing it again.

Three years ago, my mother and aunt volunteered to sing at the local nursing home, a place optimistically called the Primetime Living Center.

They recruited their cousin Gene to play lead guitar.

They soon discovered that the nursing home had a sound system—three mikes and a mixer board. However, on Saturday, the day they played, there were no staff members available to operate the system. Therefore, because of my electronics background, I was asked to help. Also, as my mother pointed out, she, my aunt, and Gene were too old to carry equipment in and out of the building.

The point is that even though I had musical abilities, I was asked to help as an electrician and beast of burden, not as a performer.

Eventually, out of guilt I suppose, I was invited onto the stage and allowed to play my guitar with the understanding that I had everyone else plugged in and going.

So play I did, even though I had no idea what they were playing. I was a generation newer than my counterparts were; therefore, the music I had always played was actually heard on the radio.

I am reasonably certain the music my mother and aunt sang was written before radio was invented.

That's the way it went, and eventually, I learned their music. It was simple, just three chords. I learned as well, that apparently, in hillbilly music, there was no such thing as a minor chord. A person was

14

considered both uppity and stupid if they attempted to interject such a thing into the music.

However, this story is about Betty's song, so let's get back to it.

Betty was a tiny woman in her nineties with dyed jet-black hair. Betty rolled around in a wheelchair and knew everyone at the Primetime Living Center. For the singing, she placed herself right in front of the stage. After the singing, Betty hung around as I cleared the stage and commented on the music that we played offering many suggestions, not all of them complimentary.

One day she asked, "Next time, will you sing a song for me?"

"Maybe. What is it you want?" I replied.

" 'Just a Closer Walk with Thee,' " she said.

"I think we can do that one," I answered. "Next time I'll make sure we sing it."

I knew the song, which was unusual. Most of the songs requested were songs that I had never heard of. But not this one, I remembered it from *Cool Hand Luke*.

After I got home, I pulled the song off the internet and ran through it a couple of times.

I called my mother and told her about Betty's request.

During the next performance, Mom announced the song.

"This song is for Betty," Mom said. Then she and my aunt sang "Just a Closer Walk with Thee." They did a pretty decent job.

At the end of the program, as once again I cleared the stage, Betty rolled up in her chair.

"Well," I said, "we did that song you asked for. How did you like it?"

"It was good," Betty answered.

"I'm glad you liked it. It's one of my favorites too."

"Next time," she suggested, "why don't *you* sing it?"

"Betty, I don't do the singing," I admitted. "I just set up things."

"Well, I would like to hear you give it a try."

"We'll see," I said.

The next two performances came and passed. On each occasion, I suggested to my mother, that perhaps I could sing one song, that being "Just a Closer Walk with Thee."

However, by then, Mom and my aunt had claimed the song as theirs, and taking it away, was akin to wresting a chunk of meat from a grizzly bear.

Still, at the end of each session, Betty persisted. "Just sing it!" she demanded.

The next session, I entered with a plan. I set up the equipment and did the sound checks. Everything worked perfectly.

The doors opened and the room started filling up.

I messed with the mixer board, kicked a speaker, and then moved to my mother's microphone. I tapped on it furiously.

"Something's not right," I said, with a note of agitated concern. "I need to reset the system."

I took Mom's microphone and stand, moved them to the area where I normally stood.

I saw Betty wheeling her way forward.

I pretended to mess with the settings of the mixer board, then picked up my guitar and said, "Let's see how this sounds."

I started singing, "Just a closer…" I finished the song, slid the microphone back to my mother. "I think it's all ready to go," I said.

As the following months came and went, I continued using that song to set up the equipment, and it became standard operating procedure.

Then, I started sneaking in another song here and there. Amazingly, my mother, usually when she had dropped her music cheat cheats and lost her place, started requesting that I sing something.

Eventually, I was singing songs just like the rest of them, and in my opinion, doing a whole lot better job on most of them. Of course, that was *my* opinion, which was shared by Betty.

The point is, if it hadn't been for Betty's persistence, I would have never started singing.

So here it was a couple of years later, and I had a whole repertoire of songs to sing. However, our group still started each performance with a sound check using "Just a Closer Walk with Thee."

After two years, our motley group of three performers and a soundman had swelled to eight. We had added a second lead, a bass, a banjo, and another singer. We played at several nursing homes and senior centers. However, we made sure to always play on our scheduled Saturday at the Primetime Living Center.

So here we were again. I had everything adjusted and ready to go, and started the set up song, which was still "Just a Closer Walk with Thee" when, unexpectedly, my mother interrupted me.

"This song is for Betty," Mom said. I stopped and gave her a somewhat dirty look.

"Go ahead," she motioned at me impatiently.

I continued the song, but I noticed that Betty was not in front as usual. However, as the song ended, I thought I caught a glimpse of her sitting in the back of the room. She was smiling.

When we were done, I put away the equipment. Betty had already left; she probably didn't feel well. She had been sick for a couple of months, and two months ago, had missed us completely; therefore, I was a little concerned. It is a fact of life, when you play music at nursing homes, you lose a person every month or two.

Later that evening, as usual, I called my mother to talk about how we had sounded earlier in the day.

"Is Betty sick or something?" I asked during the course of our conversation. "I didn't see her sitting up front as usual, and she wasn't there as I put things away."

"Oh son," she said, "I thought you knew. Betty passed away last Tuesday. That's why I interrupted you and announced that 'This song is for Betty.'"

"No, I hadn't heard."

"Well," Mom said, "you did a wonderful job singing it. I'm sure Betty would have enjoyed it."

"Yes," I said, "I think she did...I mean I think she would have."

THE MEMORY PILLOW
LINDA CAPPS FISHER

I drove a rented Jeep past a bullet-splattered city limit sign, population 757, to the Ozarks' village I had moved away from the day after my high school graduation. The Bridget Moore CPA firm grudgingly granted family leave so I could check on my ailing mother. I hadn't been home in a decade, until the emergency phone call from old Mr. Barker, her neighbor of fifty years.

"Lueva Ellen don't seem to be herself 'zactly," Mr. Barker said in his hillbilly twang when he called me last week. "She's pert'ner actin' strange."

Mr. Barker was quite a bit older than Mother and must be in his nineties, yet he was as protective of her as if she were a fragile southern belle and he, Ashley Wilkes. I could not fathom what my mother was doing that Mr. Barker considered "pert'ner" strange considering her usual eccentric behavior.

Weeds slapped my legs as I walked up the path to the backdoor of the shabby house with its paint-blistered clapboard siding. I knocked on the thin wood frame of a torn screen door. My knock was unanswered, so I called out a refrain from my childhood, "Mother, I'm home."

Getting no response, I opened the door. My mother was hunched over a Formica dining table eating a bowl of Cheerios. Milk dribbled down her chin and splattered onto the front of her housecoat, which was wrong side out. She glanced up, bloodshot eyes looking through me. She calmly continued eating her cereal.

I trudged through piles of old newspapers and rubbish on the cracked linoleum floor. Discolored watermarks looked like pee stains on the ceilings and explained the five-gallon bucket partially filled with dirty water. This home sweet home was earmarked to be my inheritance. As the only daughter of an only daughter, my mother expected me, in due time, to live in this house which was her mother's before her. *That* would never happen.

I heaved my suitcase to the bedroom. Its bar-coded airline tag with a silver "clear" sticker, certified me a non-terrorist, bomb-free tourist.

The narrow bed in my mother's spare room looked as uninviting as a pile of dirty clothes. I would have to scrub and disinfect the room before I could sleep there without wondering what kind of microscopic creepy crawly things would attack my slumbering body in the night.

First, I tackled the bed. No amount of jet lag and mental exhaustion would allow me to sleep on a bed with covers that most likely had not been changed in ten years. Had it really been that long since I visited my mother?

The iron frame looked corroded and as untrustworthy as a telemarketer. I stripped quilts, blankets, and uncovered faded cotton sheets with a shotgun pattern of miniature pink roses. Tattered featherbed ticking rested on top of metal springs, the unforgiving coils looked like a medieval torture device.

I tossed dingy linens onto a floor yellowed with old wax and caked with dirt. I pulled a cotton pillowcase off the bolster, which lay across the top of the bed giving it a puffy-comfy look. Beneath the bolster were two feather pillows, flattened from years of being squashed by human heads and, who knows, possibly my mother's butt as she elevated it for sexual encounters with insignificant lovers.

Throughout the day, I busied myself with laundry, cleaning, grocery shopping and cooking dinner. I avoided careful scrutiny of my mother who sat in her chair staring into space unimpressed that her only child was home.

This broken woman bore small resemblance to the woman who had greeted me when I arrived for my last visit. That time, my mother flung her arms around me, drew me to her trim body, and planted a kiss on my cheek, leaving a lipstick mark.

She had pushed me to an arm's length, and greeted me with her husky voice, "Ellen! It is so good to see you, child!" From the warm motherly greeting, an eavesdropper might have missed the subtle animosity in her voice, but I heard the tone as plainly as a sour note in an otherwise flawless symphony.

Lueva Ellen had never looked, or acted, like a mother. When she was younger, she opened her silk blouses to the third button, her alabaster cleavage providing eye candy for salivating men. Envious women couldn't help but stare at Mother's amazing breasts. I'd heard rumors that when I was a baby, she didn't want to breast feed me for fear it would damage her treasures, but occasionally bared her breast in public while she pretended to offer her nipple to me.

She wore mini-skirts and stilettos to show off shapely legs encased in expensive silk stockings. She never attempted to make friends with women who hated her; instead, she was content knowing men lusted after her, and never found a man who wasn't willing to bed her. After nocturnal visits to Mother, prominent citizens stealthily fled into the darkness to their respectable wives and snooty children who thought I wasn't good enough to be in their circle of friends.

Memories crashed around me, as I held the pillow in my hand and tugged the laundered case onto it. I sat on the edge of the bed and closed my eyes. The memory of the awkward feeling of being between a girl and a woman washed over me.

I was nearly twelve, and my mother began making disparaging remarks about my arrested physical development. "I don't understand how a daughter of mine can be so flat-chested. And why do you have your nose buried in a book all the time?"

I grew up, albeit slowly, and then my mother saw me as a rival. Most of the men my mother brought home gave me the creeps, but that didn't stop Mother from turning hard eyes on me as she stood in her bedroom door, her body silhouetted by lamplight. "Young lady, you need to do your homework and get to bed."

My room was my haven, a place where I pretended my life was normal. I cranked up the portable radio and tuned it to WLS. The Beatles and Dave Clark Five helped drown out the racket of the squeaking bed and obscenities my mother yelled between orgasmic groans. The ill-fitting door with its two-inch gap at the bottom did little to muffle the sounds.

I played the radio while I slept, but one night awakened to creaking sounds as the floor groaned under the weight of an intruder. "Who's there?" I whispered.

"Just me, honey," a man's husky voice said. His breathing was labored and caught in his throat. It was my mother's latest boyfriend.

One big hand clamped down on my mouth and the other roughly pawed at my body. He hooked his thumb in the elastic of my underwear and pulled until the thin fabric gave way. I kicked and thrashed, making as much noise as I could with my lips smashed into my teeth.

The door flew open, a blinding light exposed his naked ugliness, and he jerked his hands from my body and threw them in front of his face. My mother held a butcher knife with both hands. She raised it above her head and screamed, "You bastard! Get away from my daughter. Get out, get out, get out before I kill you!"

The man cowered on the floor as my mother threatened him with the knife and kicked him in the ribs. My mouth filled with saliva and bile burned the back of my throat. I spewed stinking vomit all over the floor and into his face. He gagged and pushed past my mother while her attention was on me.

The next morning, I climbed onto the school bus, stone faced. Outwardly, I looked the same. If anyone had cared enough to look into my eyes, they would have seen the haunted knowledge that lingered behind my irises.

I became obsessed with schoolwork, compulsively studying, memorizing—only satisfied with perfect scores. So, I was the smartest kid in my class which helped make up for my lack of nice clothing, my crummy home, and my weird habit of talking to myself. No one seemed to like me. Girls assumed I had the same nature as my mother, and boys quickly lost interest because I didn't

My first serious boyfriend was a tall, thin boy named Sammy. I wove fantasies around him, designating him hero of my childish romantic stories. I chose names for our oldest child, which would be a girl, of course. I planned to name her after my mother, whom at that time, I still loved despite her faults, and for my grandma, Astoria Ellen. I always felt more of a connection with my grandma, who was as unlike my mother as a black-eyed Susan is to an orchid.

Grandma Astoria wore her Repunzel-length blond hair braided and twisted into a coronet on the top of her head. A hand-embroidered apron, covering her from chest to mid calf, protected her gingham cotton dress from spills while she cooked pots of roasting ears and iron skillets full of new potatoes fried with the skins on.

My mother didn't cook. She opened cans and bought take-out. Dishes piled up in the sink and trash overflowed with sacks and paper cups from Eddie's Hamburger House. As a teenager, I normally opened a can of Campbell's Soup and fixed sandwiches for us. I filled the sink with scalding hot water, and after I had finished my homework, I tackled the daily accumulation of lipstick stained coffee cups, old jelly jars we used for water glasses, and food encrusted flatware.

The woman sitting in the wing-backed chair in the living room could have been a stranger. Mother's stringy gray hair hung unattended in untidy knots. Instead of looking at me, she looked past me with glazed eyes. With her robe wrapped loosely around her, one pendulous breast hung out, resembling a five-day-old balloon with a few breaths of stale air left in it. I tugged her pink robe shut to cover her nakedness.

"There," I said.

Her eyes fixed on my face as she glared at me and defiantly bared her entire chest. "There!" Spittle formed on her chin from the force of her reactive one word declaration. Her eyes became unfocused and her gaze fixed on the wall over my left shoulder.

Holding her bony liver-spotted hand in mine, I led her toward her bedroom. Having used up her quota of defiance with the robe position, she climbed into bed as obediently as if she were the good child I'm positive she never was. I pulled covers over her as I would a baby, if I had one, which I didn't since I'd never had a serious relationship other than a brief high school romance with Sammy. I had prayed for him to love me back, but he dumped me for another girl.

I'm not sure which depressed me the most—thinking about the person Mother was or the person she had become. I crawled into bed, threw the bolster onto the floor, and hugged the pillow to my ear. I heard a slight rustle as feathers repositioned themselves, sounding like whispers from long ago. My longings began with wanting my Memory Foam pillow and escalated to homesickness for my tidy apartment, oil paintings, Fenton Glass collection, Waterford Crystal, and literary magazines.

An unfamiliar bed and the emotionally draining day disturbed my normal dreamless slumber. In my dreams, Grandmother Astoria kneaded biscuit dough in a crock bowl, working the sticky substance through her fingers, pinching off biscuits, rolling them in grease, and placing them onto a blackened cookie sheet. As if she were a master chef on a TV cooking show, Grandma placed the biscuits in the oven of her enamel Home Comfort wood-burning stove and immediately pulled out a pan of golden brown biscuits. Instead of her normal sweet smile, she smirked falsely like an infomercial star.

The next morning, I awakened feeling strangely exhilarated. I walked into the kitchen, tugged open a wooden drawer, almost tearing it apart when it stuck on one side. Inside the drawer was a stack of aprons, and I selected one with cross-stitched apples across the bottom. I placed the loop over my head and wrapped the long ties around my waist, whipping them into a lop-sided bow behind me. I dragged a straight back oak chair to the old-fashioned white cupboard and, using the chair for a stepladder, reached for the large crock bowl stored on top.

I worked feverishly, in a daze, cutting dry ingredients, stirring in milk, kneading, and rolling the white orbs in grease. My mother walked in behind me.

"What are you making, Mama?" she asked.

Well, finally Mother had acknowledged me and had some recognition of me, although in her befuddled state, she mistook me for my grandmother. All my life, people told me I looked like my grandmother—the same golden hair, the same diminutive stature, the same blue eyes flecked with green.

"I'm making biscuits, but where is my cook stove?"

She placed her hands on her hips and said, "Remember, Mama, we bought this electric range. See, here is how you turn it on. Let it preheat; then, we will bake the biscuits."

"Oh," I said, turning from the spot where I fully expected the wood stove to be. *I'm not familiar with this kitchen*, I thought.

I put six pieces of bacon in a skillet to fry while I waited for the oven to preheat. The smell of the hickory smoke flavor rising from the sizzling meat made my mouth water.

Forks clattered and scraped the chipped ironware plates as we dug into a full country breakfast. I hadn't eaten this much food so early in the day since I ate at Cracker Barrel on my way home after spending the night with Ed, my gentleman friend.

"You make the best biscuits, Mama," Mother said. She closed her eyes as if to savor the taste of the food, or shut out the world, or both.

"They *are* good," I said, surprised at my creativity. I had never made decent scratch biscuits in my life, but this morning I made them without a recipe.

Feeling someone's eyes boring into my back, I whirled around to see who was in the kitchen. No one. An oven mitt lay on the floor. Its silent descent when it fell off the counter must have stirred the air giving the illusion of another person in the room.

I cleaned the kitchen and muddled over plans to oversee my mother's care. I drove my rental car into town to visit the Shady Pines Home for the Elderly. A skinny girl, with spiky red hair wearing a thin white T-shirt and blue jeans that dug into the crack of her butt, directed me to the administrator's office. A bald, obese man sat behind a polished walnut desk in a leather swivel chair, which appeared to be in danger of exceeding its load limit. A brass plaque on the desk read: Samuel McClellan, Administrator. I blinked as my brain processed the information.

"Sammy?"

"Ellen! It's good to see you after all these years!" He heaved himself out of his chair and hugged me in a way that would make my chiropractor cringe. He smelled of sweat and stale tobacco smoke. "How is your dear, dear mother?"

"She's old," I said. I had always heard that when you return to childhood places everything looks smaller, but in Sammy's case, it looked a whole lot larger.

I filled out a stack of forms, and gathering up a packet of brochures, I shook Sammy's hand and left. "Thank you, God," I whispered under my breath as I closed the door behind me.

An overweight nurse with hair chopped off in an untidy line at her shoulders gave me a tour. As I pushed open the double glass doors to leave the facility, she asked, "Do you want your mother on a waiting list?"

"Waiting list?" I gulped. "How long is your waiting list?"

"If we classify her as 'urgent'—about six weeks."

I felt my shoulders droop as I digested the information. By the time I could settle my mother in the nursing home and winterize her house, I'd be forced to beg my obnoxious boss for an extension of my leave-of-absence.

That night, I dreamed about my grandmother again, but this time I *was* my grandmother, and my mother was a little girl.

"I don't want to go to Grandma's wake," Lueva Ellen said in the shrill high-pitched whine of a child used to getting her way. Her dark hair was pulled back into pigtails and her blue polished cotton dress poofed out over several layers of petticoats.

"Lueva Ellen, you hush this minute!" I said in an unusually stern voice.

Soon, I, as Astoria, peered at the face of my own beloved mother. She wore a heavy dark dress and the warm glow of the lamps denied color to her pale face. Her mouth curved in an unnatural position and her flattened features failed the oft-mentioned "natural" appearance, and instead, her corpse looked…dead. Lueva Ellen began to scream and tugged at my arm.

"What is wrong with you?" I whispered loudly, noticing aunts and uncles looking at us with the same disgust they would have for a pile of dog poop on their doorstep.

Lueva Ellen stopped screaming, her blue eyes huge on her small face. "Mama, she wants to take me away."

Suddenly my body was cold and I began to shake. I knew she spoke the truth because I felt it in the prickles running up my neck and onto the top of my head.

She jerked from my grasp and bolted for the door. I chased her as she shot headlong into the street. The sound of squalling tires was followed by a sickening thud as the truck hit my daughter.

"Oh, God! My baby is dead!" I screamed.

Young Jimmy Barker jumped out of his rusted Ford pickup. "She ran right out in front of me!"

My baby, my baby. I grasped her still body to my bosom, as if to suckle the baby she once had been. Her blue eyes opened and she said, "I'm all right, Mama."

I felt hands on my shoulders and a voice whispered in my ear, "It is not for me to take her over to the other side. You do it, daughter, when it's her time." I turned, but no one was there. Jimmy Barker carefully picked Lueva Ellen up off the pavement, her dress saturated with motor oil. Underneath her lay my mother's right hand black glove trimmed with simulated rabbit fur. I wasn't sure how it had gotten there, but I left it since my mother wouldn't need it anymore, and I had no idea where the mate was.

I awakened face down on the feather pillow and couldn't breathe. I sat up in bed and flipped on the light. I stared into the mirror that loomed above the cherry dresser situated at the foot of the bed. The mirror's wavy surface distorted images on a lesser scale than mirrors at fun houses, and my heart pounded at the image reflected there. I swore my grandmother's face was peering back at me. I grabbed my glasses from beside the bed to get a better look. When I saw the reflection of *my* face and *my* golden hair, and not hers, my racing heart returned to its normal pattern, and I no longer felt throbbing in my jugular.

Dawn was a half-hour away, but wide-awake, I decided to brew coffee. I padded to the kitchen, the linoleum floor cold against my bare feet. I measured coffee and filled the basket of the old perk pot. I sat it on the wood stove, where amazingly, a fire burned. I settled into a rocking chair in front of the warm blazing fire and dozed off.

"Coffee?" My mother stood in front of me, her pink robe gaping open, holding a cup of coffee in her outstretched hand.

"Thanks," I said. I was sitting in a kitchen chair, leaning on the table, ridges on my cheek and wrinkles on my forearm. I rotated my head, and heard a crunching sound in my ears, as I attempted to relieve the crick in my neck. My mother replaced the carafe under the Bunn coffeemaker.

"Imagine my surprise to find you here this morning, Ellen!" My mother pushed the words out in her raspy voice.

"I've been here two days," I said.

"Well, where have you been hiding?" My mother hugged me. She smelled musty, and I decided she needed to bathe today.

I saw Grandmother's crock bowl on top of the cupboard. How had my frail mother managed to put it there? I puzzled over yesterday's scratch biscuits, hazy as to how I had morphed my ability to slam cans against the counter into the feel of dough on my hands. Had it not been for two biscuits sitting on the counter, I would have convinced myself I had dreamt the culinary experience.

I warmed the leftover biscuits in the microwave and scrambled eggs. Mother and I ate in silence, and before we finished our meal, her eyes stared vacantly at her plate. She did not speak another word that day.

Old Mr. Barker called to check on my mother and remembering last night's vivid dream, I asked, "Mr. Barker, do you know if my mother was hit by a car when she was younger?" I instantly felt foolish for being so influenced by a dream.

I felt less foolish when he told me he had hit her with his old truck the night of my grandmother's wake. He said. "I wuz jest shore I'd kilt her. I al'us felt 'sponsible fer her af'er that."

I waited until gathering darkness signaled evening was near before I ran water into the claw-foot porcelain tub for Mother's bath. Whippoorwills called and although everyone said they were calling "Whip poor Will" it still sounded like "purple rim" to me. Purple rim didn't mean anything and my mother used to laugh at my insistence that this was the sound the birds made, but then I didn't see what whipping poor Will had to do with bird calls either.

I helped my mother navigate the step to get into the tub, which was perched on top of large footed legs. As soon as I finished scrubbing her, I wrapped a pristine white terry robe around her.

I poured a cup of chamomile tea and after she sipped it dry, she began to nod off. I helped her to bed, and then I retired for the night.

I fell asleep and awakened to feel gentle hands stroking my hair.

"Ellen, wake up." I opened my eyes to see moonlight glinting off my grandma's crown of braids, creating a gleaming halo.

"Grandma!" My voice sounded childlike and when I reached out to touch her, my hands were the tiny child hands I used to have.

"Granddaughter, I have come for Lueva Ellen."

"Grandma, I'm afraid," I said, forcing my sandpaper tongue to form the words.

"Don't be afraid, dear. It's time."

Her voice faded, and her image evaporated. I lay there staring into the darkness, deserted by the moonlight of a heartbeat before. My body was paralyzed and I couldn't move. I heard my mother calling out, "Mama! Mama!" I heard murmuring voices and a sound like helicopter blades slicing through air, faster, faster, faster. As the sound faded away, I heard my own raspy breath against the feather pillow.

After struggling several minutes, I was rewarded with a slight movement of my little finger on my right hand. I concentrated on moving my whole hand, and became aware of all my body parts. My sleep-induced paralysis gave way to normal movement and minutes, or possibly hours, later I rolled over in bed, one leg flopping off the side.

Through my open window, a cool breeze blew across me, chilling my exposed limbs. The night was filled with the country sounds of crickets chirping and the low-pitched drone of the bullfrogs in the pond.

I lay on my side, trying unsuccessfully to shake off the fear brought on by the nightmare. The pillow whispered in my ear. "Your mother is gone, but she is fine."

To reassure myself that I had been dreaming again, I crept into my mother's room. The moonlight illuminated her face, her mouth agape as if she were snoring, yet there was no sound. Taking baby steps, I moved closer, and closer, toward her bed. A cold draft surrounded me, the air a frigid breath. Concerned about my mother's comfort, I walked to the window to shut it, but it was already closed.

I wandered back to my mother's bed and switched on her Tiffany lamp. Her lifeless eyes were fixed on the ceiling, and when my reluctant fingers grazed her face it was like touching a Saran wrapped package of refrigerated liver.

Not knowing what to do, I dialed 911 and shouted at the dispatcher, "My mother is dead!" My hysteria spent, I waited. I roamed aimlessly through the house, weeping, and turning on every light.

Mentally, I began selecting items for the auction. I doubted the house would bring much, but a developer could doze it and build characterless houses on five-acre tracts.

I called Ed and told him my mother was dead. Before I hung up, I said, "I love you." It was the first time I had uttered those words during our five-year relationship.

I contemplated the bed where the indentation of my body was still visible. The sad feather pillows on the narrow bed accelerated my desire to sleep in my own king-sized bed with my memory pillow. I mean, Memory Foam pillow, which only remembered how I wanted my head positioned at night.

I gathered up the pillows and pushed open the backdoor of my mother's house, the damp, dewy grass cushioned my bare feet as I strode across the lawn. I stooped and picked up a left-hand leather glove trimmed with rabbit fur.

I unlatched the lid of the galvanized garbage can and dumped glove and pillows into it.

The pillow's frantic whispers echoed through the night imploring me to retrieve them. Finally, the screaming sheriff's car barreled up the gravel lane and drowned out their plaintive sounds.

FIGHTING THE DEMON
JIMMY CAPPS

There were three of us. An old priest, a young priest, and me. We were equals, all in the same boat. In the same boat figuratively as well as literally, because we were in a wooden boat, me manning the oars, as we moved through a dark, stormy night toward our destination.

We were strangers, but each aware of our purpose, and each equally responsible for our assignment. We were there to fight the Demon.

I suppose the priests were chosen because of their traditional role as demon fighters, but why was I there? It was a mystery; I'm not even religious.

Perhaps the demons I fought in my nightmares had qualified me. God knows I've had enough of those. Or, maybe I was the only one available on short notice.

We came ashore on a small rocky island off the coast of Massachusetts. While walking to the rendezvous point, we discussed the matter of my selection. It was apparent that the priests viewed me as a poor choice. I agreed. However, the selection process was not ours. Sometimes these things don't make much sense.

Whatever the reason, our course was set. We would face the Demon, one at a time.

The Old Priest chose to go first. After all he was the most experienced, and in our eyes, the most likely to succeed. The Demon, confidant in its power, allowed us that choice. Therefore, he faced our best.

The Young Priest and I waited unable to help. The battle raged around us. It seemed endless. However, it was not, and eventually, it was over.

The Old Priest had done an admirable job. He succeeded in holding the Demon at bay. However, the price was great. We could see the pain and damage inflicted upon his being. True, the old man survived, but as far as the future went, he was finished.

We both knew the beast would come again, and soon. What would be our strategy? The Young Priest was insistent. He would do it, and although ready for the task, he was extremely frightened, I could tell. Still, he felt obligated to face the Demon and could not be persuaded otherwise.

The Demon had other ideas. For the next attack, it did not allow us a choice. It did the choosing.

The Demon chose me. Why, I don't know. Perhaps the struggle with the old man had taught it to avoid Roman Catholic priests. I suspect it saw me, a non-participator of any religion, as easy prey.

Therefore, when the next attack came, I was the victim.

It swarmed upon me like a cold, dark cloud, howling like a thousand winds. Swirling, pulling, and blistering my skin. It pulled me downward, ever accelerating, into a bottomless pit. I knew my destination…hell, not the fiery hell of the Bible, but a black hole of hell—sheer terror.

Through thousands of prior encounters fighting the demons of my dreams, I knew I must turn my fear into anger. I had to be careful, for this is a dangerous tactic. Uncontrolled, my anger would assist the beast. Controlled, it could defeat it.

Using my anger, I fought free. Cursing, kicking, and screaming. Amazing even myself, I proved stronger than the Demon, much stronger.

I quickly gained the upper hand and punished the Demon as it howled in bewilderment and pain. As the presence of the Demon dwindled, I became aware of the priests. Both were amazed at my success. Caught up in the glory of my victory, I cursed and admonished the Demon as it fled in terror.

My intent was prideful: to show the priests the strength of my character, my goodness. For surely mine must be greater than theirs; I alone had vanquished the beast.

Suddenly a realization came upon me. Had the Demon won by default?

True, I was stronger and had beaten it; however in the end, the Demon had exposed me for my vanity.

THE SEVENTH AND EIGHTH GRADE BASKETBALL GAME
LINDA CAPPS FISHER

"I know I'm going to be late," I said, looking into my husband's eyes. Was it my imagination, or was that an exasperated look on his face? "Besides, I bet Crosby told me to be there thirty minutes before his game starts because he knows how I am."

I waved my hands and blew on my freshly polished nails. "I'm almost ready. I really want to be on time to watch Crosby play." I grabbed my Kansas City Chief's jacket and gently touched Josh's picture. "I'll be home by 10:30," I said.

Walking to the car, I thought about how much Josh would have enjoyed watching Crosby play. Our grandson made the basketball team last year, but we didn't get to see any of the games. Josh teetered between this world and the next after suffering brain injuries in a traffic accident. I spent my evenings with him until his death. Now, the games gave me a few hours of respite from my empty home.

I crossed the railroad tracks and squinted to read the street signs to avoid looking at the trio of crosses beside the road where a family died last winter. They were a morbid reminder of the crosses on I-70 east of Kansas City where a drunken driver crossed the median and struck Josh and his band head-on. Josh's cross was simply marked "The Fiddler" summing up his life as a member of the band. Loyal fans heaped flowers and teddy bears near the crash site.

After one painful visit, I used Highway 50 as my route to the city. In my memories, The Fiddler danced across the stage, the fiddle bow held delicately in his large hands—the sheen of sweat on his brow emphasized the radiant fervor that blazed from his cobalt eyes.

At the back of the gravel parking lot, I squeezed my car into the lone empty parking space that, unfortunately, was flanked by two huge pickups. Now, I wondered if I could open my door wide enough to get out. Oh, well, there was always the passenger side. I looked at the dried mud covering the entire truck and decided that wasn't an option.

The evening was mild and felt more like a balmy spring day than a January evening. I decided I didn't need my coat after all, and the extra half-inch might be the difference between being on time or missing part of the game while I looked for a parking space on a side street.

I successfully maneuvered through the narrow opening and crossed the parking lot. When I opened the double doors to the gymnasium, game noises filled the air. A woman with improbable red hair wearing a white Tiger's shirt collected the two-dollar admission. Tiny Winnie the Pooh Band-Aids were slapped haphazardly on the backs of her hands. "My granddaughter thought my age spots were owies," she said.

I stood in the doorway and searched the crowd for my son. A girls' game was in progress so I knew it would be a while before Crosby's game.

The bleachers were packed and I couldn't spot my family. I watched the game from the doorway. The Tigers versus the Tigers. The Tigers in the white uniforms were the home team and the purple Tigers were the visitors.

A referee blew his whistle, "Blue!" he shouted. *Blue?* Was he colorblind? Only a man would call *that* color blue. The game was nearly finished and the scoreboard read four to two.

I rummaged through my purse for my cell phone. Just when I decided I had left it at home, I grabbed it immediately before my purse fell off my shoulder onto the floor. I called my son, and he answered my question by standing up and waving. I walked on the bleacher seats like a high school kid and settled in next to him. A loud foghorn buzz vibrated the building signaling the end of the girls' game.

The boys' teams jogged onto the court for warm-up. Crosby, still waiting for his growing spurt, was the shortest player on the B Team. His white uniform hung loosely on his slender body. His oversized hands and feet reminded me of a puppy destined to be a big dog someday.

The buzz reverberated through the building and the A Team took the court. The B Team crowded into a designated area of the bleachers waiting their turn to play. The game began with the squeaking racket of athletic shoes pounding up and down the court and the referee's shrill whistles. The strong smell of buttered popcorn made the gym smell like a theater.

Cheerleaders assembled on both sides of the court, the home cheerleaders close to us. Our cheerleaders huddled in a group, adjusting their short skirts, blonde ponytails bouncing up and down as they talked. They ignored the game. The only cheerleader paying attention stood outside the huddle. She outweighed the others by fifteen pounds and her uniform was subtly different from the others, perhaps to accommodate her bigger size. Her dark ponytail and plain face made her look like a misfit among the popular girls.

A little girl walked around the edge of the court. Her chestnut hair was pulled back in a French braid that had loosened, and hair flew around her small pale face. She wore an oversized burgundy sweater and black and white checked pants tucked inside knee-high black boots. The boots' glossy newness indicated they had been a Christmas present. She took big steps as if she were splashing in mud puddles. She marched toward the ragged line of cheerleaders who clearly did not know what to do.

"Defense!" bravely yelled a confused cheerleader as the home team clamored down the court with the ball, passing it, passing it, passing it again until finally they threw it to a purple clad Tiger. The little girl strolled past the cheerleaders, dragging her coat, high-stepping around the court.

The game consisted of a lot of running up and down the court, dribbling and passing, but not much scoring. The referee whistled a time out and the home team cheerleaders shook their pom-poms yelling "T-I-G" and the crowd responded "E-R-S." The purple cheerleaders sat on the floor and slapped time with their hands and the visitors' section of the crowd stomped their feet to the rhythm.

The little girl zigzagged past the opposing side's benchwarmers and dropped her coat in a far corner. She passed in front of us again— her indulgent neglect set her apart from other spectators. People bustled back and forth, but she ignored the crowd, the referees, the pounding feet of the players, and the two squads of lackluster cheerleaders.

Three home cheerleaders twirled their skirts around their skinny waists. The chubby dark-haired cheerleader raised her arms as gracefully as a gymnast preparing for a floor routine. Once the floor was clear, she tumbled down the court doing a series of handsprings in tandem with a blonde cheerleader. Her skill outshone the blonde. A woman wearing a shirt with "Cassie's Mom" plastered across the back said, "She learned that at Tiffany's Dance and Cheer." I was certain that one of the two cheerleaders was named Cassie.

The little girl disappeared on the far side of the court as she detoured through the lobby. I watched the game. Finally, the home team made a basket after the ball skidded around the rim like an out of control gyroscope and plunked through the net. The cheerleaders didn't seem to notice.

The buzzer sounded for halftime, and cheerleaders bounced to the lobby for refreshments. The game resumed and the girl proceeded up the sideline in front of the bleachers. She had removed her boots and now shuffled along, bare toes sporting bright red nail polish. She stared straight ahead, oblivious to everything except her progress around the court. I seemed to be the only one fascinated with her.

My grandmother instinct was to say, "Put on your boots. Let me comb your hair. Sit by me; you don't have to be alone in this crowd." The A game ended and the cheerleaders walked off the court disdaining the time to cheer for the B team.

"I'm going to get something to eat before Crosby's game," I said. While I waited for a cold cheeseburger and a warm soda, I noticed the little girl dragging her coat, her bright toenails tucked inside the black boots. She pushed the door open and disappeared into the poorly lit parking lot. No one seemed to notice that a child had left the building.

Carrying my soda and burger, I pushed through the door, but she had been swallowed up by the night. It was a small town. *Safe. A town where a tiny girl might walk from school to home if she lived close by.* I shook my head.

I returned to the bleachers to watch Crosby's game. The coach was talking on a cell phone, obviously no more interested in the B Team game than the cheerleaders were. Six players ran onto the court but the referees and the coach did not notice. Finally, a voice boomed from the bleachers, "Six white Tigers on the court!" One of the players ran off the court, and the coach decided to end his conversation and resume coaching.

Crosby was an aggressive player and stole the ball. A player on the other team fouled him. My son and I cheered with more enthusiasm than professional cheerleaders when Crosby made both free throws. The game finished in a loss for the home team, but we heaped hugs and congratulations on Crosby.

I pulled out of the parking lot and headed for home. In the quiet moment, images of the little girl intruded on my thoughts, and I sent up silent prayers for her safe journey home.

I drove around the gentle sloping loop that skirted the town, taking the scenic route to my silent home, delaying the time when I would crawl into bed for a night of restless sleep. As I neared the railroad crossing, the arms dropped, lights flashed and the lonesome whistle blew a warning.

I drummed my fingers on the steering wheel in time to a sixties rock tune playing on the radio. Moonlight glowed on the three crosses I had effectively ignored earlier. Hollowness settled in my chest when I dredged up the memory that this tragedy occurred the same night of my husband's accident.

The train lumbered on the tracks, screeching, banging, and clanging a monotonous rhythm. Without understanding why, I grabbed my emergency flashlight and crunched through dead leaves littering the ditch to take a closer look at the crosses. The smallest cross had a picture on it. I leaned in close, adjusted my bifocals, and sucked in my breath. My flashlight illuminated the smiling face of the dark-haired cheerleader.

A breeze stirred up the dried oak leaves and chilled me. I called my son as I walked toward my car. "Who was the dark-haired cheerleader? You know, the one that did the handsprings."

"Geeze, Mom. Are you losing it? Cassie is the only one that tumbles and she's a blonde."

"Not her—the heavyset girl with her. The one with dark hair."

"Only one eighth grade cheerleader tumbles since Melissa Snow died in a car wreck near the tracks."

"There are three crosses. Who else was killed?"

"Her mom and dad."

"The whole family died?"

"Her little sister was in a coma for weeks. She was the little girl that kept walking around the court tonight."

Fiddle music drifted through the air. "Mom, are you playing Dad's CD again?"

"You know how much I love his music," I said, avoiding a direct answer. I clicked off the phone and listened as the poignant melody of my husband's signature tune echoed through the darkness. I stood beside my car, rubbing my upper arms to warm them, until the sound faded away into the sighing of the wind.

The train chugged into the night. Feeling strangely comforted, I climbed into my car and bumped over the tracks toward home.

THE DEAD IN THE WATER
JAKE COBB

COLUMBIA MISSOURI, PRESENT DAY

The man sat in the waiting room of the Harry S. Truman Veterans Hospital. He had completed an appointment and was waiting for his doctor to bring him some additional information.

As he waited, he walked to the second-story window and looked out across the parking lot. A young woman crossed the lot. She looked familiar, but he couldn't place her, his mind being preoccupied with other concerns. Still, the sight of her unconsciously jogged his memory.

He returned to his seat as his mind began to wander.

He began to recall events long past, events that may, or may not have been, related to his recent problems. As it turned out, they were, but he did not know this at the time. In fact, his problems had begun long before he was born.

~ 1 ~
ELISABETH

December 10, ninety years ago:

Jakob looked out across the swollen river. Chunks of ice floated down from somewhere upstream. He was worried about trying to cross it. His boat was solid, but he was a poor swimmer, and it was December. If his boat capsized, and he didn't drown, he could still die from the cold.

He turned his mind from the river, to troubles at the house.

Elisabeth was getting worse. He was sure that she had the flu. In November, they had made a trip to Lebanon to buy supplies for the winter. Lebanon was a long trip; however, there were people of his faith there.

He liked to see people of his own faith. They brought back a feeling of familiarity. Unfortunately, except for business transactions, he was not permitted to talk to them. He and Elisabeth were shunned from all social communication.

While in Lebanon, Elisabeth made a special request, one that Jakob reluctantly agreed to. Jakob guessed this was when she caught the sickness. Elisabeth wanted to see a motion picture, and like most things Elisabeth wanted, she got. Elisabeth thought the movie a wondrous event, although she could not read the words. Jakob could have read the words for her, but chose not to. To Jacob, the movie was a waste of thirty cents.

He was sure that's where the sickness came from. There were too many people crammed inside the theatre, like hogs in a pen; too many degenerate people. Elisabeth must have breathed their foul air and contracted their sickness.

Now Elisabeth was sick, very sick.

In Lebanon, there was medicine for this sickness called the flu. Lebanon was a long way in mid-winter. It would take two days to get there and two days to get back. He could not leave Elisabeth and the baby alone for four days, and she was too sick to make the trip. Jakob had another option. The town of Palmer was just across the river. He could go there and be back in the same day.

To get to Palmer, he would have to cross the river, the swollen, cold river, and there were other problems with this plan, problems other than the possibility of drowning. Jakob did not like the town. He had gone there before. The people were not good to him, and they did not like the way he talked. They called him a traitor.

If he was an American, they asked, why was he not in the war, fighting the Germans? Was it because he was a German himself, they accused.

"No," he said, "I am not a German." He tried to tell these people of Palmer. "I am an American. I was born in Pennsylvania."

Jakob's English was poor, and the more he talked, the more he convinced them that he was a German.

"Fighting a war is against the way of the Lord," he had said.

He tried to explain all these things, but to speak the English was awkward. He could read the English, but speaking it was a different matter.

Elisabeth could read neither English nor Deutsche. However, she was a much better speaker of the English than he was, but of course, she could not go with him, she was sick.

As Jacob recalled that day, he knew that this day would be the same, but he had to go. Despite these problems, he knew that he must take the chance. He must cross the river. He must talk to the English. Elisabeth needed the medicine.

He returned to the farmhouse and informed Elisabeth of his decision to cross the river.

Elisabeth was sick, but fully aware. She knew the dangers Jakob faced, but she did not try to stop him. To serve her was his duty and that was as it should be. It was he, who came to her home in Indiana to work for her husband. It was he, who had told her those bad things about her marriage to Peter Stevens.

"Having three wives is against God's law," he had told her. "Having three wives is against the laws of Indiana," he had said.

"You are not married in the eyes of the Lord," Jakob confided, "Nor are you married in the eyes of the State of Indiana."

She was a girl when she married, just fourteen; she didn't know the law. She had never gone to school. She only knew what her stepmother told her and her stepmother said to marry Peter Stevens.

Elisabeth had pleaded with her, "He is an old man, and he already has two wives."

"He is a wealthy man," her stepmother countered. "You will be well taken care of."

"How can I marry one who is not our kind?"

"You can marry because I have given permission," she said. Then she insisted, "You will marry Peter Stevens."

Her stepmother was unyielding. She wanted Elisabeth out of her house.

If her father had been there, things would have been different. He would not have allowed her to marry the English, but he was gone. What else could she do?

A year into the marriage, and one miscarriage later, Jakob Hess came to work at Peter Steven's farm.

As Elisabeth grew to know the handsome young Dutchman, she began to conjure a plan. Elisabeth was not without resources. She was a remarkably beautiful girl.

"You could take me away," she told him. "Take me away and make me your wife."

So he did, and they took a horse and buggy as well, Elisabeth's, she claimed. Hence, their thievery and adultery brought shame onto their people.

Back then, Elisabeth thought Jakob stupid. In fact, she thought all men stupid—stupid things to be manipulated. Jakob, it turned out, was neither as stupid, nor as easily manipulated, as she had believed.

Her plan was that they would move to the big town where they could start a new life. They would live among the English in Evansville, Indiana, and there they would make a home. That was Elisabeth's plan. What other option was there? They were shunned among their own kind.

Instead, Jakob moved them to Missouri, to Lebanon. Elisabeth decided that was fine. She liked the train ride, and Lebanon was a nice town, and as Jakob had pointed out, there were people of their own kind there.

At first, they were welcomed, but soon news of their sins followed them to Missouri. Once again, they were shunned.

That was when Jakob found this god-forsaken cattle ranch, where he could be the caretaker for the English. He traded his labor for the use of a broken down house and a pittance of a salary. They were poor, and they had no friends.

Elisabeth was worse now than before. She knew now that it was better to be the third wife of a rich man, than the only wife of a poor man.

"I hope the fool drowns," she said to herself, as Jakob left to cross the river. Instantly she regretted her wish, as she contemplated her and the baby's fate should Jakob not return.

But alas, her wayward wish was granted.

Jakob made no return from the river. Perhaps he was lucky and died quickly. Elisabeth was not so lucky, two weeks later, she ran out of food.

Delirious with starvation, and suffering from the flu, she managed to walk to the river, hoping to find help. Of course, there was no help. She sat on a log and cried.

For a while she prayed, then stopped. Eventually, she cursed God, then cursed her religion, and of course, both her husbands, but she saved most of the cursing for herself.

She could hear the baby crying all the way from the house. She had to get back. She had to get to her feet. However, she could not.

She slid off the log and into the frozen mud.

As she died, she worried about the baby.

During the following weeks, coyotes and vultures consumed her flesh. Later, the spring floods washed her bones down the Osage.

~ 2 ~
JESSE

Early summer, mid-1970s:

Jesse was driving a beautiful handmade hydroplane. The boat glistened of white and aquamarine blue, trimmed in red. The motor hummed the tune of a perfectly running two-stroke. He had the throttle only half open, and it was still scary fast. The sun was near the horizon and reflected a golden band across water that rested as smooth as glass; it seemed he was the only person on the lake. He thought that both lucky and unusual.

He noticed that he had traveled up the lake several miles. He had never been this far before. How far had he gone? He looked for a mile marker until he found one, the 70-mile marker. Gee, he must have been daydreaming. He really was a long way up the lake.

Jesse turned back toward home and opened the throttle. The small hydroplane nearly jumped out of the water. The little 12-foot boat, powered with a 40-HP motor, was a thrill to drive. Now, wide open, the boat skimmed the water at over 60-MPH. At this speed, he would be home well before dark.

Jesse marveled again at how fast the little boat was, much faster than he thought it would be; the shoreline became a blur. He came around a wide muddy point where he saw a large table-shaped rock high above the lake.

"That's Devil's chair-back," he thought, but had no idea how he knew the name of the landmark.

Suddenly, out of nowhere, he ran into a huge swarming cloud of bugs, big ugly cicadas, thousands of them. Immediately, the small boat became plastered with dead and dying cicadas. Jesse skirted the beach on the shallow side of the lake.

Jesse tried to cut the throttle, but it was unresponsive, apparently held wide open as a huge gunk of bugs clogged the throttle linkage. Jesse slapped at the bugs to clear the throttle. Then, as inexplicably as the bugs had appeared, an old wooden boat lay directly in Jesse's path. He veered violently toward the beach, barely missing the old boat.

"This can't be happening," he thought.

The hydroplane, still traveling at full throttle hit a partially submerged log and went airborne. Jesse separated from the boat as it flew through the air. Jesse and the boat, both on slightly different trajectories, cartwheeled through the air.

"This is not real," Jesse insisted.

Jesse hit the water in a downward spiral, feet first. The water was shallow with a deeply silted bottom. Jesse entered the water with such force and at an angle that he buried himself into the silt bottom.

He tried to move his arms; he couldn't. He tried to move his legs; he couldn't.

He had a feeling of the surreal. "This is a dream," he told himself.

"No it's not!" he replied to his own observation. "You've just been knocked stupid by the impact. If you don't get out of this mud, you will drown!"

He struggled violently to get free. However, the more he tried to move the more tightly he became bound.

"Think! Think. It's a dream, open your eyes, and take a look," his mind screamed.

"No, you dummy!" he screamed back. "This is real; I'm stuck in the mud!"

Jesse fought harder, but he continued drowning, sinking into a mindless blur, every part of his body was in a crushing, agonizing pain.

"Think, think, think, are you really drowning, or is this one of those seizure things? No!" Jesse screamed. "I *am* drowning, If I don't get out of this mud, I'm a goner." He fought, but to no avail.

He heard a voice; it might have been his own.

"Open your eyes Jesse, take a look."

He tried to open his eyes, but his eyelids were glued shut.

"It must be the mud!"

He tried again. His eyes opened and he could see. What was he seeing? It was an odd shape. It was part of his pillow. Beyond that, he could see the old rusty ceiling fan and the wood stove on the southeast wall of his cabin.

"Damn!" he cursed himself. "I'm having one of those miserable stinking dream-paralysis things. Damn, I hate these things. Well," he conceded, "at least I'm not drowning."

He relaxed, and that was a mistake. Immediately, he fell back under the control of the dream, which quickly morphed into something else. Now he was in an ambulance. He was very cold.

"Is this the one?" a voice asked.

"Yeah, that's the one," a second voice answered.

"What happened to the others?" voice number one asked.

"Still in the pond," voice number two replied.

"He looks normal."

"Can you believe it? He was deader than a hammer," voice number two commented.

"Wake up!" Jesse screamed to himself. "Wake up!"

Jesse slowly sat up on the edge of the bed, he felt as if he weighed a thousand pounds. His head buzzed as if it was full of bumblebees. Slowly he regained his strength and senses.

"That's what I get for taking a nap when I should be working," he thought.

He seemed to have the sleep problem either when he had too much sleep or not enough. Now, during the early days of summer, with no real job, too much sleep was the norm.

He walked to the mirror that hung above the sink. "Man," he said to the guy in the mirror, "you look like crap."

Jesse's brown curly hair stuck out in every direction. It hadn't been cut in two years. His pale blue eyes were slightly bloodshot.

"Oh well," Jesse said aloud.

He pulled himself together, went out to the porch, and settled into a rocker. There he sat, admiring the scenery. As he sat, he drank a cup of leftover coffee.

"Yes," he thought, "I like it here, at the lake, even if I am living in an old shack."

Jesse had moved into the one-room cabin at the completion of the spring semester, just a few weeks earlier. True, this was a god-forsaken place, but the cabin was his while he sat out the summer semester. And, other than taking a free vacation to Vietnam, he had nothing better to do.

When he had arrived, the cabin was in total disrepair. He was sure he had been ripped off. Since then, however, he had changed his mind. He had begun to enjoy working on the place, making it livable.

Apparently, the cabin had belonged to a man named Zimmerman. Jesse never knew the man, or his story. He didn't even know his name, until he had moved in and found some of his things. Jesse had rented the cabin, sight unseen, through an agent in Kansas City for $500.

The ad read, "Small cabin and workshop on a secluded part of the Lake of the Ozarks." It went on to say that the renter would have the use of the cabin, workshop, and a boat.

The first time Jesse read the ad, it had interested him. He had found the classified section of the paper sitting in the hallway outside his dormitory room. Someone had circled the ad in red magic marker.

He also found the same ad again, with the same red magic marker, in a newspaper at the library. When he won the money, and saw the ad again, while in the actual process of winning the money, he concluded that it meant something.

About the money, the fact that he had five hundred dollars to spare was a miracle in its own right. Was it fate or just dumb luck that the WHB radio operator called his dormitory? In addition, that he had answered the telephone at all was a stroke of luck. Generally, he was never near the telephone, but this time, he was waiting for a call and answered it. The last part was that he actually knew the answers to the questions.

"To whom am I speaking?" the man on the other end asked.

"Jesse Messenger, who is it you want to talk to?"

"You will do just fine," the man said, and continued. "This is Wild Bill, from WHB radio, World's Happiest Broadcasters, have you heard of us?"

"I've heard of WHB," Jesse answered. "Are you a salesman?"

"No, I'm a broadcaster, and you are on the air."

"Right now, I'm on the air?" Jesse asked.

"Yes, how would you like to play 'Ten Questions' with us? You could win up to five hundred bucks, if you answer all ten questions."

"You've got a player here, Wild Bill. Hit me with the questions."

"Okay Jesse, first question. In what state is Mount Rushmore located."

"South Dakota." He had just read an article in a magazine about Rushmore. "Gee that was easy," Jesse thought.

"Right! That's one for fifty dollars. Here are the next four questions, fifty dollars for each right answer. Which presidents are sculpted onto Mount Rushmore?

"Washington, Jefferson, Lincoln, and Roosevelt. Teddy Roosevelt, not Franklin."

"Jesse," Wild Bill said, "You have won two hundred and fifty dollars. Do you want to take what you have won, or continue into round two? From this point on, if you miss an answer, you win nothing," Wild Bill cautioned.

"Fire away, Wild Bill." As Jesse waited for the next round of questions, he was momentarily distracted by an ad that was tacked to the wall next to the telephone. It had been cut from the classifieds. It read, "Secluded part of the Lake of the Ozarks."

"That's strange!" he thought. "There's that same ad again."

The idea of spending the summer on the lake appealed to him. Some time ago, Jesse had spent two summers with his grandfather on the Grand Lake of the Cherokee in Oklahoma. The old man was a fisherman; he ran trotlines, nets, and traps, most of them illegal. He was a real fisherman, not one of those "fancy Dans" with the expensive boats, big lures, and life jackets.

Wild Bill came back into focus. "Okay," Wild Bill said, "questions six through nine. Name four of the five Marx brothers. And you may quit at any time, if for example, you only know two of the brothers."

"Man, how lucky can you get," Jesse said to himself. His crazy roommate was a Marx brothers' fanatic, and talked endlessly about them.

"Okay," Jesse said, "I understand. Well here goes, Groucho and Harpo of course, they're the easy ones, and Chico, that's three, and Zeppo and Gummo. You know something, Wild Bill, I believe that's all five. I believe you owe me five hundred bucks."

As it was, Jesse was right. He won the money and visited the real estate company.

Back at the cabin, Jesse arose from the rocker, and walked to the workshop across the yard. He considered his projects for the day.

A hydroplane sat on a platform of sawhorses. Jesse admired it; it was a beautiful little boat, built of plywood and fiberglass. Jesse knew from photos he had found in the cabin, that once, long ago, the old man who lived here had raced these hydroplanes. This one must have been a leftover from that era.

The lady who rented the place to him had been very specific. "Any of the equipment at the place you are renting—you can use. If there is any gas left in the fifty-gallon tank, use it up, or it will just evaporate." Therefore, he had set to work.

"Man," he thought, "I would like to see this thing run."

It was a beauty and if he could just get the motor to run, all the boat needed was some sealant and paint. The motor was a broken down forty-HP Scott. Off and on, all week, Jesse had worked on the motor. He was a decent mechanic, and thought he had the problems figured out, but was wrong. So he stopped working on it, for a while.

The other boat, the one tied to the small dock in front of the cabin, was a johnboat. It was ugly. Even worse, it was slow and ugly. However, the five-horse Johnson that powered it ran fine. It was his working boat and his main transportation.

Today, like every day since he had arrived, Jesse planned to take the johnboat out to explore the area. It was a good running boat and he was glad to have it.

Luckily, the owner, Zimmerman had left him decently prepared to navigate the lake. First, there was a fifty-gallon tank of gasoline, nearly full. Then, there was the map.

A map of the lake printed in 1935 was tacked to the cabin wall. Zimmerman had noted the exact location of his fishing lines on the map. The map served that purpose well and Jesse found those trotlines. The features of the lake, that is the geography, were the same as in 1935, but names had changed. While navigating the lake, Jesse spent most of his time trying to figure out where he was.

Jesse was amazed at how easy it was to get all these little coves mixed up; they all looked alike. The very first day he had explored the lake, he found a small waterfront store. Since then, he had been unable to locate it. The amazing thing about living on a lake was that sometimes a place that was only a mile away by land, might be twenty miles by water, or vice versa.

Jesse needed to find that store again. He had eaten fish for two weeks and had used up all the coffee. Worse of all, he had a serious craving for a Pepsi Cola. So, he went looking for the store.

In the middle of the lake, while chugging along in the johnboat, another boat came flying around a corner and passed Jesse in a flash. Jesse recognized the driver and tried to wave him down.

~ 3 ~
ROBBIE, LILITH, AND MELISSA

The young man in the other boat was Robbie Driscoll. Of the local residents, Robbie was one of the few that Jesse knew. Robbie had picked Jesse up while hitchhiking on the Falcon Point Road. That was shortly after Jesse had caught a ride with the preacher.

Jesse had chosen to hitchhike from Kansas City to the lake, and since he did not own a car, that was an easy choice.

Just south of Marseilles, while walking along Highway 105, Jesse got drenched in a downpour. Then out of the fog, coming Jesse's way, was an old hearse. It stopped.

"I hope he doesn't know something that I don't," Jesse thought as he opened the door to the hearse.

The driver, who looked a lot like Porter Waggoner, introduced himself as Seth Hopkins. He was a minister of the Gospel. Sitting beside him, was his companion, Sister Ruth. They were on their way to a revival.

 Sister Ruth slid over next to Seth, and Jesse climbed in.

"Where are you going, son," the preacher asked.

"Lake Road 13," Jesse replied. "I've never been there, but it's off Highway 105, about 15 miles south of Marseilles."

"Well I don't know exactly which one is Lake Road 13," the preacher replied. "All them side roads are scattered up and down this here road, so we will just be watching the signs till we find it."

"This is quite some car," Jesse noted.

"Yes it is," said the preacher. "It ain't no normal hearse, it's a Buick, a 1960." Bought it off an undertaker whilst preaching a funeral in Chillicothe. Best car I ever owned, it makes for a right fancy station wagon."

Like a mute, Sister Ruth, a heavyset girl with one blue and one brown eye sat silent the whole time. She might as well have been a mannequin.

Fifteen miles later, at the bottom of a long grade, the preacher eased onto the brakes, and came to a stop beside the highway.

The preacher stared down a winding dirt road. The sign said Lake Road 13. There were also several big ugly signs advertising developments.

"This here is Falcon Point Road!" the preacher declared solemnly. "Lake Road 13 is the Falcon Point Road." He said this with some concern.

"This is my stop then," Jesse replied. "I thank you for the ride."

"You shore you want off on this here road?"

"Yes sir," Jesse replied.

"God be with you then." The preacher pulled away, leaving Jesse standing on the dirt road.

Jesse walked nearly five miles down the gravel road before he saw his first vehicle. Up ahead, he heard more than saw, a brown car enter his road from a smaller side road. It swerved around onto the main road and went on ahead of him.

A few minutes later Jesse walked past the side road. There was a sign indicating that a town called Palmer could be found somewhere down the road.

Nearly a half-hour later another vehicle came along. It was a young man and a little boy in an ancient pickup truck.

The driver stopped. Jesse noticed that the truck didn't have doors, windows, or license plates, but it sure beat walking.

The driver introduced himself as Robert "you can call me Robbie" Driscoll. Jesse introduced himself. He learned that Robbie was returning from the small town down the road he had passed.

Riding in the pickup truck, and sliding over next to Robbie, was a young blond-haired boy in Big Smith overalls. The boy, with his bright green eyes, struck Jesse as odd. He stared straight ahead with a blank expression.

The driver, Robbie, put his hand on the boy's head and ruffled curly blonde hair. "Try to pretend she's not here."

Jesse realized then, that the boy was actually a girl.

"Melissa, Missy for short, she's a neighbor girl," Robbie said. "She's special, a savant, I think it's called. She won't talk, not to you anyway. Most of the time, she won't even talk to me. Don't take it personal."

Jesse explained where he was going. Robbie said that he knew the place and would take him there.

Three miles down the road, they came upon a young woman standing beside a broken down Studebaker. Jesse recognized it as the car he had seen enter the road ahead of him earlier.

"Melissa's sister," Robbie said. "Serves her right."

Robbie pulled up beside the Studebaker. The girl was redheaded and freckled. She stretched tight both her white shorts and a blue tube top, her best features emphasized by the tube top.

Oddly, an ominous impression flashed through Jesse's mind.

"Looks like your car won't run," Robbie said to the redhead.

"Well goodness gracious, it's Sherlock Holmes," she answered sarcastically.

Robbie put his truck in gear, and the truck started moving forward.

"Hey, hey, hey!" she said. "Just a joke. It appears that I ran out of gas. I can't believe my old Granny don't keep it full."

"What's the deal with Melissa?" Robbie nodded his head in the direction of his young passenger.

"What do you mean 'What's the deal?' It's just my idiot sister, that's all."

"You're a real piece of work, Lilith. How could you leave her behind?"

"I saw you in town and knew you would give her a ride." Lilith smirked. "Maybe make a woman out of her, since you missed your chance with me."

"Jesus, Lilith, she's eleven years old. If you were a guy, I swear to God, I'd kick your butt. I may anyway."

"Oh, I'd like that. How's about just a spankin'?" she said. Robbie shook his head in disbelief.

By then, Lilith, had turned her attention to Robbie's passenger. "Who's this riding with you, Robert?"

"Jesse, Jesse Messenger," Jesse said.

"Hi," she giggled. "My name is Lilith, Lilith Michaels. Did you notice, we've both got the same first and middle names. The crazy one there, between you two, is my sister. I guess, oops, I forgot and left her behind, sorry sis.

"Say, Robert," she said, "I'm real sorry and all that apologetic stuff. Now can I please have a ride home? I can just scooch in there, right between you and Mr. Jesse. Missy can ride in the back."

"I'll give you a ride, but it's you that can climb in the back. Missy can stay right where she is."

"Screw you, Driscoll," Lilith said. "If I ride in the back, then Missy rides in the back too." With that, Missy wiggled out of the seat and climbed into the back of the truck.

Later that evening, after taking the girls home, Robbie delivered Jesse to his cabin.

Back on the lake, Robbie had spotted the slow moving johnboat and recognized the young man waving at him. He pulled up next to Jesse and shut down his motor.

"Say, city boy," Robbie said, "are you lost, or what?"

"I'm not lost," Jesse said. "I can find my way home, but I can't seem to find what I am looking for."

"Almost lost then?"

"Something like that," Jesse said, then went on to explain. "There is a little store on the water around here somewhere, back in a cove. And, I need some food."

"Well for one thing, you're going the wrong way. Follow me."

Jesse turned 180 degrees and followed Robbie's boat around a bend, around another, into a big cove, then into a side cove, and there it was.

The store was called JR's Marina and Bar.

In a five-minute dissertation, Robbie revealed all that was to know about the establishment.

It was owned and operated by Junior Ryder and his wife, Irene. They were both in their fifties. Junior imagined that he looked like Bing Crosby, and that was a stretch, but that's what Junior thought. Irene was too vain to compare herself to any real person, but Robbie thought she looked like the bad witch in the Wizard of Oz.

Their store was located in the worst part of Falcon Point development. Robbie noted most people believed that any part of Falcon Point Development could not possibly be worse than any other part. There was a worse part, and this was it. As far as JR's patrons, most customers came here simply to get drunk, but the store did have a decent supply of groceries.

Robbie said he had to go check out a boat down the lake a bit, but would be back in a half-hour or so. He would like to talk with Jesse some. Maybe do some business if he would wait there at JR's dock for him. Jesse agreed.

Jesse tied his boat to the dock, and walked the rickety walkway to the store.

The store sat on pilings sunk into the mud. A floating dock that served as a bar fronted it, a sign boasted Cold Hamm's Beer.

The establishment had seen its better days and smelled of rotting mud and fish. Behind the store was a large parking lot, mostly empty. In the corner, nearest the store, and under a sycamore tree, squatted an ancient silver travel trailer. Robbie had identified it as the living quarters for the Ryders.

As Jesse entered the store, he saw a large sunburned man in a brown shirt, eating lunch at the counter. An older, skinny woman worked behind the counter. She sat in a high-back wicker chair, a Pall Mall cigarette dangled from her face.

"Hello," Jesse said as he walked to the bar. "I'm Jesse Messenger." Jesse extended his hand in turn to both the man and the woman. Both returned his handshake. "I moved into Zimmerman's cabin, about a mile down the lake."

"I'm Irene. I run the joint. This here is Red Schultz, the local game warden. Pleased to meet you."

"You any kin to Zimmerman?" Red Schultz asked.

"Nope," Jesse replied. "I rented the place from a newspaper ad in the Kansas City Star."

"He was a good one, a strange one, but a good one," Irene added. "I'm real sorry that he died."

"Went missing," Red corrected.

"Sorry, I never knew him," Jesse said, "but I'm glad he was well liked."

"I need to get some groceries," Jesse said, then walked into the store section and stocked up on essentials. He returned a few minutes later and put them on the counter. "I was wondering about the name of this place. Is there a JR?"

"Oh yeah," said Irene, blowing out smoke, and pointing her thumb in the direction of the trailer, "he's still sleeping it off."

"Oh. Do you have a cold Pepsi in your cooler there?" Jesse pointed at the rusty horizontal Coca-Cola cooler behind the bar.

"Got Coke." Irene pulled a cold bottle of Coca-Cola from the cooler.

"That'll do." Jesse set aside a box of Cheez-its, while Irene rang up his purchases.

Jesse paid his bill and took a seat at the bar next to Red Schultz and ate his lunch of Cheez-its and Coca-Cola.

"Say," Jesse asked, "do either of you know who the girl is that lives over across the lake, right across from the Palmer arm? She dresses like a Mennonite."

"Where exactly are you talking about?" asked Red.

"The other side of the lake, down about five miles."

"Huffman Bend," Red answered. "I don't think anyone lives over there."

"That whole place is deserted," Irene added. "I believe that's where Zimmerman was born though, before the lake, when it was a river."

"No Mennonites, Quakers, or people like that?" Jesse asked.

"Nope, nope, and double nope," answered Red.

"Hey," Irene said, "there are girls on this side of the lake. Come the Fourth of July, you'll be tripping over them."

Red cut in with some advice, "Huffman Bend is the most tick infested, rabid area of the whole Lake of the Ozarks, and it's private property. So, you don't need to be wandering around over there."

Irene muttered, "That's right," in agreement.

Red had observed Jesse's boat upon his arrival. "By the way," he said, "it looks to me like that boat of yours is fitted out for trotline fishing. The question is, are you fishing this summer?"

"Yeah," Jesse said.

"I mean with trotlines, like Zimmerman did?"

"Yes, and I may be hunting too. I've got both licenses, if you need to see them," Jesse answered.

"The state doesn't require a license to drink soda-pop and eat crackers," Red laughed. "Are you running with that Driscoll boy?"

"I know him. I wouldn't say I was running with him."

"How many lines do you have, anyway?" Red asked.

"What do you mean 'lines'? My understanding of the law is that I am only allowed one," Jesse answered with a grin.

Jesse paid his bill and headed for the door.

"You're right, one trotline is the law," Red reminded Jesse as the door closed behind him.

Jesse walked down to his boat, and right on cue, Robbie docked his. He checked out Robbie's boat. Compared to Jesse's relatively neat boat, Robbie's boat was a mess.

Robbie's boat was a thirteen-foot, aluminum V-bottom. Bolted to the back, for power, was a 25-horse Wizard. It was at least ten times faster than Jesse's boat. Robbie had his boat cluttered with an assortment of fishing equipment.

Jesse's first thought was that Robbie was a real fisherman.

"Is that damned old fat ass Red Schultz in there?" Robbie asked.

"Sure is," Jesse answered.

"I think he has the hots for old Irene," Robbie said.

Jesse thanked Robbie again for the ride he had been given.

Robbie noticed the fishing gear in Jesse's boat. Soon they were talking about fishing. Robbie was amazed that a slicker like Jesse knew anything at all about trotlines.

Jesse said that what he did know was Grand Lake of the Cherokee stuff, things he had learned from his grandfather. Both Jesse and Robbie guessed that Grand Lake of the Cherokee stuff was probably pretty much the same as Lake of the Ozarks stuff.

As it worked out, Robbie's prior fishing partner, his older brother Sonny, had taken a paying job. Now, Robbie could use a hand to help catch bait. And, by the way, he could also sell any fish that Jesse caught, with just a small commission, and Red Schultz could go screw himself. Was Jesse interested?

"Sure, why not," Jesse replied.

"Old JR gets some of our bait too," Robbie informed Jesse. "Old JR's got a top-notch throw net, but he's too damned old and blind to throw it. So we made a deal. I use his net and catch bait for both of us."

"So what do you want me to do?" asked Jesse.

"Well, when we see the shad schooled up, just row the boat close to them. Then, I'll throw the net. It's a piece of cake."

Robbie retrieved JR's top-notch net from a beer cooler on the dock, where it was hidden.

"Great place to hide a fifty dollar net," Robbie laughed. "Old JR's not that smart. I told him, 'What if someone steals the cooler?' But he said, get this, 'Don't care if they steal the friggin' cooler, it ain't worth nothin' nohow.' Then I said, 'but the cooler's got the net in it.' I don't think he ever figured out what I was trying to tell him. Let's go get some bait. Come on, and follow me," Robbie said as he pushed off and departed. Jesse followed.

~ 4 ~

THE QUAKER GIRL

Later that week, just before dark, Jesse worked on the hydroplane. As he rebuilt the carburetor, he thought about the girl he had seen while fishing, the mystery woman.

Jesse didn't have much luck with women. In his life, what he could recall of it, he had serious relationships with only two girls. With both, he felt as if he had been shot in the stomach. The first desperately wanted to be engaged and was willing to lie, cheat, and connive to attain that status; the second, ironically, already was.

Between his two serious relationships, the girl who wanted to be and the one who turned out to be, Jesse had a string of short term, casual girl-companions. After this latest fiasco, the one with Camille, he felt burned and swore to avoid women. However, as many can attest, that is a difficult task.

Now he had seen this girl across the lake, and she was intriguing.

When he first saw her, he was in his boat, repairing Zimmerman's lines. Zimmerman had three lines, two more than the state of Missouri, or old "fat ass" Red Schultz allowed. All of the lines were in various stages of disrepair, having been in the water unattended for an undetermined amount of time.

Jesse swore that when he left the lake, at the end of the summer, he would bring the lines in, because leaving trotlines in the water unattended was a hazard to both the fish and the line. On this particular line, the one off the point at the end of Huffman Bend, Jesse was replacing rusty hooks. He had been working for nearly half an hour when he spotted her. It was as if she had appeared out of nowhere.

She was on the flats at the end of the point, about two hundred feet away. Jesse stood in his boat and watched her. She walked along the beach, moving closer to Jesse, then stepped up onto a huge driftwood log.

He could see her clearly. She was standing there, looking out across the water. She was beautiful, dressed in dark, old-style clothing. She appeared as if she had just stepped out of a 1920s movie. She wore a strange little cap, like a Quaker cap, but not quite. As she gazed out over the water, she removed her cap to reveal her hair clearly pinned in a bun. She unpinned her hair and shook it out. Her hair fell nearly to her waist and was dark reddish brown. She turned and looked directly at Jesse, for what seemed like an eternity.

Jesse found this fascinating. Why was she doing this? Was it for him? Or, was she simply tired of her hair being up? Did she even see him?

Then, just as quickly as she had appeared, she jumped off the log, turned, and disappeared. Jesse dropped the trotline into the water, his boat drifted slowly out into the lake. Where had she gone?

Then he saw her again, she was already nearly a eighth of a mile away, and going away quickly. She was walking up the ridge that ran parallel to the lake. He wanted to catch her, but if he did, what would he say? Should he beach the boat and chase after her? No, she would think he was a nutcase.

He lost sight of her, then he saw her again, she was even farther up on the ridge. She was walking with purpose. Jesse used his oars to coast along the bank below the ridge. Occasionally, he caught a glimpse of her as she walked through the trees. Then she was gone.

Jesse awoke at five a.m. with a headache. He assessed his headache and decided he needed to eat breakfast. Hunger, he concluded, was why he had the headache. Despite his hunger and headaches, he did like living on the lake. As he thought about it, the bachelor life was probably the best choice for him. Still, he wondered, how would it have been if he and Camille had made a go of it?

Bachelor life had its advantages. It was simple. There was nothing complicated about living on the lake. He didn't have to go to work, he didn't have to go to school, and all he had to do was make enough money to feed himself, which reminded him again that he was hungry. He knew he would have a decent breakfast this morning, because he had been invited to eat with Robbie Driscoll's family.

At daylight, he was out on the lake running his lines for the early morning check. He took off three fish and re-baited with cut perch. He met Robbie at a pre-arranged meeting place.

At the end of a cove, Jesse found Robbie waiting in his truck. From there, they drove a couple of miles, over the hills, to the Driscoll farm.

The Driscolls lived in a hollow where they raised hogs, cows, and chickens. The family men were also commercial fishermen, which would have been an honorable occupation if not for being illegal. Theirs was a typical Ozarks farm, an old house, a large barn, and several outbuildings.

When they arrived, Ma Driscoll was setting up breakfast. Robbie introduced Jesse to the family. The family was comprised of Robbie's older brother Sonny, who was pleased to meet him, Pop Driscoll, who didn't say much, and an uncle, who was Ma Driscoll's mother's brother, Jack McDoogle.

Ma Driscoll was delighted to see Jesse, and asked him a multitude of questions.

After breakfast, Pop and Sonny Driscoll left for work.

Mother Driscoll, Uncle Jack, and the boys visited for a while. Ma Driscoll talked about the Driscoll family and her parents' family, the McDoogles. As they talked, Uncle Jack sat and shook his head in agreement with anything that Ma said.

According to Ma, the Driscolls and McDoogles had lived on the Osage since it was homesteaded in the early 1800s, sometimes living upriver, sometimes down-river, but always on the river. Ma Driscoll spoke of the Osage as if it was still there, spinning along somewhere down under the lake.

The men had always been fishermen. Five generations had fished the Osage, then the Lake of the Ozarks. Unfortunately, somewhere between the third and fourth generations, commercial fishing had become illegal. The Driscoll's had kept fishing just the same, taking their chances with the law.

According to Uncle Jack, "All we done was catch fish and sell to people who weren't smart enough to catch their own."

Jack conceded that catching fish to sell was a dying business. Catfish farms were selling fish cheaper every day. "It's getting to the point that a good honest poacher can't make a living no more."

In fact, as they all pointed out, Pop Driscoll, and now Sonny, had totally quit fishing to work construction. However, Robbie still practiced the craft.

During the conversations, Jesse learned that the Driscoll's had known Zechariah Zimmerman, Jesse was curious as to how Zimmerman had died.

Jack McDoogle said something interesting, or strange, depending on a person's point of view. "Don't necessarily know that he did die. He just disappeared. People assumed that he fell in the lake and drowned and that could be. His boat, the johnboat you are using now, was found adrift."

"Where is your family?" Ma Driscoll asked.

"My father died when I was young. He was killed in the Korean War. My mother and sister died in an auto accident three years ago. I lived with my grandfather until he died last year. Now, I'm pretty much on my own."

Jesse realized that he had given Ma Driscoll more personal information than he generally gave out. Jesse knew that he simply could not answer most of the questions people asked him; therefore, his general mode was avoidance.

Jesse changed the subject by asking a question about the girl he had seen on the other side of the lake.

Ma Driscoll seemed interested but offered no explanations.

Later that day, as Jesse ran his trotlines, he thought about the life the Driscoll family lived. Then, a thought crossed his mind. In another life and time, he would have been content just to be a farmer.

~ 5 ~
THE FARM

Jesse dreamed of faraway places and of a different time.

He awoke with a start. Most of his dreams, he could not remember, but this one he could recall.

In the dream, he was sitting in a college class. The man conducting the class was Professor Messenger. Jesse wondered, was he a relative, or was the name just a coincidence?

The professor seemed to be intelligent, but Jesse guessed that this man might be a nut case. For example, look at this class. What kind of professor teaches classes on such a ridiculous subject? The occult and ghosts—all that supernatural bunk.

Jesse sat at the back of the classroom, intentionally avoiding contact with others in attendance. He had a notebook for notes, on which he drew pictures.

On his right side sat his former girlfriend, Camille. For some reason, that's exactly where he expected her to be. Camille ignored him, as if he didn't exist.

The other girl came as a total surprise. He had not noticed her enter the room, or take a seat. It's as if she had just materialized out of thin air.

She sat in the seat to Jesse's left. She never said a word, but smiled sweetly at him. For reasons, unexplainable, Jesse was immediately both attracted and alarmed by her. "Strange," he thought, "she's not my type." Amazingly, Camille ignored both of them, but then, she was like that.

Jesse's first impression was that the new girl was beautifully understated, and dressed in what could be described as "upscale Amish."

Professor Messenger droned on. Inexplicably, Jesse became distracted from the girl and focused on the Professor's words. The professor described a bizarre neo-religion theory as to what happens to the spirit when a person dies.

"When the body dies," the professor said, "the spirit separates from the body. It floats like a piece of paper above the ground, sometimes moving across the earth. The spirit exists in two dimensions. It is not composed of matter, as we know it; therefore, it remains invisible and undetectable on earth.

"A computer-like device, let's call it a mechanism of God, sweeps the surface of the earth collecting spirits for recycling. It covers the entire surface of the earth every forty-eight hours.

"The two-dimensional spirits float parallel to the surface of the earth. This is natural and is necessary for the collecting device to detect and collect spirits.

"Occasionally, for various reasons, a spirit becomes flipped into the vertical. When a spirit is vertical, the collecting device cannot detect it, and therefore misses it. The result is, that spirit is left behind.

"A vertical spirit, the ones missed and left behind, exists out of their natural orbit. These spirits become marginally interactive with the natural world. This is what we know as a ghost.

"In order for a spirit to move onward, it must be turned from the vertical to the horizontal.

"If a human can concentrate hard enough, they can mentally penetrate this dimension and correct an errant spirit."

The upscale Amish girl stood and interrupted the professor. She was visibly angered. Although her English was slightly broken, her question was easily understood. "Are you one of those?" she demanded. "One of those that does this thing. This thing that is none of their business."

Jesse and the professor answered with one voice.

"Yes!" they both said.

"Gee," Jesse thought, as he awoke with a splitting headache, "that was a strange one." He shook his head; the details of the dream that were so clear just moments earlier, had quickly faded.

"Lizzie," Jessie called, as he sat up on the edge of the bed.

"In the kitchen," she yelled back.

Jesse dressed and walked into the kitchen. Lizzie was fixing breakfast. Jesse assessed his wife, she wore a simple cotton dress and apron, and she was barefoot. She was a beautiful woman.

"I just had another of those dreams," he said. "You were in it. Well I think it was you, but I don't know if it was really you, there were other people."

"My husband does have the strangest of dreams," Lizzie said. "In this dream, were you living again in that little house?"

"No," he said, then reconsidered. "Come to think of it, I was in that little house again, earlier in the dream."

Jesse sat down at the kitchen table. As he sat there, he examined his work-hardened farmer's hands. In a sudden flash of memory, he could see them tying hooks onto a line.

"It seems like I was a fisherman."

Lizzie walked behind him and massaged his shoulders. "What is it you want to do today?" she asked.

"I would like to go for a ride around the property," he replied.

After breakfast, Jesse walked around the farmhouse trying again to familiarize himself with his surroundings. This routine, he had to do daily. All that he could recall were recent events, just the last couple of weeks it seemed. It was difficult at times, but Lizzie was always there to help. What would he have done without her?

He knew he had a memory problem. Lizzie had explained that the accident had nearly killed him. The accident, she said, was how he had lost his memory.

He went to the barn and saddled the horses, at least he could still remember how to do that. Just last week, it seemed he couldn't even ride—or was that yesterday? He recalled Lizzie showing him how to saddle the horses and teaching him to ride. No, that was last week, or was it last month? He knew that it was in the summer, but it seemed to him, all his memories were in the summer.

Of course, there must have been a winter, because that's when he went through the ice. That's when he had his accident. Occasionally, in a dream, he could recall going through the ice, but he just could not remember anything else from before. Oh well, best get the horses ready.

Jesse brought the horses around to the front of the old frame farmhouse and tied them to the rail. The house was old, it needed repair, and he would have to work on it.

How was it they had come to live here? He tried to remember what Lizzie had told him. Was this her parent's house? Is this where she was raised? How did they get here, where did he come from, how did he meet her? He would have to ask her, but he asked her so many questions, apparently the same questions that he had already asked so many times before. Then he would forget again. Lizzie was tired of his constant questioning.

"Lizzie," he yelled into the house, "I'm ready to go!"

"Okay," she answered, "I will be right out."

Although Jesse's memory was faulty, he did know that Lizzie had been sick. As he recovered from his accident, he knew that Lizzie had fought off the flu. He was not sure that she had fully recovered.

"Lizzie," he said, as she came out of the house. "You really don't need to go with me, if you're still sick."

"I will be fine," she stated.

They rode up the west ridge trail for nearly a mile. They stopped high on an overlook. The view was beautiful, and below they could see the river. Lizzie said it was the Osage.

Jesse could see a few houses on the other side of the river, but theirs seemed to be the only place on this side of the river. "It must be a big farm," he thought.

Jesse dismounted his horse and walked along beside him. Lizzie did the same.

"Lizzie, did we ever have a car?" he asked.

"Of course not," she replied. "Those things are the devil's contrivance."

Jesse made a mental note, "I guess there is not a road here good enough for a car anyway."

"We have always lived as God intended. Cars and electricity are the crutches of sinners."

"Lizzie, did I ever see a doctor?" Jesse asked.

"No," she said, "I prayed endlessly for your deliverance; you were gone. The Lord brought you back to me. Doctors are useless."

Lizzie stopped walking, and started to cry softly. "The baby died," she said. "Doctors couldn't save the baby." Lizzie continued to cry. "Husband, please, can you not just be content to be here with me?"

"Yes, I am content, and I am sorry that I made you cry." Jesse mounted his horse and pointed it toward a small valley leading away from the river.

"Let's ride down through that bottom to the south," he suggested.

"Dat vould be fine," Lizzie answered. Jesse wondered where the Deutsche accent came from, but said nothing. They rode on, after a few minutes Jesse ventured another question. "Just one more question."

"Yes, husband."

"Just how big is this farm anyway?"

"It is big," she said. "Very big."

"Do we have cattle?"

"If you want cattle, we have cattle."

"I want cattle."

"Do you want a lot of cattle, or just a few cattles?" she asked.

"I want a lot of cattle."

"That is a good choice, husband," she replied with a smile, "because on this ride today, you are going to see very many cattles. Your cattles."

~ 6 ~
A COUPLE OF SÉANCES

Jesse sat on his porch rocking in his chair. He was waiting for Robbie and Sonny Driscoll to arrive. He was going with them to an Independence Day celebration at a little town a few miles away. Jesse had never been there, since he could only travel to those places easily accessible by boat, and this place was not. Therefore, he looked forward to the opportunity to go.

It was nearly dark and had been raining for hours when the Driscoll boys arrived to pick him up.

Sonny, Robbie, and Jesse rode crammed into the cab of Robbie's pickup. They splashed through the mudholes and ruts that laced the dirt roads to the small town of Palmer, as they headed to the annual Independence Day party.

"Do you think anyone will be there?" Jesse asked, as Robbie slid the truck around a muddy corner.

"Why wouldn't people be there?" Robbie asked. Robbie was the talkative one. He was a dark-haired version of his older brother, Sonny. Both boys were considered good-looking young men.

"Well, because of this crappy weather," Jesse stated the obvious.

"No," Robbie answered, "we drive in this crap all the time. Besides, there ain't nothin else going on."

"That's for sure," thought Jesse. This whole place had been like a ghost town since he had arrived. Robbie had assured him that the pace would pick up again as the Fourth of July approached. Jesse was yet to be convinced.

"Hey, did you hear the news?" Robbie spurted out with glee. "That old shit head, Red Shultz is being transferred out, to some lake down south."

"I wouldn't be so happy," Sonny said. "No tellin' who they may replace him with. By the way," Sonny said to Jesse, "we were asked not to bring you along."

"Really?" asked Jesse. "Who would do that?"

"Lilith. For some reason, she thinks you're bad for her mojo."

"Bad for her mojo?"

"Yes, bad for her mojo. That's what she said."

"She learned all about you, and your effect upon her mojo, by conferring with her Ouija board." Robbie laughed

"Yes sir," Sonny said. "She thinks you're a regular boogeyman."

Jesse recalled that first day hitchhiking and laughed. "I think that was funny when you made Lilith ride in the back of your truck.

"What? You made her ride in the back of your truck!" Sonny laughed. "What the heck is wrong with you? You know," he added, giving Jesse a slight, all knowing, elbow to the ribs, "that girl should be giving him rides, not the other way around."

Robbie was a little peeved, then ignoring his brother, he said to Jesse, "My big brother is a gutter-minded hillbilly."

"Yes sir," Sonny piped in, "and damn proud of it."

"Lilith is just a little too weird," Robbie said as Sonny passed Jesse a can of Old Milwaukee.

"Yes weird," Sonny said. "A weird little honey, built like a brick outhouse, and hot to trot."

"How about I fix you up with her, big brother?" Robbie asked.

"Hey, I'd take her in a minute, but she's a little too young for me. Besides, it ain't me she likes."

Sonny spoke to Jesse, "In case you ain't figured it out yet, Robbie here has the chicks crawling all over him. But he's too goody-goody to take advantage of his assets."

"That girl is the devil," Robbie mumbled.

Like Robbie, Jessie had no desire to associate with Lilith Michaels. He had run across her a few times since he had met her. At first, she was semi-cordial, lately though, her mood had turned nasty.

For one thing, Lilith liked to mess around with Ouija boards, and Jesse had learned to be wary of those things.

He recalled attending a party when he was in college. It was a couple of weeks before Psycho had gone crazy, back in the good old days, when Jesse was dating Ms. Camille Guerin.

Jesse had escorted Camille to a fundraising bazaar at the Sigma Kappa Sorority house on campus. It was the annual Halloween Bazaar. It was a chaotic scene where several events were underway simultaneously, one of which was a séance.

Upon arrival, Camille commented, "It looks to me like a few people here are stoned out of their minds."

Jesse replied, "We won't stay long."

Soon, they ran into Psycho, who was definitely impaired. Psycho grabbed Jesse's arm. "Come on, you gotta check out this séance!"

Jesse and Camille followed Psycho to the gathering. The "medium" conducting the séance was a young woman named Sarah, whom Jesse knew, though not well. Sarah had a partner who assisted her with the Ouija board pointer. They placed their fingers on the pointer and began.

Camille, who had never witnessed a séance, was sincerely unimpressed. "This is absurd," she said.

Despite Camille's skepticism, sure enough, Sarah made connections with the dead. She had contacted a mischievous, foul-mouthed spirit.

Camille soon grew bored. "This is a lot of idiotic bullshit."

"Of course it is," Jesse agreed.

"Let's see what else this joint has to offer."

She and Jesse left the séance and migrated to the second floor of the sorority house. There a Bingo game had been scheduled; however, poker had prevailed, which was more to Camille's taste.

Meanwhile, back at the séance, the spirit turned nasty as it began terrorizing the attendees. The attendees were primarily a captive audience of Sigma Kappa hopefuls, who were afraid to be afraid.

Psycho, attending the séance by choice, and a self-proclaimed expert on the occult, deduced that the séance had gotten out of hand, and the errant spirit must be dealt with. Psycho knew just the man to do it. Jesse Messenger.

Jesse was a local legend in the small circle of the occult. Jesse had "the gift." His possession of the gift was odd, because Jesse did not believe the occult was real. He rationalized it as subconscious manipulations. He did, at one time, think it entertaining.

For others, Jesse's gift was more than entertainment. Psycho, for one, thought that Jesse was chosen.

Of course, Psycho was called Psycho for a reason.

Psycho found Jesse and Camille sitting at a card table. Camille was playing poker and winning. Upon arrival, Psycho appeared agitated, excited, and impatient, all of which, was "normal Psycho" behavior.

Psycho leaned over and spoke into Jesse's ear. "Come on," Psycho said, "that Sarah bitch has stirred up a real honest to God hellbender. You need to come downstairs and send that thing to hell."

"Look, Psycho," Jesse said, "I'm with Camille. Can't you take care of this?"

"You know, sometimes, these things scare me to death. Come on, you can take care of this. It would be easy for you." Psycho stopped and shuddered slightly.

"Psycho," Camille said, as she checked her cards, "what is your real name anyway?"

Psycho stood for a moment, as if she had forgotten her real name. "Jane Sikorski," she said.

"Jane," Camille said, "can you give me a minute with Jesse."

The tall, skinny girl with a chronic sniff backed off several feet. She stood there, looking out of place in her army surplus jacket. Jane, putting on a show of agitation, stood impatiently shifting her weight from one foot to the other.

"Is that girl in love with you, or what?" Camille asked.

"Not quite," Jesse answered. "More likely, she would be in love with you, if you get my drift."

"Well then, for God's sake, go get rid of that boogeyman for her."

Jesse returned with Psycho to the séance. At the séance, Sarah's collection of future Sigma Kappa's seemed just a little spooked.

Jesse asked what was going on.

Sarah explained how they were having fun asking the spirit about boyfriends, ball games, and fun stuff like that. Then the spirit started with the creepy stuff, like dying, and being killed or mutilated, and other disgusting things. It had just ruined her séance.

"Now," she said, "we are all kind of spooked."

"Who did the spirit say it was?"

"Martin!" Sarah said.

"Call Martin up for me, will you?"

"No," she said, "I've had enough of him!"

"Do it!" Jesse demanded.

Sarah and her partner operated the Ouija board, asking for the spirit Martin. Soon they had a response. "Got him," Sarah said.

Psycho stood there smiling, and then said to no one in particular, "Just watch this!"

Jesse put his hand on Sarah's shoulder.

"Hello, Martin," Jesse said aloud, "let me introduce myself." Jesse closed his eyes and stood in silence. He appeared to be in a trance. After about thirty seconds, he opened his eyes. "He's gone, but just to be sure, try to call him back."

They tried, but could not.

"Jesse killed that mother!" Psycho stated.

Before leaving the room, Jessie offered some general advice. "You all should just leave this stuff alone."

As they rode along, Jesse recalled a week earlier, when he had attended an event with the Driscoll boys. The beach party. Actually, it wasn't much of a beach, just a dried up gravel bed in the back of a cove. They had ignited a gigantic pile of driftwood and drank beer.

Soon various denizens of the area started arriving.

One of the McDoogle boys brought a half-gallon of moonshine, which had the potency to intoxicate at least two dozen grown men. Soon another showed up with another jug of shine.

"Damned hillbillies," Robbie said. "I wouldn't drink that crap if I were you. I used to drink it, but not since I saw it being made."

"So," Jesse asked, "McDoogles are hillbillies, but Driscolls are not?"

"No. Let me explain. Driscolls, we are hillbillies. I ain't trying to deny that, but the McDoogles, by-golly, they are really hillbillies."

"Can you clarify that just a little?"

"What I mean to say is this—we Driscolls are hillbillies, that is true, and proud to be, but the McDoogles, by-golly, they are real hillbillies. I mean, dirt floor hillbillies."

"Thanks for the explanation."

"Say," Robbie said, "do you know the difference between a good hillbilly and a bad hillbilly?"

"No, what's the difference."

"Well, if you piss off a good hillbilly, he will wait till you are out of your house before he burns it."

Jesse's mind drifted back to the memories he had visited earlier that evening. Back then, when he attended college, especially before he hooked up with Camille, Jessie thought messing with the occult was fun, cheap entertainment. Jesse, and a few of his friends, especially Psycho, made the rounds.

However, last winter, Psycho went off the deep end and had a nervous breakdown. She was carted off to the loony bin never to be seen again. Since then, Jesse had quit the occult. He decided that the dead, were best left alone.

It was past dark, when Jesse and the Driscolls arrived at the Independence Day party. The place was hopping. The party had the look of a circus, literally. Three large tents were pitched down the center of the main road. The tents even looked like circus tents and may have been at one time.

Various degrees of entertainment and drunken pandemonium were simultaneously evolving. Jesse was astounded; he had never known these things took place, way down here in the sticks. There must have been a hundred people gathered: drinking, smoking dope, thumping on guitars. They ranged in age from senior citizens to pre-school children. It was festive chaos. Furthermore, there was not a cop within twenty miles.

As they walked through the crowd, Jesse caught sight of Lilith. She was dressed as a fortune-teller, or a belly dancer, or maybe as a fortune telling belly dancer. As Jesse had suspected, she had brought an Ouija board and had gathered a group of followers, possibly inspired by a liberal doping of marijuana.

Robbie and Jesse slid by Lilith's séance, unseen. Another tent served as the musical nerd tent. A small band of country jammers who were aggressively massacring Elvis songs occupied the tent. Jesse lingered, borrowed a guitar, and joined the massacre. Robbie moved on.

When the guitar players moved on to massacre Hank and ET, Jesse migrated down to the town's lakeside pier. He stood and looked out across the lake at the reflection of the moon across the water. He wished Camille were here with him. He wondered what she was doing. He wondered what was across the lake, on the other side.

For some oddball reason, he had developed an urge to check in on the séance. He walked back into the crowd, blending into the fringes of the circle surrounding the séance. He sat down next to Melissa Michaels.

"Hello Melissa," Jesse said.

"They don't like you," she said. These were the first words Melissa had ever spoken to Jesse.

"Who doesn't like me?"

"Them." She pointed toward Lilith and the girl working the Ouija board with her.

"Oh, well." Jesse didn't care if Lilith and her friend liked him or not. They were not who Melissa meant, but she said no more.

Meanwhile, Jesse eavesdropped on the conversation of two boys sitting next to him.

"She's moving it," one said.

"It's all fake," the other agreed.

Lilith threw up her hands in frustration. "It's gone," she said. "You nonbelievers caused it to go."

Then she noticed that Jesse was sitting next to her sister.

"Or some other *thing* scared it away."

She went back to work with the Ouija board. "Is there a spirit here that wants to talk to me?" she asked aloud. The board remained mute.

Repeatedly, she tried. With each attempt and failure, people got up and left the séance. This was devastating for Lilith, who cherished being the center of attention. However, she had an ace in the hole, a surefire way to call spirits, and she used it.

"Melissa, you get over here and work this pointer with me."

Obediently, Melissa moved to sit with Lilith at the table. Melissa took the pointer, and it started floating over the board. Soon they contacted a spirit.

"It's a girl," Lilith said. "Anyway, that's what it claims, but these spirits, they lie, so you can't really tell. It might be a dirty old man."

Lilith asked the spirit some typical chitchat questions. She noticed, to her approval, that she had now gathered a bigger crowd.

Soon however, the spirit had a request. She, the spirit, started making messages to the effect that she wanted to communicate with a boy.

There were several young men available at the séance, so Lilith found one to join her at the Ouija board. Melissa, her task complete, went back to sit with Jesse.

The spirit apparently did not like Lilith's choice in men. It said he was stupid, to bring another one. This was hilarious. Lilith played it up, everyone laughed.

Lilith found a different young man. The spirit said the boy was a spoiled little fool. "Get another one."

Lilith and her followers thought this was a riot, and it was getting better. The laughter drew in more spectators.

The next guy, was little Billy Smith, from the good part of Falcon

Point, as if there were a good part. The spirit refused to acknowledge him.

She, the spirit, asked for the "other one."

By then, the séance had evolved from funny, to creepy. None of the guys wanted to take Billy's place at the Ouija board, so Lilith left him there. He just sat there, grinning at her like an idiot.

"There is no other one," Lilith stated.

"LIAR!" it said.

"I want to talk to a different spirit!" Lilith said aloud.

"NO!" the pointer nearly exploded, pointing at the "NO."

"THE OTHER ONE. NOW!" The board spelled out the words with violent movements of the pointer.

Jesse felt his skin start to tingle and his head throbbed. He knew for whom the spirit was asking.

Just then, Lilith vomited. Billy Smith started to cry hysterically, but he could not let go of the pointer.

"NOW! NOW! NOW!" It spelled out. Then it stopped, and very slowly, it spelled out: "I AM WAITING."

"Enough of this!" Jesse said as he stood and walked over to Lilith and Billy. He pulled the board from their grasp. Jesse's arm felt as if he had encountered an electrical shock as he grabbed the board, but he held tight.

He took the Ouija board and walked away, leaving the group behind. Only Melissa followed. They walked to the end of the pier overlooking the lake. Then, like a giant Frisbee, Jesse sailed the board out into the darkness.

~ 7 ~

QUESTIONS?

Jesse dreamed of a party with many people. He awoke with a splitting headache.

Jesse had so many questions he wanted answered. However, Lizzie was difficult. She sidestepped or ignored most of his questions, even simple questions like these.

Where do we get our food?

How long have we been married?

Where are my parents and family?

What religion are we?

What year is it?

Then of course, there was the taboo question, the one that he had asked Lizzie once. It had put her in a foul mood for the rest of the day.

It started with a simple question. "Lizzie, do we ever have company?"

"Of course not," she stated. "We have been shunned, husband. We are not allowed company."

"What did we do to be shunned?"

"We cannot speak of this," Lizzie replied. "Do not ever ask again!"

What was the motive for withholding information? He was growing suspicious of his own wife, surely, that must be a sin.

In all things, except Jesse's questions, Lizzie seemed sincere and genuine. Jesse was convinced that she loved him. He justified her avoidance of his questions in that she must be shielding him from something. Perhaps, he was not ready for things that she thought.

While Lizzie fixed breakfast, he walked around the farm taking his morning inventory. The horses, chickens, and cattle seemed healthy. However, he noticed something new.

"Lizzie," he asked, upon his return, "who painted the house? Yesterday, the house looked old and needed painting. Now it looks great."

"Husband, your memory does this to you," Lizzie explained. "The house was painted last summer. Yesterday, the house was just as it is now."

Jesse ate his breakfast without further comment about the house. He did compliment Lizzie on the quality of her breakfast: bacon, eggs, biscuits, and gravy. Lizzie was an accomplished cook.

He thought about his wife. Lizzie was exceptionally beautiful, almost movie star material. Then a question crossed his mind. What is a movie star? How did that definition even get into his head?

Oh well, she was a wonderful cook, and so very good to her

husband. It was unreasonable that he should have these doubts, but he did. Sometimes he felt as if he did not even know her.

Then there was the lovemaking. Shouldn't a man and woman who have been married for many years feel familiar with each other, even if he had a memory problem? Why then, did he feel, as though it was illicit, as if she was a stranger? Why did he feel, afterwards, as if he had sinned?

Jesse couldn't overcome those nagging feelings that something was wrong. He put those thoughts aside and made plans for the day.

"Let's ride the south ridge," Jesse suggested, as they finished breakfast.

"As you wish, my husband," Lizzie responded.

So they rode the south ridge. After some distance, they could see a small village across the river. It was up a creek bottom, nearly a half-mile from the river itself.

The village was too far away to see anything specific, other than a dirt road going up a hill. The road looked like a red string wiggling up the hillside. The houses were tiny specks, too distant to see any detail.

Still, Jesse knew, this was a place where other people lived, unlike this side of the river, where apparently, only he and Lizzie lived.

"What is that town," Jesse asked.

"I do not know what that town is called," Lizzie replied. Then she added, as an afterthought, or perhaps an explanation as to her ignorance of its name, "It is on the other side of the river."

Jesse and Lizzie rode down and around the south ridge, on their side of the river. It was a beautiful property. His creeks were clean, his pastures cleared, the trees grew tall, and even his house was painted. To top it all off, it was a warm summer day and Jesse rode a splendid horse. All of this, while enjoying the company of a beautiful, considerate woman. A thought crossed his mind. "Did I die under the ice? Is this heaven? Now that was a stupid thought," he said to himself. He felt more alive now than he could ever recall.

"Now *that* was also a stupid thought," he reconsidered. "If I can't remember anything else, how could I tell the difference?" He concluded that he could not, but that he would not worry about it.

"Accept it as it is," he told himself. The fear that this whole place was not right still nagged at him.

They returned home. Jesse put away the horses.

Lizzie sat in a rocker on the porch knitting. During their ride, Jesse had noticed that Lizzie had been coughing all day. Now as they both went inside, he thought she looked sick, very sick.

"Lizzie, you don't look like you're doing so well."

"No, no, I vill be fine," she said.

"Lizzie, what happened to the baby? Why did it die?"

"A baby?" she said. "What makes you think there was a baby?"

"I thought," he said, then stopped. He was going to say, "Because you said so," but he thought better of it.

"Lizzie," he asked instead, "do we have a boat?"

"Yes," she said, "a fine rowing boat. Down by the river, it's tied to a tree."

"I think I'll row across the river to that little town. Maybe I can get some medicine for your sickness?"

"If you brought back medicine, does that mean that I would take it!" she snapped.

He wanted to row across the river. He felt he needed to get to the other side; he had to get medicine.

Jesse's mind raced. "Lizzie needs medicine. The flu had killed so many people. She has the flu. I know she has the flu."

She spoke softly, "It is better to stay here on this side of the river, husband." Lizzie sounded fearful. "This I tell you for your own safety. You, of course, cannot remember, but those people are not of our kind. They will treat you most cruel if they find you on their side of the river."

"Well," Jesse said, "I will look the boat over to see if it still floats."

"My husband must make up his own mind," Lizzie said. "It is not a wife's place to tell her husband what he can, or cannot do."

Jesse had already made up his mind. He would find the boat and get it ready. If Lizzie did not get better by tomorrow, he would row across the river. He would see for himself just what type of people these were, those that were on the other side of the river.

Surely, those people across the river would not deny him medicine for a sick wife.

~ 8 ~
LETTERS

The little girl stood knocking at his door; it was Melissa Michaels. She had a letter in her hand. Tonight, like the first time he saw her, she was wearing Big Smith overalls.

He noted that actually she was a pretty girl. He had also heard stories about her, that she had a photographic memory. Apparently, she knew everything that was in the *1962 World Book Encyclopedias* that were in her grandmother's house. She also had memorized *Webster's Dictionary* and the *King James Version of the Holy Bible*.

Although she had never said so, and would never say so, Missy liked Jesse. She liked him a lot, although it wasn't the way that she liked Robbie; Robbie made her tingle all over. With Jesse, it was different, he was like a big brother, and like her, he had a gift.

"This came to my grandmother's house, by mistake," she said. "It's from your guardian."

Melissa stood there for a minute, still holding the letter; then she began speaking again. "I think you need a guardian. I'm a guardian, you know, but I'm just not *your* guardian. I can help, but you really need your own guardian."

"Thanks Melissa," Jesse said. "Can I get you anything, a drink of water?"

"Nope. I'm good." She turned away and walked down the road.

As she left, Jesse wondered why she would think the letter was from his "guardian."

"Oh, there's the reason," he said to himself, as he turned the letter over. It had been sent in a "Guardian" envelope.

He didn't know that he could receive mail down here. What was his mailing address anyway? He sat on his porch and looked at the return address.

He wasn't anxious to read this one; it had to be bad news.

Jesse set the letter aside. He pondered the story Mrs. Driscoll had told him the last time he visited the Driscoll house. She did know something of a girl who lived across the lake, of a girl who dressed like a Quaker. She had heard it from her Great Uncle William McDoogle. Old Blind Bill, as most people called him. He had been dead many years now, but he used to tell a story that left many people thinking he was crazy.

He claimed to know a couple who lived across the lake many years ago, when he was a young man, back when he had his sight. Germans, he called them. He said the woman could speak decent English, but the man was hard to understand.

Bill sold them supplies occasionally. He would bring things over from Palmer. He said the couple would not go into town. The wife was a real looker, according to John, and somewhat of a flirt.

They both disappeared one winter. Probably just left, but rumors began to spread that something bad had happened. During the following years, several people claimed to have seen the woman in the woods. Some say she never left, that her husband deserted her, and then, she just hid in the woods.

A strange thing, some say they left a baby. The baby was found alive, nearly starved. It was taken in and raised by a German family in Cole Camp.

Years later, after he lost his sight, he claimed that while sitting by the lake, a woman approached him. The woman held his hand and spoke to him with a slight German accent. He said he couldn't prove it, but he knew that it was the same woman to whom he had delivered supplies years before.

"It smelled like her," he said.

"I suspect Old Blind Bill was near senile by then," Ma Driscoll said, "but that was his story. I thought you should know. You know, there is an old graveyard over there."

She added, "Maybe what you saw was someone come down there to decorate graves. It was near Memorial Day when you seen that girl. Folks around here decorate graves on Memorial Day."

Jesse considered everything: his sighting, his dreams, the séance, and Old Blind Bill's story. He concluded that what he had seen that day across the lake probably was just someone visiting a grave.

There was another curious item. His grandfather's letter, it was a letter concerning an incident that involved Jesse when he was a small child.

Jesse found the letter earlier that year, when he brought his grandfather's things back from Oklahoma. For Jesse, the letter was the first and only evidence he had that his grandfather had once lived on the Lake of the Ozarks.

His grandfather's letter was lying on the desk with the "guardian" letter. Jesse picked it up and reread it.

It was to Jesse's mother, dated November 22, 1963. It had never been mailed.

Dear Mildred,

In response to your question, yes I do recall an incident concerning your boy. I have never told anyone this, and am not sure I will mail this letter.

It was before Jack went off to the war, back in the days, when you still talked to me. Jack and I had taken the boy with us on a venture across the lake.

We went in the boat. Me, Jack, the boy, and Jack's dog. We crossed over to the other side of the lake. The deserted side.

Jack took his dog and rifle and went into the woods to hunt squirrels. The boy, who was maybe three, stayed with me on the shore. We fished for bluegill along the bank.

I had brought a blanket that I spread beneath a sycamore. The boy and I napped. I don't know how long I slept, but when Jack came back from squirrel hunting, the boy was missing.

I was lying there stuck in one of those damned seizure dreams, when Jack found me and shook me awake.

I remember that I was desperate to find the boy. In the nightmare I was having, I had seen a witch come to the blanket and take the boy away. I could see her as plain as day, but was unable to move; that's the way those nightmare things are.

However, we did find the boy and he was just fine. He had been playing in the sand just around the corner from where I was sleeping.

There are a couple of reasons that I remember this, even now, years later. For one, it was how frantic I was to find the boy. In my half awake, half-asleep state, I really thought a witch had taken him.

But the other thing was this, when I asked the boy what he had been doing, he said, "I was talking to the girl."

"What girl?" I asked.

"The pretty girl," he replied.

Of course, at that, I thought that maybe, there really was a girl on the beach, that maybe I really had seen a girl, that it wasn't a dream.

I looked up and down the beach and in the woods. Jack thought I was nuts. Of course, there was no girl there on the beach. The whole place was empty for miles around. Jack told me not to worry about it.

"He makes stuff up," Jack explained. "He even thinks he has a pet monkey at home."

"The pretty girl was bad," the boy said.

The letter was unfinished, and unsigned.

"I wonder what part of the lake he lived on?" Jesse said to himself.

He put away his grandfather's letter. He picked up the other one. The one that he was anxious about, but not eager to read.

Camille Guerin was the last person on earth Jesse had expected to hear from. He opened the letter and read it. Her letter was remarkably simple and to the point. It was not the news he had expected.

Dear Jesse,

I got your address and directions to your cabin from your aunt in Kansas City. I will be down to see you as soon as I can work it out. I would like to spend some time with you. Remember, you asked me to. You do remember asking, don't you?

See You, Camille.

P.S. I gave the ring back.

Gave the ring back, what did that mean? The fact that she had kept her engagement from him had really pissed him off.

She didn't say when she was coming. How old was the letter?

Jesse checked the postmark. The letter had been sent over a week ago. How did it end up at the Michaels' house?

He reflected on Camille. She was truly one of a kind. She could have been a fashion model, except she wasn't very fashionable. She was a stunner and even in ragged jeans and a sweatshirt, she stood out. Jesse thought she looked like she belonged on a horse, maybe as the barrel-riding rodeo gal at the county fair.

Camille's father was a big-shot lawyer and he had hoped she would follow his example. She wanted to study archeology, but settled for a degree in history; she planned to teach. Her career choice was a disappointment to her old man.

Jesse wondered if she had found a teaching job yet.

Camille was easily the most unexpected girlfriend that Jesse could have imagined, so therein lay the problem. Was she ever his girlfriend, or just a means to get through college?

There were too many doubts involved with their relationship; Jesse's analytical mind had problems with loose ends. Camille was older than he was, and above his social class. He should have known there was a catch.

Of course, Camille dealt with her own problems. Her friends thought she was foolish for getting involved with Jesse. She had a man, one with social status and a future. Why was she messing around with a low-class kid like Jesse Messenger?

They made sure that Camille knew their viewpoint, although in the end it was a moot point, because as it turned out, no one could tell Camille Guerin what to do.

Jesse recalled their meeting; it had been in algebra class. Jesse liked algebra and sat near the front of the class. The students that struggled tended to sit in the back, which was where Camille originally sat.

One day, half way through the semester, Jesse found Camille sitting in the seat next to him. The boy who had previously occupied that chair was irritated, but not so much as to confront Camille. It would have made no difference anyway, and he knew it.

Camille introduced herself to Jesse, and said, "I've noticed that you're really good at this stuff."

"And I suppose you're not," Jesse answered.

"Awful," she replied, "and I need a math class. This was the only one that fit my schedule."

"So," Jesse said, with a smile, "you didn't sit here because of my handsome looks and charm."

"Oh yeah," she said, "that's the main reason. But I thought, since I'm here, because you're so handsome and all, that you might help me learn some algebra as well."

One thing led to another, as they often do, to the extent that by the time school was nearly out for the summer, Jesse considered Camille to be his girlfriend. He suggested that, during the summer, she might spend some time with him.

That was his plan, but not entirely hers. Jesse had become totally infatuated with Camille, right up to the point where she disclosed a slight complication. She could not spend the summer with him, because she had prior wedding plans.

Jesse was stunned, but he didn't make a scene. He didn't ask her to choose, and he didn't say goodbye. He just left. He never expected to see her again.

Jesse turned in for the night, as he lay there thinking of Camille, he closed his eyes and drifted off to sleep.

~ 9 ~
THE ICE

It was winter. Most of the old timers said that this was the coldest winter they had ever seen. Robbie and Jesse walked on the ice.

"I've never seen the entire lake frozen over," Robbie commented. "I bet the ice is a foot thick."

Robbie carried a chainsaw, while Jesse carried fishing poles.

"Who would have thought we could go ice fishing on the main lake?" Jesse said. "Back in the cove, yeah, but out here on the main channel, no way."

Robbie started the chainsaw. He dipped the tip of the blade into the ice. The tip bit and ice chips flew.

After a few minutes, the chainsaw had sliced a square hole into the ice. They measured the thickness of the ice, not nearly a foot as Robbie predicted, but a good solid six inches. Where they fished, the ice was safe, but they didn't catch any fish.

"Let's leave the chainsaw and fishing poles on the bank and walk up to JR's," Robbie suggested. "It's less than a mile on the ice, and it seems solid everywhere."

They walked along on the ice until they were almost to JR's. Jesse looked out across the big cove between them and the store."

"Are we going to walk around the edge of the cove, or try to cut straight across the middle?"

"I don't know." Robbie looked up the cove, then across it. "It's sure is a lot closer, cutting straight across."

"Maybe an extra mile around the edge," Jesse said.

"Well," Robbie commented, "last week, Sonny and I walked straight across, and the ice was as solid as a rock. But we did have that one warm day."

"One warm day," Jesse said, "should not make a difference, as cold as it has been since then."

"What really makes the ice dangerous," Robbie observed, "is the current under the ice. It can eat through the ice, bottom side up."

"The cove is not on the main channel," Jesse said, "so it shouldn't have a current. Besides, we fished on the main channel and it had plenty of ice."

"I think we're okay," Robbie said.

"Let's do this. We will spread out about sixty feet apart and go slow. If we hear any cracking or anything strange, we backtrack fast."

Jesse crossed the ice first. For nearly two hundred yards, the ice was solid. He was halfway across while Robbie followed behind.

Suddenly Jesse heard a rifle shot. "Oh, no!" he thought. "That wasn't a rifle; that was the ice." Jesse froze in his tracks; he took one step backward, then another.

The sound Jesse heard next was ominous—a series of loud pings. *PING. PING. PING.* Eight loud *pings*, some as far away as a half of a mile.

"We're in serious trouble," Jesse mumbled.

Immediately, a huge, hundred-foot-long rift cracked beneath Jesse's feet. Now the ice was pinging like popcorn. Jesse had to make an instant decision. He stepped back. The slab of ice he stepped on started to sink into the water. Jesse spun around and made a desperate run for the bank. It was too late, the slab tipped. He fell prone on the ice and slid back into the water.

Jesse knew he was in dire trouble. The broken slab of ice had dipped into the water, but luckily, it still supported his weight and he had not slid under the ice. If he had, it would have been all over.

So far, his luck held. He was in the water, and in big trouble, but he was still on top of the slab. Inch, by inch, the slab continued to sink. Within seconds, he would slide off the slab and into the water, then he would drown.

Desperately, Jesse breaststroked and scissor-kicked; slowly he gained elevation on the ice. The slab quit sinking. He made a few feet, then again, a few more. Then a thought crossed his mind. "Maybe I can roll out." Jesse tried to roll up the incline of ice and water like a log. Amazingly, this worked.

He could see Robbie desperately trying to reach him, crab crawling down the ice.

"Get back!" Jesse screamed. Jesse rolled up a little farther.

Robbie continued to crab down the ice.

"Get back!" Jesse screamed again. "I'm going to be okay." Jesse had now rolled out of the water and was slowly making his way up the incline. His wet clothing apparently gave him traction as it froze momentarily to the ice.

Then to his horror, Jesse heard the *ping* of more breaking ice. He saw Robbie slide away from him, toward a second crack in the ice. Robbie was desperately clawing at the ice. Then, Robbie disappeared from Jesse's view. Jesse heard him go into the water.

Jesse crawled farther upon the ice shelf. He sat up to look for Robbie. There was no Robbie.

Jesse, still soaked, fell back on the ice in utter exhaustion. He looked at the clear blue sky. The clouds were magnificent. He passed out.

He awoke sometime later, how long, he did not know, but it could not have been very long. He knew that he must get moving or he would die of exposure. He knew this, but he couldn't move. "My God," he realized, "I have lain here too long, and I have frozen to the ice. *This can't be happening!* This is not fair. I fought too hard to get out of the water. I can't just lay here and freeze."

He tried to assess his situation. He had been in the water only a few seconds; in fact, his inner clothing was not soaked, just wet in a few places. His outer clothing was wet and had frozen to the ice. Even his hair was frozen to the ice. He was disoriented and couldn't think straight. "I'm in shock," he thought. What a stupid way to die.

"Robbie!" Jesse screamed. Where did Robbie go? Was Robbie with him on the ice, or was he by himself? Who was Robbie? He could not focus. Why was he on the ice?

Oh now, he remembered. He was crossing the ice because he had to get medicine. He had to get medicine for his wife; she had the flu. The flu had already killed so many people that he couldn't take the chance. He would have to trust the doctors. He would have to visit the others. He would have to cross the ice. He had to get medicine or she would die.

Then he saw someone gliding across the ice toward him; it was Lizzie. She could save him, he thought. She could break him free from the ice.

"Don't step on the crack!" he screamed. In his mind, he screamed, but in reality, only a muffled groan came from his lips.

"Why are you out in the cold," he thought. "You're too sick to be out in the cold."

She glided toward him. Was she on ice skates? How did she glide toward him? Yes, she was on skates, pulling a sled.

He passed out again. Next, he was being pulled along on the sled. Back toward the wrong side of the lake.

"*Clop, clop, clop,*" her skates rang out as she raced along the ice, then sped across the ice faster and faster.

"This is the wrong way," he mumbled as he realized they were going away from where people lived.

"No, no, no," Jesse said, as he suddenly realized that he was dreaming.

"Wake up!" he screamed. However, that was not to come.

He was in an ambulance. He heard two voices.

"What happened to the others?" voice number one asked.

"Still under the ice," voice number two replied.

"What about this one?"

"Back from the dead."

"Wake up!" Jesse screamed. Jesse lost control of his dream again as he slipped backwards, spinning into the blackness.

Sometime later, maybe seconds, maybe hours, he awoke. He was in his cabin, and it was almost dark. He could see the woman. She was in the cabin with him. Who was she? He should know. *Think.* The name Lizzie popped into his mind. Who is Lizzie? Jesse couldn't recall anyone named Lizzie.

The woman was looking through his things. Reading his mail, looking in his cupboard.

The woman stopped looking through Jesse's things and came back to his bed. She tended him, checking his fever. Was she real or a fabrication of his dream?

This woman looked familiar.

"Oh, that's it," Jesse thought, as his mind settled on an explanation, she was the Quaker girl on the TV commercial, not real at all. He reminded himself that this was just a dream. Did Robbie go through the ice? No, that was a dream too, or was it? He simply could not tell; his mind was playing tricks on him.

The woman/Quaker girl sat beside him and dabbed his forehead with a wet cloth.

"This is just a dream and I will wake up," he said.

"No, husband," the woman replied, "this is real. Perhaps the other is just a dream. I must get you home. This is a dreadful place."

"Wake up!" Jesse screamed. He tried to shake his head. His head moved a little. It was still dark in the room. Perhaps the woman could not see that he needed to wake up.

"Shake my head!" he said to himself. "Then I can wake up."

"You must stay with me, where it is safe," she reassured him. She cradled his head in her lap.

"Shake your head, and wake up!" he screamed to himself.

However, the woman held his head tight. He couldn't move his head. Jesse came to a terrifying conclusion, "She doesn't want me to wake up."

Suddenly the small cabin filled with a bright intense light. Another presence had entered. The woman/Quaker girl faded away from his vision as another form replaced her.

"Who are you?" Jesse screamed. This time he knew the words actually had come out.

"Damn it, Jesse, it's Camille," the figure answered. "Now, wake up!"

Camille pulled Jesse to an upright position. As usual, when awaking from one of these episodes, Jesse's head felt as if it were a hive to a thousand bumblebees.

"Jesus," he said, "that was a bad one; a horrible nightmare."

"Nightmare, talk about nightmares!" Camille replied. "I just drove down fourteen miles of gravel road. That's enough to scare the crap out of a Baptist preacher."

"Camille," Jesse said, "you know I admire you and all, but if you are ever going to be a schoolteacher, you have to quit talking like a sailor."

~ 10 ~
HEADACHES

Melissa liked walking the road. She was walking the road when the yellow car came by. The car stopped. The woman driving the car said she was Camille Guerin. She said she was looking for a man named Jesse Messenger.

Melissa nodded in acknowledgement that she knew Jesse.

"Can you show me where he lives?" Camille asked.

Melissa nodded in agreement to that as well, and entered the yellow car to ride along, to show the way.

Melissa instantly liked Camille. She had never seen a woman this beautiful. She had brown eyes and brown hair. Melissa wondered if she was an Indian.

"Yes she is, she is an Indian," Melissa decided. "Part Indian, probably part Cherokee. Yes that's what she is, part Cherokee," and, indeed Camille was.

Melissa could sense that Camille was special. Camille was of the white light, like herself. Jesse and Robbie were of the blue light, and this lady must be Jesse's match. Blue lights always needed a white light to make them complete. White lights were special; white and blue lights together were especially well matched.

She thought about the lights. Most people were sheathed in a yellow or green light, or none, and some were smudged with ugly colors, like black and red, bad people. Her sister Lilith was a greenish orange. That was not good, but not terribly bad.

Melissa pointed the way to Jesse's but rode along in silence. She was afraid to say anything. What if she said the wrong thing, and this beautiful woman would not like her?

"You sure are a pretty girl," the lady told her. "What is your name?"

Melissa did not say her name, she just smiled, but not outside where the lady could see, just on the inside. Melissa knew who this lady was; this was Jesse's guardian. This was the one Jesse was supposed to be with. Maybe Jesse didn't know it, but Melissa did.

As soon as Camille pulled into Jesse's cabin, Melissa stepped out and walked away.

"Hey, wait, I'll drive you home," Camille yelled, but Melissa kept walking. Soon, she was out of sight.

"I wonder who that little girl was," Camille thought as she entered the cabin.

"Who are you?" Jesse had screamed.

Camille and Jesse talked most of the morning.

She explained to Jesse that she wanted to stay with him through the week. Then, she would need to go back to the city to clean up some details. After which, she would like to come back to close out the summer.

She had a teaching job waiting for her near the college. Perhaps they could work something out, live together while Jesse finished his college, who knows.

Jesse liked the idea, the bachelor life, which he had liked at first, was not so great after all.

Right now, Jesse was more concerned about the immediate future. Perhaps Camille should not be here. He was conflicted and tried to explain. Camille did not comprehend his concerns.

"So, explain again," she asked, "why you don't want me to stay?"

"Of course, I want you to stay," he said. "But there are some strange things going on. I don't want you to think I am crazy."

"Crazy doesn't bother me," she said. "Stupid, I can't stand, crazy, that's okay."

"Seriously Camille, weird things are happening here. It may not be safe." Jesse shook his head. "These headaches and nightmares are driving me nuts."

Camille wondered if something really was going on, or if he just wanted her to go away. After all, he had taken the whole thing badly. She decided to throw her cards on the table.

"Hey look," she said, "I am so sorry that I didn't tell you the truth before, but what is done, is done. If I could undo things, I would. I'm here now, and I have brought my things. I have committed to you. If you want me out of your life, tell me so. You don't have to give me some bullshit story about weird things happening."

"No, I mean it, Camille." Jesse walked to the porch and vomited stomach acid. "Damn, this headache is killing me. You know, I just feel very strange, like I'm losing it, and these headaches will not go away. Then, I made things worse. The other day I was at a party where some people were messing around with the supernatural crap, and like a dumbass, I got messed up in it. That's about when the headaches started."

"Maybe you're diabetic. Maybe your blood sugar is low, or maybe you're having diabetic seizures. I can take you to a doctor." Camille gave Jesse a sideways glance. "And, as I recall, back in college, you messed around with that supernatural crap. And I thought you quit all that nonsense."

"Yeah," said Jesse, "I did quit."

Jesse started a pot of coffee. "Another thing, a while back, when I first came down here, I saw this girl, actually a woman, a Quaker I believe, on the other side of the lake in an area where no one lives. Since then, I've had nightmares constantly. And this woman is always in them. It's like she is stalking me, but I just can't recall the details."

Jesse sat down next to Camille. "Damn, I'm beginning to doubt that she is real. Maybe I dreamed the whole thing up in one of my hallucination nightmares and simply confused reality with a dream."

Upon first seeing Jesse, Camille had noticed he looked severely fatigued. She had said nothing, but was immediately concerned. She had volunteered at the old folk's home, and that's what Jesse reminded her of, an old person facing death. She decided she should stay as long as she could, go back to the city, do her business, then return as quickly as possible.

"So, you're having fantasies about some other chick, I guess I can live with that. Unless she shows up here, that is."

"You see," Jesse said, "that's the problem. You don't believe in ghosts."

"No!" Camille said, "I don't believe in any of that crap. Ghosts, bigfoot, or little green men."

"Really? Not even little green men?"

"Not even. Next time you see Miss Ghostie, tell her I'm not running from any friggin' spook."

Jesse was starting to feel better already. Camille was good for him it seemed. Camille unloaded a bag from her little square back Volkswagen.

For the next three days, Jesse and Camille hung around the cabin. It was as if Jesse had taken a miracle cure. He looked and felt so much better.

"I need to take you to see the Driscolls," he said, but they never got around to it.

Too quickly, it seemed, Camille had to leave. There was business to attend to in KC. Also, she would look for an apartment. She assured Jesse that she would be back as soon as possible. After which, she planned to move, with Jesse, back to Kansas City.

That is what she wanted. She told Jesse that he had a week to think it over. A week to decide if that is what he wanted as well.

Then she left.

Jesse found Robbie at the usual places. Robbie listened as Jesse related the unexpected return of Camille.

"I guess you will be heading back to the big town come September."

"Maybe before that," Jesse answered.

"Shit a brick. Everyone is going somewhere except me."

"What do you mean?" Jesse inquired.

"Well," Robbie answered, "first of all, Lilith's grandmother sent her back to Oklahoma to stay with her parents. I guess she got too wild and hard to handle. No loss there, Melissa is still here. Then, Sonny and the Old Man took a job up on the river above Warsaw. They will be there till winter."

"Well," Jesse said, "you have to go where you can make a living."

"Yeah, I know. Even heard that old J.R. has his place up for sale. Damn, don't know what I will do about a throw net if he leaves."

"Maybe you could buy it from him, if he does go."

"Well, I just don't like it. This friggin' place is getting to be a ghost town."

Later, in the evening, Jesse sat alone on the porch. The rocker rocked, his brain worked, and he thought about things that he probably should have just let lie.

He tried in vain to recall the accident, the real one, not the one that he dreamed about with Robbie, but the real one. If only he could remember. However, to Jesse Messenger, life before seventeen did not exist.

He only knew the story from what he had been told.

It was early February. They had gone to town to buy groceries. While they were shopping, a sudden winter storm blew in. The icy roads were covered with a fresh layer of snow.

On the way home, his mother lost control and went over an embankment. The car rolled onto its top, ejecting Jesse into a snow bank. It continued to slide, upside down, across a field and onto the ice-covered surface of a small lake, where it broke through and sank.

Jesse, his fall cushioned by the snow bank, was not seriously hurt. He ran after the car and went into the water in an attempt to rescue his mother and sister. It was an impossible task, as the water was twenty feet deep.

Jesse came to the surface, but missed the opening in the ice. He drowned, while looking at the blue sky through the clear ice.

Twenty minutes later rescue workers cut through the ice to rescue him. Miraculously, they revived him and he survived. His mother and sister's bodies were recovered an hour later. They did not survive.

He went inside the house and slept.

Jesse awoke with a splitting headache. He had been up most of the night tending Lizzie. They were in the middle of a torrential storm, and Lizzie was afraid of storms. She had been running a fever all night, and he thought she was getting worse.

Jesse wished his memory would return. He hated depending on Lizzie. He hated this dismal little farm. He hated this old dilapidated cramped up house. He had a lot of work to do, if it would just stop raining.

Did it always rain here? It had rained everyday he could remember, and Lizzie was so grouchy, she complained constantly about the rain. In fact, she complained about everything.

This morning was different, maybe she had gotten better in the night. She was out of bed before him. Perhaps she was on her way to recovery. Maybe she would be in a good mood. She was fixing him breakfast, which was certainly an improvement.

Yesterday, they had argued about him crossing the river to get medicine. Maybe there would be no need for that now.

Even with his faulty memory, he knew that Lizzie was sick. He assumed that was why her behavior was erratic. She had explained to him that sometimes she was a bad wife. If he would just wait, she would be better, and then she would be a good wife. This, of course, made him feel guilty about his resentment.

"Lizzie, how are you doing this morning?"

"Husband, I am doing very fine," she said, "and no more talk of medicine."

"Yes," Jesse thought, "she is better."

Lizzie brought him his breakfast, eggs and bacon with biscuits and gravy. Jesse realized that Lizzie was really a good cook, and just look how considerate she was of his needs.

As Jesse ate breakfast, Lizzie washed the iron skillet in which she had cooked his breakfast. Jesse noticed that she was sniffing, but not coughing.

"Yes, I think she's better," he said to himself.

Lizzie walked behind Jesse, stood behind him, and massaged his shoulders. It felt good. She stepped back, and retrieved something.

"I'm so happy she is better," he thought.

Jesse felt his head explode as Lizzie knocked him out of his chair with the iron skillet.

Like a madwoman, Lizzie pounced on him.

"WHO IS SHE? WHO'S IS DAT VOMAN!" Lizzie screamed as she hit Jesse in the face with the skillet.

Jesse's head throbbed, and he bled from a large gash, but he managed to escape Lizzie's blows.

He rolled away and tackled her legs. Jesse dragged her to the floor and rolled her to her back. She hit again with the skillet from the prone position. He pulled it from her grip.

"Lizzie!" Jesse screamed, "There is no other woman!"

"I seen her!" Lizzie screamed, *"I seen her!"*

Jesse guessed that the fever had taken her. She was totally out of her mind with the sickness.

Lizzie screamed in a language Jesse could not understand—was it Deutsche? No, it was not a language. Was it tongues, like those overcome by religion?

Jesse held Lizzie flat on her back. Still she kicked at him and spat at him. She switched back to English.

"I will hurt you!" she screamed. "You are a bad husband!"

Crying and frothing at the mouth, she screamed at him. "You Better be good to me, Jakob!"

"Jesse," Jesse said in confusion, "my name is Jesse."

Lizzie wailed at Jesse while banging the back of her head against the floor.

"Jesse? What is Jesse? You are husband!"

Suddenly Lizzie's body relaxed, as the seizure passed. She fell into a heavy sleep.

Moments later, Jesse brought a pan of water and a towel to her side and slowly revived her. He noticed that her fever was beginning to break.

Jesse held her. His gashed head dribbled blood, and his ribcage stung with pain where she had kicked him. Still, he tended to his wife.

Lizzie slowly came around. An hour later, she was calm, like a person who had worked hard, and needed rest. The rain outside had stopped and the sun began to shine.

"Husband, I think I was very sick. Did I hit you?"

Jesse said nothing as he dabbed at her forehead with a wet towel.

"Husband, that was not me. I am not like that. I would never hurt you. That was not me."

"Lizzie," Jesse asked, "what is my name?"

"Your name is husband," she said, while looking at Jesse as if he were an idiot.

"No," Jesse said. "What is my name?"

"Jesse. Your name is Jesse. It is Jesse."

"What is my last name?"

"It is the same as mine," she answered. "This name, you must remember yourself. This is caused by the accident. I will not tell you your last name."

"You know my last name then?" Jesse continued.

"Of course I do."

"What is it then? Answer me."

"I will not. Why are you doing this to me?" she asked. "When it is you that does not even know your own name. I had to say your first name was Jesse for you. I will not say your last name for you. You must remember it yourself."

"My name is Jesse Messenger," Jesse answered in frustration. "My name is Jesse Messenger."

"So it is," she replied with a satisfied smile. "And my name is

Elisabeth Messenger." She repeated the name two more times, as if practicing. "Elisabeth Messenger, Elisabeth Messenger."

Jesse walked down to the river.

After weeks of rain, the river was in flood stage with brown turbulent water. It was not a safe time to be on the river, but Jesse knew that he must cross it. He had to get medicine. Right now, Lizzie was better, but he knew the worst was yet to come.

~ 11 ~
THE MESSENGER COMETH

Camille sat in the waiting room at the Marseilles Clinic while Jesse was with the doctor. Early that morning she had returned to the cabin to find Jesse seemingly beat up.

Jesse was unable to explain his condition to Camille.

"When I woke up, I felt as if I had been beaten over the head with an iron skillet."

He knew something was wrong, and that it was not getting any better. Consequently, he agreed to do as Camille insisted. She loaded him into the Volkswagen and drove him thirty miles into Marseilles to see a doctor.

"What's going on?" the nurse had asked.

"I don't really know," Camille said. "He has an enormous knot on the back of his head, and his ribs and back are bruised."

"How did that happen?"

"Well, Jesse or I honestly don't know. Last week, while I was gone, he trimmed a tree behind the house," Camille explained. "He told me, that he must have fallen out of it, although he doesn't remember falling out."

Later, as Camille quizzed the doctor, she ventured questions of a different nature. "Jesse had a terrible dream last night. He has terrible dreams all the time. In the dreams, he becomes paralyzed. He wakes up, but can't move."

"The medical term is sleep paralysis," the doctor explained.

"Unusual, but nothing to be concerned about. The person wakes up, but can't move. I suppose it's very disturbing."

"Jesse told me people think they're being visited by demons and hallucinating things."

"Oh yes," the doctor answered. "In the old days, people believed they were being possessed by demons. Now, they think they are being abducted by UFO's."

The doctor turned to Jesse's immediate problem and its treatment. He addressed Camille. "Jesse has a large knot on the back of his head. He took a severe blow, I assume from the fall. You didn't hit him with a skillet, did you?" he asked jokingly.

"I, sir, have no acquaintance with skillets, or any other cooking utensils," Camille answered.

The doctor continued, "None of his ribs are broken, but several are bruised. He will be in pain for the next couple of weeks. I am giving him a prescription for Vicodin. Oh, by the way, tell him to stay out of trees."

As they drove back to the lake, Camille told Jesse of how she had found his cabin on her first trip to the lake. She asked Jesse if he knew who the sweet little girl was that had directed her to his house.

Camille described her to Jesse.

"That's Melissa," he said. "Melissa Michaels. When I first saw her, I thought she was a boy."

"A boy?" Camille laughed. "What kind of idiot would think she was a boy?"

Lizzie did not like the boy. Was he real? Sometimes she could not hear what he was saying; sometimes she could not see him clearly. One thing for sure, he was beginning to annoy her.

What did he want? He came when her husband was away. He would not come into her house, but would stand outside the door and try to tell her things. Things she did not like. She was not sure that the boy was real.

"You must go home," the boy had told her.

"What do you mean?" she had screamed back at the idiot boy. "I *am* home!"

Now she wondered if he was outside again. Lizzie pulled the curtains back from the window and checked the yard. She half expected to see the boy. Thankfully, this time, he was not there.

He was a strange boy, the boy in blue overalls, him with his pretty face. That boy knew things that little boys should not know.

He claimed that he was warning Lizzie, but that's not how Lizzie took it. She took it as it was meant, a threat. She did not like the boy.

"You must come home to your kind," he had said.

That was a stupid thing to say; she always stayed with her own kind.

Who was this boy, she wondered, where did he come from? Why did he show up when her husband was gone? This boy was angry with her; she knew that. Something told her that this boy was dangerous.

The boy instructed her, "You cannot have this man. An angel has found him."

Lizzie wondered about the crazy things the boy said. What did any of it mean?

"An angel?" she asked herself as she envisioned an image of white light.

She tried to reach the boy but couldn't. If she could catch him, she would twist him into a stick and poke him into the earth. She would show this boy that Elisabeth was not to be threatened.

Camille and Jesse sat on the porch and talked. It was early in the afternoon—too hot to work, and too early to go to sleep.

Camille commented, "It's hot as hell down here."

"Camille, do you think you could stand the life of a fisherman's wife?"

"I think," she answered, "a person doesn't have any idea what they can stand, until they have to stand it."

"Not much of an answer, but I don't think I'm cut out to be a career fisherman anyway. Or a poacher, I guess is the correct term."

"Maybe we could get into some other illegal activity."

"Perhaps, I'll just be content to live off your salary," Jesse said. "Maybe get a job, when I'm thirty-five or so."

"How is it, do you think, that we ever met? An accidental meeting in algebra class, or were we destined to be together?"

Jesse thought about Camille's question, but no ready answer came to him. He would have been content to sit and philosophize all afternoon, but he had work to do. He had three trotlines in the water, and he needed to bring them in.

Jesse launched the boat, and got to work. It was a long exhausting day, getting all the trotlines pulled out of the water and stowed. While stepping out of the boat, Jesse slipped and fell; this aggravated his rib injury. By the time he returned to the cabin, he was in severe pain.

Jesse, an oddity among his peers, had never done drugs. He had gotten drunk once, the experience had made him so sick that afterwards, he never drank more than a couple of beers at a time.

Jesse hated the idea of taking painkillers, but the pain was getting worse. He read the instructions that came with the pills. "Don't operate machinery, don't consume alcohol. May cause drowsiness."

He thought, "This should not cause me any problems." The pain in his ribs was killing him.

Camille convinced him that he needed the sleep. She said he should just take the damn things. After all, she would be there.

Jesse took the pills. He slept. He dreamed. It was a pleasant dream.

He was sitting in a college class. The man conducting the class was Professor Messenger. Jesse sat in the back of the classroom drawing pictures in his notebook.

On his right, sat Camille, on his left sat the girl from the Quaker Oats commercial.

They could not see each other.

"I've had this dream before," Jesse said aloud to the class.

The professor ignored him.

"I've had this dream before," Jesse said to Camille. Camille ignored him as well. "Dammit! Are all you people deaf? Or, are all you people dead?"

"Young man," the professor said.

"Yes," Jesse answered.

"You have not had this dream before, this is an original."

"Okay," Jesse said, "let's get on with it then."

"Not so fast cowboy, I must tell you something."

"Okay," Jesse said.

"Did you notice that these two girls can't see each other?"

"Yeah, that's kind of weird."

"That," the professor emphasized, "that probably means something."

"What?" Jesse asked. "What does it mean?"

"Damned if I know, spaceman, I'm just a character in your dream."

"If you can't help me, then get the hell out of here."

Jesse surprised himself. He didn't normally use foul language, but then, why should he feel guilty for using foul language in a dream. It was a weird world. Jesse guided his dream into another direction. It led down a winding country road. It was October; the leaves were pretty.

Jesse arrived at a sleep state between being awake and being asleep. It was similar to the sleep paralysis nightmares, except different, it was pleasant.

"Strange dream," he thought, "perhaps it is the drugs." He drifted through time and space gathering speed, gathering power. The sensation was exhilarating. He surged through matter as if it were air.

His mind expanded until all that he had ever learned was suddenly available. Then much that he had never known, he suddenly was capable of deducing. Mathematical formulas, scientific equations, laws of physics, principles yet undiscovered were clearly apparent.

"I must remember this; this is important," he said to himself.

"You will not remember," a voice whispered.

"Why not? And who are you?"

No one answered.

Jesse gradually began to feel as if he was acquiring an overwhelming power.

"It must be the drugs," he told himself.

"It is not the drugs," the voice told him. "It is, however, time to do what you do."

"Who are you?" Jesse asked. No one answered.

"Did Camille say that?" Jesse wondered.

He knew she was in the room with him, perhaps talking to him in his sleep. Maybe reading a book aloud. Perhaps the radio was on, but it did sound like Camille's voice.

"Why would Camille say that?"

Jesse knew he was asleep, but his mind and thoughts were clear, not clouded like a dream. Even in a state of sleep, he was looking for logical explanations. The "why" of what he was experiencing?

Then inexplicably, it was there. He felt the burden of a great understanding come over him.

I am *The Messenger*, he realized.

He could see it now, as if a great cloud of amnesia had lifted. He knew who he was, what he was, and why he was what he was.

He was the avenger, Jesse the Messenger, sent to dispatch a wayward soul to hell.

Jesse stood in front of an 1880's farmhouse.

"Lizzie! Get out here," he called. Lizzie came to the door.

"Yes husband, what is it that you want? Do you want me to cook you supper? Do you want to go riding? Whatever you want," she said, taking off her cap, and shaking out her long beautiful hair. "Whatever you want, it is yours."

Messenger was unaffected.

Lizzie stared at her husband. She could hardly recognize him. It seemed that he had changed. Something was terribly wrong.

Was this that evil little boy's doing?

Had that other woman infected her husband?

Yes, that was it. He didn't know what he was doing. He had become infected by the light. He was out of his mind! He was there to harm her. *Yes, yes, yes!* She realized he was there to harm her.

The Messenger knew his duty; there was a process, a semi-formal process. The proper steps must be taken. He recalled the last process, in a different time and place; it had been flawless. He had processed an entity called Johan the Babbit.

"What is your true identity?" The Messenger had demanded, as he addressed the Babbit entity.

"Who asks?" it answered.

"I am the Messenger. It is not your place, to ask of me, yours is to listen and receive judgment. What is your true identity?"

The entity was compelled to answer.

"I am the Babbit, Johan," it answered.

"Johan Babbit," said Messenger, "you are guilty of existing in a realm beyond your entitlement. Johan Babbit."

"Yes," it answered.

"May you serve Lucifer in hell."

Messenger reached out to the entity. It did not resist; it could not resist.

He took its form in his hands. He twisted the form. It howled in pain. He twisted the form into the shape of a rod.

He placed the rod into the earth.

Messenger held a silver hammer in his hand. He struck the rod. The entity, Johan the Babbit, was delivered to hell.

Now he stood as Elisabeth faced him.

"What is your true identity?" Jesse demanded.

"I am the wife of Jesse Messenger," Elisabeth answered. "I am your wife, and why are you treating me this way?"

"I am the Messenger," answered Messenger. "It is not for you to question. It is for you to listen and receive judgment."

"How can you be like this, husband?" Elisabeth pleaded.

"Elisabeth, you are guilty of interfering with the natural process. Elisabeth, you are guilty of existing in a realm beyond your entitlement."

"Wait," Elisabeth, cried to the Messenger, "I will serve you, you are my master. Have pity on your poor wretched wife."

"Elisabeth," said Messenger.

"Yes," she trembled.

"May you serve Satan in hell."

Messenger reached for her; she did not resist, she could not resist.

He took her form in his hands.

He twisted her form as if she were a towel from which he was wringing water. She howled in pain. He continued twisting; the entity tried to escape Elisabeth's form. It crackled and sizzled like frying bacon but could not escape.

Lizzie was terrified. Why was her husband doing this evil thing to her? She cried in pain as the torture continued.

Why, why, why? Then it came to her. This was not her husband. This was a demon disguised as her husband. This is how demons get in; they come disguised as a loved one. She must resist.

Messenger continued twisting, twisting, and twisting. Elisabeth's form was now the shape of a rod, she continued to howl in pain.

Messenger took the rod and stuck it into the earth.

He held a silver hammer in his hand. He swung the hammer. The rod was gone.

Messenger was troubled. Was the rod properly driven, or did it disappear at the instant he swung the hammer?

Had she escaped?

Perhaps it was all just a dream.

Jesse awoke suddenly. What was that dream? He was forgetting the details already. He was some sort of avenging angel.

Oh well, it was just a dream, it really didn't matter, it was a wonderful morning, his headache was gone. He stretched, Oh, his ribs were still plenty sore. Camille was asleep.

"Wake up," he said.

"Why?" she asked.

"I don't know. I just think we need to leave today, get back to the city."

"I'm ready to go right now," Camille suggested.

Jesse had a final request. "Before we go, I need to say goodbye to some people, and I want you to meet them." Jesse described the Driscoll family to Camille. "So, we will take the boat over to this little Marina, JR's, where we can eat lunch. Then, we will go meet the Driscolls."

"That sounds good to me," Camille said.

Jesse and Camille took the boat out onto the lake; however, it turned out not to be as simple as Jesse had described.

"Damn," Jesse said, "I don't remember all these houses."

Quickly, Jesse became hopelessly lost in the maze of coves. He realized that he had generally traveled as a passenger with Robbie.

Perhaps he should have paid more attention. Now all these coves looked alike.

After nearly an hour on the water, Jesse's bruised ribs began to ache. It was blazing hot and the August sun was exacting its toll.

"Camille, I'm sorry, we have to go in. It's just too hot out here, and we have got a long trip ahead of us."

They returned to the cabin and packed. Jesse winterized the boat, locked the workshop and shutoff the water. He locked the cabin and put the key on top of the doorjamb.

They loaded into the Volkswagen and drove away.

"I wish I knew how to get to the Driscoll farm by land," Jesse said, "but I've only gone there by water."

Camille drove without comment, jamming the car into second as they climbed a hill.

"If you want to," he said, "we can make a trip down here next summer. Then, we could take the time to find everyone."

Camille said nothing, but glanced into her rearview mirror.

~ 12 ~
2003

Jesse pecked out his daughter's number on his cell. She answered.

"Hello sweetie," Jesse said, "I'm here in town, at the hospital, doing the same old stuff. I should be through by noon. Can you meet me for lunch?"

Jesse had left his house on the Gravois Arm of the Lake of the Ozarks early that morning. It took a little over an hour to drive to Columbia. He was familiar with the drive, having once lived in Columbia. He and Camille had only recently moved to the lake, just before she got sick.

Although he didn't enjoy going to the hospital, it would be a good opportunity to see his daughter.

"Sure," she replied. "How about Jimmy's Deli? It's close to campus. Do you know where it is?"

"Oh yeah, I know it. That sounds fine," Jesse answered. "See you around twelve."

As he waited and considered his current condition, he reflected on his life.

It had been a productive life.

They had toured the country while Jesse put in twenty years. After the Navy, Jesse taught electronics at the community college. Camille taught history; then she wrote a series of children's books. Along the way, they raised a family. As it turned out, they had thirty-two years.

When Camille died of the flu, her death was totally unexpected. If Jesse had died, it would have been easier to accept. He had a multitude of ailments, but Camille was always so healthy. How could a person die of the flu in this day and age?

Jesse was devastated at the time, and he was still trying to get over it, but probably never would.

Today, Jesse's appointment was for a MRI. It was the fourth MRI he had undergone, and he hated them. This time it was his brain, which reminded him of an old joke. "They examined my brain and found nothing."

All joking aside, he hated the procedure. It meant he had to go all the way into the machine. For a person who had once claimed that he was not claustrophobic, Jesse certainly hated sticking his head inside that tunnel.

The doctor had returned with a folder in his hands.

"Did you have a brain injury as a child?"

That question was a dead giveaway that something was amiss.

"When I was sixteen, my mother and sister drowned in an auto accident," Jesse answered. "They died in the water, under the ice."

Jesse stalled momentarily in his recollection. "The thing is, I drowned. Apparently, I died in the cold water and was revived. I guess I was lucky to be wearing a large insulated coat, it kept me from sinking to the bottom of the lake."

"Really?" the doctor said. "You hear about that, but the fact is, it's very rare. I mean it's rare for someone to actually be revived. Especially, when, gee, what was that, forty years ago?"

"Well," Jesse said, "my mother and sister did not survive. Also, I guess as a result of the cold water, I developed amnesia. I have never recovered memories from before the drowning.

"Gee, that is unusual as well; however, I don't believe the drowning caused the problem I see in the MRI films," the doctor said. "This looks like you had a concussion to the back of the head."

Jesse thought for a minute, then remembered something. "You know, when I was about twenty years old, I had a strange incident. I believe I fell out of a tree and cracked the back of my head."

"Now that accident could account for this," the doctor commented.

"The weird thing was that I lay around in my house for several days, and had no recollection of it. Not until my wife returned, well she wasn't my wife then, but she was the one who found me."

"There has been some fluid leakage in the back area of the brain," The doctor said. "I have to tell you, this is not good. If you're okay with it, I'm going to send you to a very good neurologist at Walter Reed Hospital in D.C."

"That's fine," Jesse said, "go ahead, and set it up."

As Jesse sat and digested the news, he recalled the summer at the cabin. Because of his injury, he had hallucinated people, and places, that did not exist. It had taken him several years and more than a few visits to the shrink before he could accept reality.

He and Camille made a trip back to the Lake of the Ozarks four years after they left. The old cabin had been torn down, the lot being more valuable than the cabin. A new large lake house stood in its place.

However, that was not the problem. The problem was with the people. Jesse could not find anyone he had known.

He looked everywhere and asked around. He checked with the local law enforcement. There simply was no family named Driscoll.

Robbie, Sonny, Ma and Pop Driscoll did not exist, nor did Uncle Jack McDoogle.

There was no Lilith or Melissa Michaels. There was no Irene or JR Ryder. There was never a game warden named Red Schultz or a man named Zimmerman. The town of Palmer was under the Lake of the Ozarks, and had been for fifty years.

These people, the shrink assured Jesse, were simply manifestations Jesse had created to replace the family that he never had, probably brought on by the trauma of the fall. These, she said, were the parents he had lost, the little sister that had drowned in the accident, people he had known but had forgotten.

Both he and Camille agreed to accept this explanation. It was better than the alternative.

There was a loose end left dangling, something never resolved. It was with Camille. She had seen one of Jesse's hallucinations, a little girl in denim overalls.

Jesse jumped back to the present. That stuff was all water under the bridge, too long ago to worry about. He had learned years ago not to question those kinds of things. He just lived life to the fullest and tried to be content.

Just then, the doctor returned with information about Walter Reed Hospital. He said that Jesse would receive instructions in the mail.

Jesse was done at the Harry Truman Veterans Hospital. His next stop was at Jimmy's Deli to see his daughter, Kathryn. She was a lab technician at the University Hospital, and Jesse made sure to visit her, if possible, when he was at the VA Hospital, which lately, seemed to be often.

Jimmy's Deli was a short walk from the hospital. He left his car in the parking lot and walked. He liked walking. He walked down the sidewalk in front of a large complex of dormitories and classrooms.

He must have entered the university campus just as the last morning class ended. The sidewalks were suddenly full of students.

A young lady walked just in front of him. She seemed familiar, but then, as he grew older, almost everyone seemed familiar. She, however, seemed an oddity. He thought it nice that people of all faiths were attending college nowadays. Years ago, a Mennonite woman would never have gone to college.

As the girl walked down the sidewalk in front of him, she suddenly took a right angle and walked out across the campus into the crowded courtyard. Suddenly, she stopped and turned back toward the sidewalk. Back toward Jesse. He could see her clearly. She just stood there, looking out across the campus.

Jesse concluded that he had been mistaken, she wasn't Mennonite, she was odd though. She was beautiful, dressed in dark, old-fashioned style clothing. She appeared as if she had just stepped out of a 1920s movie. She wore a strange little cap, similar to a Quaker cap, but not quite. Jesse had an odd sensation of déjà vu.

As she gazed out over the courtyard, she removed her cap, to reveal her hair clearly pinned in a bun. She unpinned her hair and shook it out. Her hair fell nearly to her waist. It was dark reddish-brown. She turned and looked directly at Jesse, for what seemed like an eternity.

"Holy crap," Jesse said aloud, "this has happened before. When did this happen?" The girl turned and walked away.

"God my head hurts," Jesse said.

The girl walked into the crowd. Occasionally, Jesse could see her walking through the trees that lined the courtyard. Then she was gone.

"This has happened before," he said to himself, his head throbbed. "Who is she?"

He heard a voice in his head. "I've been waiting," it said.

Jesse struggled to shut it out. "No!" he said aloud.

Later that afternoon, Jesse made the return trip home, home to his big empty house.

That evening he sat alone on his porch in a rocker. A porch was one of the specifications he had required when the house was built. It was a grand house, way beyond Jesse's needs. It had cost a small fortune, nearly three-quarters of a million dollars. What the hell, it was just money. He and Camille had both been successful, especially Camille.

At least she went out in style.

Now, Jesse wondered what he would do with such a big house.

"God, I wish I could do it all again," he said to himself that night, as he lay in his big empty bed.

Jesse slept. He dreamed. He was in an ambulance. He heard two voices.

"What happened to the others?" voice number one asked.

"Still under the ice," voice number two replied.

"What about this one?"

"Back from the dead."

Jesse awoke with a headache.

He wanted to stay in bed, but he had to get up; there was so much work to do. He rolled out of bed, pulled on overalls and laced up his high-top work shoes.

Jesse walked into the kitchen and operated the small hand pump. As he pumped water into the wash pan, he marveled at the convenience. He had installed the hand pump last week. It brought water up from the cistern. Before the pump was installed, he had to carry the water into the house with a bucket.

Still, so many other things needed fixing.

He stared at the man in the mirror. The man in the mirror had shoulder length brown hair. His pale blue eyes were slightly bloodshot.

"How old do I look?" he thought. "How old am I? Thirty, thirty-one?"

This was just the way it was. The accident caused it. Jesse had no memory of it, but knew what happened from what his wife had told him. He had gone through the ice; he had survived but lost his memory.

For Jesse Messenger, life before the accident did not exist.

He walked into the kitchen. His wife was preparing breakfast: bacon, eggs, biscuits, and gravy. He was a lucky man; she was not only beautiful, she was a marvelous cook.

"How was the trip to the city?" she asked.

"It was okay, but I was gone much longer than I wanted to be."

"Well," she said, "it is a long trip, all the way to the city and back. I did not hear you come in last night."

"No," Jesse answered, "I didn't want to wake you. You were sleeping so well. I think you must be better now."

"Oh yes," she said. "I haven't been this well in years."

Jesse sat down and began to eat. His wife stood behind him and massaged his shoulders. For some reason, this made Jesse uncomfortable. He reached back and took one of her hands.

"Sit with me," he said, as he moved her around to his side. She sat at the table.

"Lizzie," he said, "how old am I?"

"You are twenty-six," she said with a smile, then laughed. "My husband does ask the silliest questions.

A PRISONER OF MY DREAMS
LINDA CAPPS FISHER

I'm not clairvoyant. Awake, I am as oblivious to the future as everyone else. But when I sleep, the future unfolds like a Chinese hand fan, revealing mysterious patterns hidden among the folds.

I didn't just wake up one morning to discover an uncanny ability—oh no, it was gradual. My first inkling that my dreams could change the course of my life involved lost homework. The teacher assigned every other problem—the ones not answered in the back of the book. Math was never my strong subject, and I struggled over the assignment during fifth period. Only two problems remained, and they were bonus problems. I wasn't sure I wanted to waste time finishing them.

At bedtime, I decided to tackle the bonus problems. With my plummeting grade point average, the extra points would guarantee a passing grade. I couldn't stand another year with Mrs. Downing.

I slid the book out of my backpack and opened it to retrieve my paper, which should have been folded in half, marking the assigned page. It wasn't there. I searched my book, notebook, backpack, and under my bed. The paper was gone.

"Time for bed, Clarinda," Mom called. She sat on the sofa watching *Law and Order* on A&E.

"I'm looking for my homework," I said, as I ripped through a stack of papers.

Mom leaned against my bedroom doorframe. "Let me guess—math."

"How did you know?" I asked.

"Clarinda, did you finish your homework?"

"Of course, I did."

"Go to bed," she said. "It will turn up."

I dove into my waterbed obsessing over the math homework. In my Technicolor dream, I drifted through the double doors of East Brook Elementary, down the hall, past the bald custodian, who whistled a jaunty tune as he buffed the floors. I paused in front of my locker and worked the combination, spinning the tumblers: turn right, whirl left, *click, click.* My homework lay in the bottom of my locker between my history text and a library book. Now, how did it get there?

The next morning, with the vision fresh in my mind, I pulled my homework from its hiding place. Unlike ordinary dreams, Technicolor dreams were vivid, and true.

I found Jimmy Dority's lost German shepherd, Angela Steven's scarf, and then I guided the Morton County sheriff to the basement of the old Tellis place where the body of two-year-old Bobby Tubbs was hidden. The dreams began to scare me, and I wanted them to stop.

Finding a dead child destroyed the fun of amazing my friends with my talent. Yet, the solution to daily mysteries was revealed through dreams as amazing and unwanted as a litter of stray kittens. I became secretive about my dreams, letting people think I was merely lucky.

I grew up and married a charmer whose touch made me tingle and who filled my heart with love and lust. Daniel made me fly like an eagle high above a cliff to sail through life on wings of happiness.

Then, in a dream, I opened the door of Room 217 at the Rendezvous Inn. I swallowed bile as it rose in my throat. Daniel's strong hands rubbed his co-worker's back, a white circle around his finger, his wedding ring tossed carelessly on a scarred walnut end table. She turned, peeled off her prim blouse and tweed suit, and wrapped skinny arms around his neck. I heard his thoughts and felt his guilt.

After I divorced Daniel, I dreamed the Lotto numbers, including the power ball. At the press conference, I held an oversized check representing my $6.5 million after-tax winnings, and a reporter from KYTV questioned me about the significance of the numbers.

"Nothing special," I said. "I just dreamed them up."

It seemed like an innocent remark to me, but with my newfound fame, it wasn't long before folks started recalling the dreams of my youth. Then, my ex-husband authored a book about life with a woman who dreamed the future.

Requests poured in from around the world. For $10,000, I processed one request per night. NBC wanted to do a reality show, and hey, why not. My lavish lifestyle dwindled that measly $6.5 million at an alarming rate.

The President of the United States called me. After our private conversation, I slept with a focus on his sorry state of the union and faltering popularity. An unbidden Technicolor dream revealed an unfolding assassination attempt. I phoned the White House with the plot, names of those involved, and their plans to blow Air Force One out of the air. The president was grateful, fawning even. He invited me to the White House and I accepted. Once you have all the money you can spend, power becomes more important.

Powerful, I was. I became chief advisor to the president. The press called me his friend and spiritual advisor. The president's approval rating shot to an all time high as he heeded my advice, or dreams. I was on the payroll, making more than the Man himself.

Then, the war dreams began. Not just any war, but *The War*. Destruction that made the twin towers pale in comparison. New York, Chicago, Kansas City—all destroyed. This gray-tone dream wasn't the Technicolor of a prophetic dream, but it wasn't ordinary either. What did it mean? The President gathered his war council together and they met with me to analyze this new dream and its importance.

"If physicians study you while you sleep, we may untangle the meaning of this dream," the prez said. He depended on me. My responsibility was to save the world, literally.

"I want to understand this dream too, Mr. President."

I was ensconced in a secret place, the lavender room. Dr. Arana, a renowned neurologist, studied my brainwaves. The doctor's young Chinese assistant, Quon, strapped me to a gurney and attached electrodes to my head. The electrodes were connected to a top-secret computer that translated my dreams into holographic images.

The doctor medicated me into a perpetual dream state, and dreams tumbled through my brain even when I forced my eyes open. He phoned the president with news of upcoming tribulations foreshadowed through the Technicolor dreams.

I knew Dr. Arana was evil, and he knew I knew, from the holographic images of my Technicolor dreams. Quon seemed to be kinder and more sympathetic, but he followed the doctor's orders.

My survival instinct kicked in, and I willed myself to end the Technicolor dreams. I closed my mind to the news blasting twenty-four hours a day to stimulate my dreams. My body ached from being strapped to the gurney. I refused to eat, so researchers inserted a feeding tube.

I lay there for two weeks before the Technicolor dreams stopped. They morphed into gray-tone nightmares that made me moan and cry with tears slipping down my cheeks.

"Why so sad?" Quon would ask. When Quon monitored my condition, he would brush the tears away; otherwise, they dried on my face making my skin feel taut.

Dr. Arana awakened me. "Clarinda, what do these dreams mean? They are hazy and gray. I can't interpret them."

"I don't know," I lied, my tongue felt thick, and I could hardly form the words. By now, I knew they planned to hold me captive indefinitely.

"I can't dream like this," I said. "The Technicolor dreams are gone. I have to be in a bed, without these electrodes." My health had deteriorated, and my heartbeat became irregular. Surely, my captors would not allow me to die.

The doctor advised against it, but the president, desperate to know how to avoid the future holocaust, ordered him to remove the electrodes. Of course, they could put me back in the lavender room at any time.

That night, I slept in a real bed without drugs. I began to feed the doctor a mixture of true and false dreams, trying to dream my way to freedom. I felt like a caged bird at the mercy of my keepers.

Eventually, they allowed me outside for exercise under Quon's watchful eye. I made friends with him, and my dreams told me he would help me escape. We fled, and spent nights in cheap motels, paying cash, until I dreamed our escape route to Hong Kong.

My hotel room overlooked the green and blue water of Deep Water Bay. I sympathized with the bird in the gilded cage when it chirped its protest of captivity.

My Technicolor dreams revealed Quon's betrayal. He had negotiated a multi-million dollar settlement to sell me to China, the highest bidder. If his plan worked, my freedom would be short lived, and I would once again be a prisoner of my dreams.

I took the bird from the cage and placed it on my arm so we could escape together. I heard the thud of boots in the hallway and knew it was too late for me.

I opened the window and tossed the bird toward freedom. After taking a seat on the sofa, I opened a Chinese hand fan and calmly studied the mysterious folds as the door crashed down and greedy hands tugged me toward enslavement.

THE RED VELVET DRESS
Linda Capps Fisher

Memories of the enchanted evening turned nightmare assailed Sara when she brushed the sleeve of the red velvet dress against her cheek and squeezed her eyes shut. In her memory, she heard the orchestra, tasted the wine, and smelled Bruce's aftershave as she nuzzled his neck.

The wind had created tiny swirls in the Kansas snowfall the night she wore the velvet dress—the night of beginnings and endings. The furnace hissed as it attempted to counteract the draft from the window.

Her upstairs apartment had been cleaved from a house that sagged beneath its own weight. She had pranced around modeling the dress for her best friend, Melissa. "Imagine finding this elegant handmade dress at Clarissa's Vintage Shoppe. I wonder how that happened."

"Maybe the girl who wore it broke up with her boyfriend and couldn't bear to look at it again," Melissa said. Sara rolled her eyes at Melissa's penchant for making up stories about everything.

"I can't believe my luck. When Bruce invited me to the New Year's Eve Gala, I wondered what the heck I would wear." Sara struck a pose in front of the mirror and admired the daring neckline that left her shoulders bare. The dress fit perfectly, skimming Sara's slim body. With her raven hair piled on her head, the KU student looked regal.

Sara pushed back the lace curtains and watched for her date. Since the beginning of the semester, she had admired Bruce for his quick grasp of chemistry. He was unaware of how appealing his rugged good looks were to her. She trembled each time he smiled his lopsided grin or gave her a conspiratorial look with his chocolate brown eyes.

"Quit chewing your nails, Sara. You'll ruin the manicure I gave you," Melissa said. Sara yanked her fingers from her mouth, hiding her hands behind her back like a six-year-old scolded by her mother.

"There he is!" Sara slipped on a wool coat, picked up her dainty high heels, and grabbed a beaded handbag. Her boots clomped on the wooden steps as she rushed down the stairs to meet Bruce. Bruce placed a strong arm around her waist and escorted her down the snow-covered walkway to the car. When he opened the door, warm air and Christmas music blasted from the Tahoe.

"You look gorgeous," he said as he buckled his seatbelt for the drive into the city.

The eclectic crowd at the Hyatt ranged from college students to national political figures. The evening whirled by in a blur of magical impressions of perfume, sequins, diamonds, and furs. Sara longed to grab the moments and clutch them to her heart.

Bruce and Sara's eyes toasted each other as they clinked wine glasses together. They shared their first kiss at midnight, a gentle melding of lips, with a promise of more to come.

Bruce waved at someone across the room. "Be right back, beautiful. I see an old friend." Sara sipped her Chardonnay and watched the buddies shake hands and slap shoulders. Each time Bruce looked in her direction, she felt a warm glow, and it was not from the wine.

A hand touched her sleeve and Sara turned to look into the sad green eyes of a middle-aged woman. "Coffee, miss?" The woman held a decanter in one hand and smoothed her white apron with the other.

"No thanks," Sara said. "I'm not driving."

"What a lovely dress. For a moment, I thought you were my niece. She had a dress like that." The waitress melted into the crowd without a backward glance.

Bruce returned with news. "The storm is worse. My friend is heading home and gave us his room."

The next morning, they ate a hearty room service breakfast of bacon, eggs, and hash browns. Sara was nauseous from the wine, but felt better after eating.

They checked out of the hotel, and Sara admitted how embarrassed she was to be wearing last night's dress. Bruce laughed at her, a devastating dimple in his cheek. "You are a grown woman now, Sara."

Bruce drove cautiously on the snow-packed streets. He walked her to the door, holding her arm to keep her from falling. He gently touched her cheek and kissed her goodbye. "I will always love you," he said, "my girl in the red velvet dress."

Sara stepped inside the foyer and stamped her feet on the welcome mat to knock snow off her boots. She turned to watch Bruce as he sped away, the tires sliding on the slick street. Sara smiled at his chivalry to save the reckless behavior until after he had seen her safely home.

Suddenly, the SUV skidded off the pavement and rolled down the embankment. Sara screamed and wanted to run to him, but her feet wouldn't cooperate. She remained motionless, frozen with fear. When the car exploded and burst into a ball of flames, she threw her hands over her face in horror.

Bruce was cremated, the funeral a thousand miles away. None of his college friends were invited, so they held a memorial service for him in the auditorium. Sara remained dry-eyed and numb, and gave no outward indication of her overwhelming grief.

When she wasn't in class, Sara retreated to her room. She left her door closed and ignored the other girls who acted as if life were still normal. In the silence, she became obsessed with thoughts of how life would have been with Bruce. Five weeks later, she realized life would continue—Bruce would always be with her.

Sara left college, moved into a tiny apartment. Luckily she found a job in a one-hour photo shop.

The red dress hung in the back of her closet, a reminder of Bruce. After her baby girl was born, she decided to sell the dress.

On her way to work, she took the dress to the vintage store, and caressed the soft material as she struck a bargain with Clarissa. She blinked back her tears as she left the shop empty handed.

She resolved to forget the dress. It had been nearly a year since Bruce died, and it was time for her to move on with life.

The photo shop was busy after holidays, especially Christmas. Sara stepped behind the counter and curved her lips in her professional smile. "How may I help you," she asked the next person in line.

Sara matched the stubs with packages of pictures and placed them in the customer's outstretched hand. The green-eyed woman snapped her fingers. "The girl in the red velvet dress. At last year's Gala, I mean."

"Yes, I was." Sara's voice rose from the tightness in her throat.

"I just had two year's worth of prints developed." She leafed through the prints checking the quality. "See why I thought you were my niece?" From the pack of pictures, she dealt a photo of a girl wearing the red velvet dress.

"This picture was taken at the New Year's Eve Gala two years ago. Her boyfriend died in a car wreck the next morning." The woman smiled sadly.

On her lunch break, Sara briskly walked the four blocks to Clarissa's Vintage Shoppe. Bells jangled as Sara plowed through the door and bumped into a dark-haired girl carrying a large bag. "Excuse me," Sara apologized. The girl laughed, and Sara felt a pang for the carefree happiness lost forever to her.

Sara jammed her gloves into her coat pockets. She riffled through the racks, frantic to find the red velvet dress.

"Looking for something in particular?" Clarissa's young helper asked as she snapped her gum between her teeth.

"A red velvet dress," Sara said.

"Sorry, we sold our only velvet dress a few minutes ago. The girl said it was perfect for the New Year's Eve Gala."

Sara ran to the door her eyes scanning the street in both directions, but the dress and the dark-haired girl were gone.

FIRE ON DECK
JIMMY CAPPS

January, Arabian Sea.

Wind and rain blew across the flight deck. I shielded my face from the exhaust blast of the F14, then dashed from the cover of the catwalk. I crab crawled along the deck, clearing an F14's danger zone, and ran to catch up with the other aircraft that had just caught the three wire.

I ran along with the Yellow Shirt as the S3, number Seven-Ten, taxied off the landing strip and made its way toward a parking area. I waved at the pilot to get his attention. He gave me a thumbs-up indicating the aircraft was still good. I called maintenance control to report the status.

"Bird Base, Bird One, Seven-Ten is on deck and up."

"Bird One," Base replied, "top 'er off and get it turned around; launch it on the next cycle. The new crew will meet you on deck. You need to clear the paperwork up there."

"Copy that, Base," I said. "Do you have the pilots there with you?"

"Standing right here, One."

"See if they want to hot seat this thing."

Seconds later Base called back. "That's a ten-four, One."

"Will do," I answered. "I have to clear it with the Big Dog."

Flight operations were underway on the carrier, only an Alaskan crab fisherman has a more dangerous job. A million things can go wrong, and if it does, there's nowhere to run. During the daylight, it's hazardous enough; however, at night it's really bad. It's too loud to hear, and too dark to see, everyone is exhausted, everyone looks the same—just a mass of shadowy ghosts, milling around.

We do have a means of identification, and it works well during the daylight, but not so well at night. We wear colored shirts that identify our roles on the flight deck. I am the flight deck maintenance chief, I wear a green shirt.

The guys that direct the aircraft around on the deck are the aircraft handlers, they wear yellow shirts. The Yellow Shirt I was trotting along with taxied the S3 to its parking spot. The Blue Shirts, these are the young guys training to be Yellow Shirts, secured the aircraft with chocks and chains.

After the S3 was secured, the Yellow Shirt passed control of the S3 to one of my ground-crewman, a Brown Shirt.

On the flight deck, during flight operations, jets land and take off under full power, the engines are roaring. Meanwhile, others sit on the deck waiting their turn; they also have their engines roaring. The noise is deafening. My means of communication was a radio built into a helmet. My crew, the mechanics and Brown Shirts, did not have radios. Instead, they wore a modified helmet with heavy-duty earmuffs. We called them Mickey Mouse ears for apparent reasons.

I put my hand on the Brown Shirt's shoulder to get his attention. I lifted his Mickey Mouse ears a fraction of an inch from his head and yelled into his ear.

"Hot seat, twelve K fuel." With those few words, I had directed him to shut down the starboard engine, but to keep the port engine running, then fill it up with jet fuel.

After directing the Brown Shirt, I keyed my radio and called the senior chief that ran flight deck control.

"Big Dog, Bird One."

The senior chief answered from the control room and the base of the island. "Go Bird."

"Dog, I want to hot seat Seven-Ten, slide it into the tanker launch for the next cycle."

"Ten-four, Bird. We need a tanker in the air as soon as possible, an F18 is out on station and needs gas. So you got the priority, I'll get the Grapes to you now."

The fuel crew, attired in their purple jerseys, arrived and connected fuel lines to the running aircraft. Everything was in hurry up mode.

The new pilots replaced the old pilots. I signed the papers certifying the aircraft safe for flight, and sent the papers with a runner back down to maintenance. We waited for the Grapes to clear. Once they unhooked their fuel hoses, we closed the door and restarted the dead engine.

I jogged around the aircraft doing a final visual inspection. I circled the starboard engine and ducked down and crab crawled under the hot exhaust. I came up on the other side and went down the tail of the aircraft, doing a quick check of the tail-hook. Routine stuff, typical of a quick, high priority, turnaround. Suddenly a voice screamed into my headset.

"Bird One, hit the deck. Hit the deck. *Fire, fire, fire!*"

I hit the non-skid, rolled off the flight deck and into the catwalk, and it was just in time. Just as I cleared the deck, a wall of flames burst from the side of the jet. I ran down the catwalk and jumped back onto the deck. By then, the Brown Shirt had signaled the pilots to shut down the aircraft.

I called flight deck control

"Big Dog, Bird One, we've had a problem out here on Seven-Ten."

"No shit, Bird, we saw it from here. Is it out?"

"Yeah, it's out, the fire crew is already on the scene."

I called our squadron's maintenance office. "Bird Base, Bird One. I need a mechanic up on deck. We've had a problem. It looks like a connector on the starboard auxiliary fuel tank ruptured. We've had a little fire."

It was a little fire, a short but spectacular fire. The exhaust of the engine first ignited the raw fuel, then blew away the flames.

I went on the radio to thank the person who had broadcast the warning. More than likely, that person had saved my life.

"Bird One here," I broadcast. "Whoever shouted out to me to 'hit the deck,' I sure appreciate it."

I waited for a response, but no one took credit. However, there was work to do, so I got to it.

At dawn, as flight ops had ceased and I waited for my day shift relief to show, Big Dog, the CAG maintenance senior chief, caught me out on the flight deck.

We walked and talked.

"Say chief," he said, "what was that about someone shouting a warning to you during the fire last night?"

"Well, I just wanted to thank whoever it was, because if I had not cleared the deck exactly when I did, I would have been incinerated."

"One of your boys up on the deck must have shouted the warning, because it didn't come over the radio. None of us heard any warning about fire, before the fire."

I thought for a second, then answered, "It couldn't have been one of my guys, only me, the Brown Shirt, and the Grapes were there, and they were all in front of the plane. Besides, the engines were running, I couldn't hear shit, except for the radio, and the call was loud, real loud and real clear."

"Well," Big Dog said, "we monitor all the radios, no one heard a thing." Big Dog laughed and said, "Must have been Old Bill."

"Who is Old Bill?" I asked.

Big Dog had been attached to the Nimitz for many years, and he had a good knowledge of the ship's history, but he hesitated. "I shouldn't have mentioned it."

"Go ahead. Tell me who Old Bill is."

"You don't want to know," Big Dog said.

"Try me."

He proceeded. "Okay, here goes. During the early eighties, Bill was a nighttime flight deck coordinator for a squadron called VA 23. It's long since been decommissioned. And he was a good one too, well respected on this ship. However, on this one occasion he went below deck to take a break and left the flight deck to his trainee, a young chief. While he was below, a Prowler crashed and a shit-load of people were killed. Several of those killed worked for him: his new chief trainee, a couple of Brown Shirts, and a mech or two. Bill was below deck and was not involved. He took some heat from the brass for not being topside, but mostly, he blamed himself. Personally, I doubt he could have made a difference, but I guess he did leave an inexperienced man in charge. Maybe he figured...hell I don't know what he figured..."

As Big Dog talked, I recalled hearing about the accident years ago when I was stationed at Corpus Christi.

"The ship returned to port. Within a couple of weeks Old Bill just up and died...killed himself, some say. Here's the kicker," Big Dog said, "supposedly, late at night, he walks the flight deck of the Nimitz."

Big Dog smiled and laughed. "Just stories you know, good to scare the newbies with.

He turned serious. "Now the accident, that was real, you can look it up. Sometimes," Big Dog added, "an old timer will come in and claim they've seen him on deck at night."

"That's all very interesting," I said, "but somebody did call out to me, and I know there is a logical explanation."

"Well," Big Dog said, "I'm sure there is, but if you see some old chief out here at night, check his float coat, see if it's got VS-23 stenciled on its back. If it does, you might want to thank him."

As I walked back across the flight deck, I thought about it. I had seen unidentified people wondering around up here late at night. I decided that henceforth, that I would stop and check those people. And if I did find one with VS-23 stenciled on his float coat, I would indeed thank him.

THE BIG RIVER CHURCH
LINDA CAPPS FISHER

Our large family packed the old country church. Cousin Charlie sat next to me in his usual spot. His brown eyes gleamed with mischief most of the time, but he paid rapt attention when Uncle Wilford began to praise the glory that awaited us in God's kingdom. Uncle Wilford delivered his heartfelt sermon in a homespun Matlock voice.

The congregation's voices lifted in praise and song, and the leaves whispered on the white oak trees in front of the plain sanctuary known as Big River Church. The folks seated on ancient wooden pews basked in God's glory when they lifted their arms toward heaven in prayer.

Uncle Wilford squeezed his eyes shut and described heaven, as if he dredged up the memory of an old familiar homestead. "When our time comes, glowing white angels will carry us on their wings to the gates of Heaven. Time shall be endless, and we will walk on streets of gold. Compared to eternity, earthly sorrows last no longer than a blink of your eye, brothers and sisters. A mere blink of an eye."

Charlie elbowed me and snickered. "Are you ready to go now, Cissy?"

I shushed him and turned my attention back to the sermon. "Amen!" and "Hallelujah!" rang out through the congregation.

After the accident, Ma had longed to return to her roots in the Ozark hills where her mommy and poppie raised their ten children. I was not pleased about moving to the backwoods until I met droves of cousins I hadn't known existed before our move. Where had all these relatives come from? I knew Ma had a lot of family in Missouri, but I had lived in Idaho my entire ten years of life, and the few relatives I had previously met still lived there.

"Cissy, meet your cousins," Ma said as she introduced me to our kin. "This is Lindsey, Madeline, Sonny, Loren, Winfred, Bonnie, John …"

"Ma, wait, I can't remember all those names!" I said that first day. Soon, my aunts, uncles, and cousins were so familiar that it seemed I had always known them.

We attended early church because my uncle preached that service. Ma's youngest brother was the only family member to become a minister, so he "married" and "buried" family members who required either service.

One of Ma's brothers played the guitar while his wife sang. Everyone joined in with, "...and when the roll is called up yonder."

At the end of the service, Uncle Wilford stood by the door and shook hands with every man, woman, and child as they filed out. He called each by name, and his beaming smile reflected his pride in his family.

The bell pealed, inviting the congregation to Big River Church for late services. We cleared out before they filled the parking lot with their Ford trucks and Chevy Blazers.

Charlie and I sprinted down the walkway through the cemetery where moss-covered granite stones, huge crosses, and marble angels stood watch over carefully manicured graves. If we hadn't been so excited, the shifting shadows might have given us an eerie feeling. Instead, we ran with the enthusiasm of youth until stitches in our sides made us pause on the bluff. Beyond the mud-slick bank, the turgid water of Big Shady River swooshed over boulders far below.

"Come on, Cissy," Charlie said. "There's something I need to do."

"Where are we going?" I asked.

"I need to go back inside for a minute."

"Charlie, you know we're not supposed to go back into the church," I said. "We've already had our service."

"It's okay," he said, "Uncle Wilford went back in."

It was Charlie's fault that we sneaked into the back of the church. We crept toward Uncle Wilford who rigidly stood in deep shadows while Brother Michael led the service.

A lady with flowing brown hair sat at the end of a nearby pew. She placed her King James Bible on the seat beside her, removed wire-rimmed eyeglasses, and dabbed her bloodshot eyes with a Kleenex. Her cheeks were chafed from her tears.

"What's wrong with her?" I whispered in Charlie's ear.

"I think someone in her family died," he said.

"That's so sad," I said. "I feel sorry for her."

Charlie walked to the end of the pew and knelt in front of the lady. He patted her face, and she smiled. My cousin could be so ornery, and his act of kindness surprised me.

The preacher droned on in a monotone. He had none of Uncle Wilford's fire, and an old man in the back pew slumped over in deep sleep. Just as his snores threatened to destroy the serene scene, the organist played the blaring prelude to a modern hymn I didn't recognize.

Charlie and I ran back outside, giggling about the snoring man. We took turns imitating his loud snorting sounds. I thought mine were the best, but Charlie wouldn't quit, and my snoring sounds were lost in laughter.

We sat on the bank throwing rocks into the river. The congregation filed out of the church, and we spied the crying lady. People gathered around her, offering condolences and hugs. "See I told you someone died," Charlie said.

The lady looked in our direction, and a peaceful look lightened her face. Uncle Wilford hovered near her for a while, but did not touch her. He smiled and walked toward us.

"Well, Charlie, are you ready to go now? You can see your mom's okay."

"Yes, uncle, it's time."

Charlie hugged me tight to his chest, and said, "Cissy, why don't you come with me?"

"I can't," I replied, "Ma isn't ready to go yet."

Uncle Wilford took Charlie's small hand in his, and they walked toward the river. At the edge of the bluff, Uncle Wilford released his hand. Charlie continued to walk into the clouds where two angels reached out to him. Charlie looked back once and waved at me.

"I'm going to miss him," I said.

Uncle Wilford placed his arm around my shoulders, and we turned toward the church. "Well, honey," Uncle Wilford said, "you know your ma isn't ready to go yet, not until your brother gets here."

"Why do you stay, uncle?" I asked.

"I have way too many restless relatives that need comforting. My work here isn't done yet." He smiled, and I knew he felt the love and need of his family.

Uncle Wilford and I strolled past the Big River Church into the cemetery. I snuffled and wiped my tears with the back of my hand.

"Don't be sad, Cissy," he said as he paused and ruffled my hair. "Your sorrow will pass, and you'll see Charlie again in the mere blink of an eye."

GRANDPA'S DOG
JIMMY CAPPS

I walk this road every day. Exercise, I need it: diabetes, high blood pressure, too much fat. All that, and it gets me away from an endless list of "need to do" stuff.

It doesn't seem that long ago that I jogged this same road. That was before the heart attack, when I actually could jog. Back then, I could jog, go to work, do the "need to do" stuff, and still play softball on Tuesday nights. Man, you sure get old fast. Anyway, I was jogging that day when I found it.

Someone had dumped it along the road. So, like a dumbass, I picked it up. I thought I would feed it, get it healthy, then take it to the Walmart parking lot. There, I could find some animal loving sap to take it, because I sure didn't need a dog.

My wife had a fit when I brought home "that stupid dog." However, my granddaughter, the light of my life, was there when I brought it in.

Jennifer was five at the time, and took an instant liking to the pup. She played with it and gave it a name. She called it "Pepper." So there I was, stuck with a dog.

I took Pepper to the vet for shots and all that stuff to make him a regular, owned dog. But I didn't like it. All the time, I kept beating myself up for not having the guts to just walk on by and let nature take its course, but I just couldn't do it. I couldn't leave the little critter to get eaten by varmints right alongside the road I jogged everyday... I mean, what would I think, every time I jogged past? I would have a guilty conscience.

I'm just saying, I didn't want the dog in the first place, but then an amazing thing happened. After a couple of months, it grew on me...it became my dog. No longer my granddaughter's plaything or a charity case, Pepper became my dog.

Pepper grew up to be a border collie and a damn good-looking border collie too. He was the best dog a man could ask for, loyal, friendly, and good to kids. Pepper was to me, what my own grandfather's dog was to him. Those two, Grandpa and his dog, were two of God's creatures that walked this very same road that me and Pepper walked, be it many years ago.

This road, the one that me and my grandfather walked with our dogs, is connected to a farm that has been in my family for years. When Grandpa came home from the Marines at the end of the big war in 1919, he bought this place for next to nothing. Since then, it has passed from him, to Dad, to me. This farm used to be big. Grandpa sold about half, Dad sold most of the rest, then after the parts that I've sold, there's not much left.

They're all gone now, except me. Dad got killed in a car wreck when I was gone to Vietnam. He was fifty-four, pretty young I guess. Maybe Dad was lucky dying quick...Grandpa was not so lucky. First, he had to bury his son, then a few years later Grandpa died too. He was old when he went, and he died slow. They say the old go quick but that's a load of crap. Grandpa took a long time going, but then, he was one tough old son of a bitch.

But I need to get back to my story. Just last month as I walked down this road, you know for my fatness, I heard a sound...like something was following me. I looked around, suspicious, some would say. I guess I am paranoid, and for sure, I was half expecting to find a FBI man trailing me, but there was nothing there.

The next day, damned if I didn't hear it again. Like something running down the road. Like a dog running.

Somewhat slowly, because that's the way my mind works, I started remembering Grandpa and his dog, fifty years gone.

I was in college at the time. During the summers and on weekends when I came home, I hung out with Gramps. He was still young then, in his seventies. They were all alive then, all living here where I live now—Mom, Dad, Grandma, and Gramps: Mom doing her social stuff, Dad trying to work himself to death, Grandma going senile, and Gramps. Gramps, he was my pal.

Gramps was one hell of a companion for a college kid. People said he was crazy, not to his face though, he would have kicked their ass, seventy years old or not. Truth is, I guess he was crazy; he claimed to have a ghost dog.

"He was the best damn dog I ever had," Grandpa claimed.

He called the dog Fritz, in honor of some poor German bastard he had killed at the Battle of Belleau Wood.

The dog died of old age when Grandpa was sixty-six years old. I was a teenager at the time, and of course, I knew everything. That was before I grew old and stupid; still, despite my intelligence, I was amazed at the way the old man grieved.

A few years later, on my trips back from college, I walked down the road to the mailbox with Grandpa. He talked about his dog.

"Come on Fritz," Grandpa would say to his dead dog.

Fritz would walk along with us. At least in Grandpa's mind, Fritz was walking along with us.

"Ain't he the god damndest dog ever?" Grandpa would say. "Ain't ever dog that would stay with you, even after he died."

I played along, although somewhat sarcastically. "You got that right Gramps," I said. "In fact, I ain't never heard anyone else ever claim the same for their dog."

"That's cause, god dammit, their dog ain't Fritz."

"I wish I could see him," I would say, and look this way and that. "Just where is he, anyway?"

"Hell, I cain't see the goddamn dog. Shit fire, he's friggin' dead and you can't see a dead dog. What the hell is wrong with you boy? Don't they teach you nothin' in that college? You feel him; you sense him. You just know he's there."

"Well, he sure is a corker of a dog," I would say, as we walked along in silence.

Grandpa pulled out a chaw of tobacco and offered me a chew. I took it every time, although I usually puked.

I remember one day as I walked with Gramps and his invisible dog, the wind blew softly through the dead leaves that littered the road. I swore I heard something walking beside us.

Grandpa laughed and spit tobacco. "You hearing things there, boy?"

"Just the wind," I said.

Now I am the Gramps, and every day I walk this same road. It beats sitting home enduring my wife's menacing glare. Today, my fourteen-year-old granddaughter, Jennifer, walks with me, which is a change, since all week she has been hanging out with Rodney, that little earring wearing juvenile delinquent that lives up the road. This morning, thank God, his mother hauled him off to stay with his dad in Jeff City.

So, as we walk, we hear the wind rustle the leaves behind us. I turn my head slightly to hear better.

Jennifer gazes my way. "What are you listening for, Grandpa?"

"Ain't listenin' for nothin' girl. Done heerd 'im," I say, as I put on my best hillbilly accent, not real, but an amusing irritant to my granddaughter. "That there is my dog," I say. "That there'd be old Pepper."

Jennifer shakes her head in dismay, and disgust; she was there that day two years ago when a gravel truck squished old Pepper. She and Rodney, who was a pretty good kid back then, helped me bury him in the backyard.

She has also heard me tell stories about my grandfather's dead Fritz of long ago and knew where this conversation was leading.

"For God's sake, don't tell Rodney about your dead dog," Jennifer says.

"Rodney, Rodney who?" I ask.

My granddaughter renews shaking her head.

We walk along in silence. Suddenly the wind rustles the leaves behind us. Jennifer turns quickly to look behind.

I laugh and spit tobacco.

"Want a chaw?" I ask my granddaughter, offering her some Beech Nut.

"No!" she says, as she gives me a devastatingly evil look, one no doubt inherited from her grandmother.

WHISTLE STOP
LINDA CAPPS FISHER

The mournful train whistle made Mattie feel lonesome. Later, she wondered whether it was her first hint of the catastrophic event a mere whistle stop away.

Mattie tugged on the collar of her itchy wool dress and pressed her nose to the train window. For thirty miles, the Amtrak chugged through rolling Ozark hills where a deer family and wood smoke puffing from the chimney of a rustic cabin had been the only signs of life.

Now, in the middle of nowhere, a cluster of dilapidated houses huddled beside a dirt road. The whistle blew and the train screeched to a stop in the shabby village. A gaunt dog trotted down the road with his nose to the ground. A skinny girl stood in the snow-packed yard of a tumbled down shanty and was proof that humans inhabited the ugly town.

Mattie guessed the girl to be her age, ten, and imagined the girl reeked of poverty. Her clothes appeared to be castoffs from the Salvation Army. Her denim coat hung to her knees and her floral dress dangled to mid-calf. One anklet was pulled up, the other gathered near the shoelaces of a scuffed grayish sneaker.

Mattie mashed her face to the window, and the girl smiled slightly at her antics. A streak of dirt slashed across the girl's cheek. Her hollow eyes scared Mattie, and she pulled back from the window but never lost eye contact.

"If I were you," Mattie whispered, "I would scrub my face with soap and water."

The girl's eyes pierced into Mattie's, and her lips began to move. Mattie heard the echo of her own words: "If I were you" bounce inside her head. A buzz silenced Mattie's ears, her head began to spin in an endless spiral, and she squeezed her eyes shut in denial of this weird sensation. A chill cascaded through her and her teeth chattered. The whistle blew and the train rumbled.

Mattie opened her eyes to see the train clanking down the tracks. A little girl, who looked exactly like Mattie, put her thumbs in her ears and waggled her fingers. She stuck out her tongue, and Mattie's mother tapped the girl on her arm and frowned at her.

Mattie knew her mother said, "Don't be rude, Mattie Jane Dawson!"

The wind whistled up Mattie's dress, chilling her. A tired looking woman stuck her head out the shanty door and yelled, "Susan, get in this house this minute! Good grief, what do you have on your face?"

Mattie was cold, confused. How was she ever going to get home? The train was gone, and she wore the rags of this Susan person.

"I'm not Susan," Mattie grumbled beneath her breath. She had already been paddled for sassing when she tried to tell these people she was not their daughter. The shanty was cluttered, dark, and crowded on the inside. The windows on the north side of the house were covered with ragged quilts instead of brocade drapes like the windows at home.

She had eaten the disgusting dinner of beans, fried potatoes, and corn bread without comment, although Mama would be upset about the lack of vegetables.

Mattie was scared and tried to do as she was told. The second paddling came when she resisted sleeping on gray sheets with Sissy, a four-year-old with a constant runny nose.

Somehow, someway, she had to get home. They might not recognize her, but she had to let them know the Mattie living with them was an imposter. The girl looked like Mattie on the outside, but she wasn't Mattie on the inside.

Mattie became best friends with Becca who listened intently to Mattie's story of being sucked out of her body and into another. Becca seemed to believe her, which was more than Mattie could say for anyone else.

She and Becca walked to school together.

"Have you found a way back yet?" Becca asked each day.

"No, but I watch the Amtrak to see whether the imposter is on it. If I ever see the pretender, I'll think of something! Surely my own mother will know I'm me."

"Tell me again how it happened. Every detail, Mattie. I will help you if I can." Becca's green eyes bore into Mattie's brown ones as if to read her soul. Becca was easily the smartest kid in the one-room school. If anyone could figure this out, it would be Becca.

"I looked out the window and said, 'If I were you, I'd wash my face' or something like that. I smashed my face on the window…" and Mattie told the story again and again, adding details as they came back to her.

The winter days seemed cold and miserable. February rolled around and Mattie had been hostage in the dismal town for more than a month. She avoided the man and woman who seemed to think they were her parents. The woman was gentle natured, but the man was surly and smelled of whiskey. He called her "Suzie-Q" and seemed to think she was his personal servant with his constant demands. "Fetch my shoes, Suzie-Q," he would order. He mostly took his anger out on the woman who bore her bruises without complaint.

Mattie silently wept her homesickness into her pillow at night. Soon it would be Valentine's Day, but she knew there would be no boxes of candy or pretty cards for her. She had found old valentines in a box beneath the bed, and last night she carefully erased the names and rewrote the names of her classmates. The big one with sparkles was for Becca.

Mattie kept watch out the smeared glass in the front door. She knew Becca would wait at the end of the path so they could walk to school together.

Becca walked with her head down, wind whipping her brown stringy hair into her face. She walked right past Mattie's door without stopping.

"Becca! Becca! Wait for me!" Mattie grabbed her lunchbox and the sack of valentines and slammed out the door.

Becca kept on walking. Mattie caught up with her and tugged on her jacket. "Why didn't you wait for me?" Mattie was out of breath from sprinting to catch her best friend.

"Who are you?" Becca asked.

"Don't be silly, Becca."

"I don't know you," Becca said. Tears ran down her cheeks.

"Becca, it's me, Mattie, your best friend!"

"My name isn't Becca and you're not my best friend. My best friend is Cate."

"You mean Kathy? I don't know any Cate," Mattie said.

"I'm going to the train station and get back on the train. I don't know how I fell off."

Mattie stepped back and looked at Becca. There *was* something different about her. "You were on the train?"

The train whistled and the ground rumbled. Becca ran toward the train, Mattie caught the tail of her coat. "Wait, Becca. They won't let you on the train without a ticket. I know because I tried."

Becca ran toward the train, waving her arms. The train didn't slow down, and Becca ran faster. She waved her arms and jumped on the tracks in front of the speeding train. The train blew its whistle and never slowed down.

Mattie shut her eyes and when she opened them, the tracks lay waiting for the next train. Becca was gone.

No one mentioned Becca at school and when the teacher called roll, she skipped Becca's name. Her desk was missing. It was as if she had never existed.

Mattie missed her. She pulled the shiny valentine out of the bag and tucked it inside her math book.

Mattie thought about Becca and how strangely she acted that morning. She wondered what had happened to her, but she knew Becca wasn't really gone, and the girl who jumped in front of the train wasn't Becca. Mattie was sure of that.

Mattie stood in the shanty yard and pulled her denim coat close for warmth. The train rumbled by and Mattie sighed, her shoulders slumped with the burden of missing Becca.

The whistle blew and the train stopped in front of the station. Mattie looked at the people on the train from habit and an unreasonable hope that she would see the girl she used to be. Her eyes focused on a girl waving frantically at her. Becca? She didn't look like Becca but a spark of Becca formed an aura around the girl's smiling face.

She pointed at a girl in the seat behind her and mouthed something to Mattie. Mattie's eyes shifted to the girl and the woman beside her. Mattie's pulse throbbed painfully in her neck and she began to breathe hard. The girl beside Mattie's mother looked at Mattie and smirked.

Becca pounded on the window, trying to tell Mattie something. Becca pointed to her eye and then to Mattie. This was becoming a frantic game of charades. Mattie knew Becca had found the key to get on the train and had located the imposter known as Mattie Jane Dawson.

Eye. You. Suddenly, Mattie knew how to force Susan to trade places. She glared into the eyes of the pretender, and chanted, "If I were you…"

The whistle blew and Mattie turned to her mother and said, "What a pitiful little girl. I'm so glad I'm your daughter." She brushed glitter off her hands and smiled at the girl peeking over the seat in front of her.

LOSING WILLIE
JIMMY CAPPS

The lady called and introduced herself as Susan McCoy, of Sun State Insurance Company, Naples, Florida. She seemed slightly amused.

"You'll never guess what was found near Highway 41 in Collier County," she said. She was right, I couldn't.

"A 1995 Harley Fat Boy," she said, "metallic blue, license number J8KSBYK."

"My bike," I yelled into the phone. "My old Harley. It's been missing for," I thought a moment, "twelve years."

"Exactly," Susan said. "It was buried in the mud at the bottom of a canal."

Susan McCoy from the Sun State Insurance Company explained that apparently, during the recent severe droughts, the canal had partially dried, and the long missing motorcycle had surfaced.

"We want to know if you want to purchase it back from us," she said.

I had received a settlement years ago; however, it was a common practice for Sun State to offer recovered property back to the original owner.

"Three hundred and twenty dollars is the salvage price. If you want it, we will offer it to you first," she said. "But you have to dig it out of the mud."

Once, long ago, I had loved that bike. I've had several since, but I guess that Fat Boy was always my favorite. It was probably a basket case, but I still wanted it, so I went for it.

"How about two-fifty?" I asked, ever the bargainer.

"Sorry we don't negotiate," she replied. "Three hundred and twenty dollars is the salvage price—take it or leave it."

"Okay, that's fine," I agreed.

I arranged to send a check, and it was mine to dig out.

I got directions to the motorcycle, and when the weekend came, I took my truck, a shovel, and a winch and headed to Collier County.

Two hours later, I came across the Collier County line. Old

memories flashed back.

Years ago, while I was in the National Guard, I spent a summer in Collier County. I was deployed to an outlying field just outside of Naples.

As I drove along, everything seemed familiar, just older and grayer. I followed the directions to the canal and found the motorcycle without any problems. There it was, rear sticking out of the mud, the rest of it still submerged. It was apparent that someone, probably the Highway Patrol, had gone into the canal just far enough to wipe the mud off the license plate. So I waded in and went to work.

As I worked extracting the bike from the mud, I saw a car coming down Highway 41. Just as it neared me, a deer jumped into its path. The car skidded around the deer and continued down the highway.

An eerie feeling came upon me—Déjà Vu. I looked up and down the highway, half expecting to see something. There was a deer crossing sign just down the road from where I had parked my truck. The sign was new, probably four or five years old.

Then I saw it—about sixty feet away, halfway between me and the deer crossing sign. It was a small wooden marker, once white, now mostly brown. It had been hit by the county mowers and thrown onto the edge of the canal.

I put down my shovel, sat on the canal bank. My thoughts raced. They centered on a day long ago. The day my motorcycle was stolen; the day I lost Willie.

It was a maintenance check flight. It had started out normal enough. Willie and I were briefed by Charley-base in the hanger maintenance center. We wanted to be thorough, so before going to the helicopter, we visited the shop and maintenance crew that had done the work.

"What have you changed?" Willie asked as we talked to the head mechanic.

"The automatic stabilization package," the mechanic answered.

"The old ASE package," Willie said knowingly.

"Yes," the mechanic answered, "that's the most logical, although it could still be a rudder servo."

"Well let's hope it's not," I said, as I put in my opinion, as if I actually knew something.

"It's always the ASE package," Willie stated, even more knowingly.

"The package we removed," the maintenance man said, "checked good. We didn't find any faults."

"Most of the time you can't," Willie said.

"Well," the maintenance man said, "the book says change the ASE package and fly it."

"That's us," Willie said, "the flying part."

Willie was sure the ASE package would fix the problem. The thing was, when it came to stabilization problems, Willie was knowledgeable. He had come up through the ranks, and that field had been his specialty.

"I've flown at least thirty of these check-flights for this same problem," Willie said to me as we walked toward the helicopter. "In all but one, changing the ASE package fixed it."

"What caused the other problem?" I asked.

"Rudder servo," Willie said. "A rudder servo is not that big of a deal to change, but they rarely go bad."

Willie Page had been my best friend since we did that tour in the desert during the first Iraqi war, the good one—old George's war, not like this last one, you know, George Junior's war.

Willie and I liked to fly together. We still flew the old Vietnam era Hueys. The other outfits had all gone to the Hawks, but Willie and I both had made an effort to get into Charley Squadron, because we liked the Hueys. Kind of stupid, I guess.

About flying helicopters, people think it's easy. I guess it does look easy, but it's not. It's best to fly with someone you trust, and I trusted Willie.

We taxied out to the end of the ramp, checked our equipment, and then lifted off. Our flight plan took us south over the Glades, then back northwest along Highway 41.

The check flight did not go as planned; slowly, but surely, the aircraft started crabbing to the right. The left rudder control felt mushy.

"Shit," Willie said, "I guess I was wrong."

"Charley-base, Charley-two-six returning," I called in. "And, we're not fixed yet," I added, as I gave Willie a dirty look.

"Roger, Charley-two-six," Charley-base answered.

A few minutes later, Charley-base called again. "Two-six," Base said, "I've got the maintenance crew here with me."

I could visualize them all standing around the radio, looking stupid. The maintenance chief had probably given them all an ass chewing by now.

"We're going to change out the rudder interlock servo. We want to do that on the ramp under power. Then you can fly it again."

By then I had landed and was rolling toward the maintenance area. What the maintenance chief wanted me to do was to leave the helicopter running, while the ground crew fixed it.

It's a little more difficult to change equipment that way, but if the engine is shut down, the helicopter has to be re-inspected and re-certified for flight. Overall, it was simpler to leave it running.

So I called back as I came to a stop, "Roger, base, will do, we are on the ramp waiting."

The maintenance crew arrived and set to work changing the rudder servo; a twenty-minute job if all went right, an hour or more, if things didn't. Then, of course, after the maintenance, we needed to do another check flight.

It should have been an easy day, our whole flight evolution, from beginning to end, should have been over in an hour, but it didn't work out that way. Of course, changing the rudder servo took longer than it should have. Meanwhile, Willie kept checking his watch while looking progressively more agitated. Then he asked a favor.

"I need a favor," he said.

One thing a person ought to know about the military. The military always wants things neat, according to procedure, no deviations, no funny business.

From the point where Willie asked his favor, and thereafter, things were not done according to procedure—a fact that would later come to surface.

"Sure," I said, "anything."

"The transmission on the Challenger quit," he said flatly. Willie drove an old 1970 Dodge, which he had restored, and it was a beautiful car. However, Willie drove hard.

"When did that happen?" I asked.

"Last night, down at Pedro's Steakhouse. I had that pretty thing Melinda what's-her-name with me, you know the brunette at the accounting office, the girl with the big tits. Well, I had to take her home in a damn taxi."

"So where is the car, and yeah she does have some big ones."

"Silicone, I think, but I don't know. Like I said, had to take her home in a damn taxi. It's at Bob's Transmission, the shop across town, so, I need a favor."

"Too bad," I said, "I'm broke."

"Don't need your damned money, Jake, I need a favor. I didn't expect to be out here on this friggin' ramp all day. I gotta get to the bank, and run a cashier's check to Bob's shop pronto. Take about fifteen minutes."

"You know," I said, "I can't let you leave the helicopter without voiding the flight plan."

"Cover me partner," he said. "Fifteen minutes, ain't no big deal, no one will care. Just tell them I had to run in and take a crap!"

I agreed. It seemed like a safe gamble. That was my first mistake.

"One more thing," Willie said, "I need your bike."

Now that really was a favor. I wouldn't normally loan my motorcycle to anyone, but Willie needed a ride, and he was my best friend. So I caved in.

"Willy, you son-of-a-bitch," I said as I handed him the key to the motorcycle, "you better not put a scratch on it, or I'll skin you alive."

Giving Willie that key was my second mistake.

In this situation, we had both broken protocol, but I was the senior officer, and it was Willie who had gone missing. Therefore, it didn't matter that we had both bent the rules. Later, when the shit hit the fan, I was the only one around to blame.

So Willie got out of the helicopter, to run his errand, and like I mentioned, you're not supposed to do that, but it happens. Sometimes, during a maintenance evolution, one of the pilots will run into the hanger to use the facilities, no one says much about it. That's what the ground crew thought Willie was doing, running in to take a leak. However, Willie's plans went further than the nearest bathroom. He left the base.

He rode my Harley out the gate, then another ten miles down Highway 41. There he got his check and ran over to the transmission shop.

Then he started his return.

Fifteen minutes, he'd said. He was gone for nearly forty.

I should have just shut it down, signed the paperwork, and filed for a new flight. But then, I would have had to have it re-inspected, re-certified, etc., in other words, a lot of work; plus, I would have to explain where my co-pilot was.

And Willie, the inconsiderate slob, he was no help. He said it would take just fifteen minutes, but that's not how it worked out.

The truth is, it was me who broke the rules. I just kept the damn thing running, idling out there in the middle of the ramp. When the ground crew finished the servo installation, it was time to fly again, and here I was still without a co-pilot.

I called the maintenance chief on the radio and made excuses, told outright lies, waiting for Willie to return. Then, finally, I gave up and called with a request.

"Charley-base, Charley-two-six, my copilot's feeling a little under the weather. Who do we have on standby?"

"Charley-two-six," base replied, "let me check."

I thought it would be nice if I could just do the flight without a co-pilot. It wouldn't be that difficult—I do it in the civilian world all the time. Of course, here, in the military world, that would be a major no-no, and I had already broken too many rules.

"Charley-two-six, Charley-base, the standby is Warrant One Mackalowski."

"Crap," I thought, "not that idiot Mack."

Mackalowski was absolutely the worst pilot the National Guard had ever certified. I was scratching my head, wondering what to do.

Then suddenly there was Willie, strapping into his seat.

Charley-base called again. "What about it, Charley-two-six, do you want Mackalowski sent out."

"No thanks, base," I called back, "My co-pilot is suddenly feeling much better. Charley-two-six, ready to taxi, call you on return, two-six out."

"Let her rip," Willie said.

We departed on our second flight. We flew out over the swamp and did some maneuvers. The old bird seemed good at first; then things began to quickly degrade. I circled back toward Highway 41 as the degradation escalated. Soon it was far worse than before.

Willie had an answer. "I'm betting one of the servo pulleys has popped a cable. They have to take the cables loose to change the servo. Getting the cables back into the right position on the pulleys can be tricky."

Willie slipped out of his seat and disappeared into the back of the helicopter.

"Wait!" I yelled, as the helicopter was becoming a handful, but he was already gone. I could hear him pounding on an access panel.

Of course, I had my own problems as I fought to control an aircraft that continued to get worse. I tried to line up along Highway 41, just in case I had to put it down. The aircraft had ideas of its own, and crabbed back over the swamp.

By now, the old Huey was in severe distress. It pitched and yawed violently, first one way, then another. I called a Mayday into Fort Myers air traffic control while looking desperately for a place to crash.

Then suddenly, I had control, not total control, but just enough to fly.

Willie fixed it, good old Willie.

"Willie!" I screamed as loud as I could. "You've fixed it. Now get up here and help me fly this thing!"

Willie never came up to help, and despite the improvement, I did crash. I guess you could call it a controlled crash, if there is such a thing. I was just a half-mile short of the airfield.

I was knocked stupid by the hard landing and still can't recall anything until after the rescue party arrived.

They could not find Willie. We thought, perhaps he too was

knocked stupid and wandered off. Search parties looked, but came up empty. The idea that he might have fallen out of the aircraft started to become a possibility. The search was widened, but to no avail.

Willie's disappearance set off an investigation that lasted all night, and, unfortunately, I was the center of it. First, at the hospital, and then again back at the base.

By the end of the night, I had told so many lies that I couldn't keep them straight. Trying to cover both my butt and Willie's while impaired with a concussion was more than I could handle.

So, finally, I just told the truth, at least what I believed was the truth.

The next morning Willie was located, nearly six miles from where I had crashed. His mangled body was found on a canal bank, near Highway 41.

He was dead.

My military career was over.

Willie had probably saved my life. If he had not gone into the rear of the helicopter and fixed that servo cable, we surely would have gone down in a ball of fire. One thing for sure, that idiot Mackolowski would never have known what to do.

In the weeks that followed, I tried, but could not convince the authorities, that my breach of procedure did not cause Willie to fall out of the helicopter. Like a big ugly gorilla in the room, it would not go away.

I quit trying, and the fact was Willie saved my life, so I quit worrying about myself, and fought to get him a medal. It was the least I could do. Eventually, I took full responsibility for everything, and got what I wanted. Willie's medal was the last thing I accomplished in my military career.

In military circles, I was known as "the man who lost his co-pilot," not a very distinguished title, and not a nickname that promotes a promising future. Eventually, I resigned my commission and became a full time civilian.

It's all water under the bridge now. I didn't mind the career change,

142

but losing Willie was something I'll never get over.

So there I was, standing in the mud remembering things.

I recalled returning from the flight. Amid all the confusion of the interrogation, the concussion, and the subsequent heartbreak of Willie's death, on top of all of that, I learned my Harley Fat Boy had been stolen.

It seemed that Willie, in his rush to get back to the helicopter, had left the key in the bike. In South Florida, a Harley with the key in it gets stolen.

I recalled Willie's mother flying into Fort Myers. I took her to where Willie's body had been found.

I recalled that while being questioned by the Collier County investigator, I overheard the county medical examiner comment, "Falling out of a helicopter does the same damage to the human body as a motorcycle accident."

I recalled that while being questioned by Army CID, I was told that none of the ground crew could remember seeing Willie entering the helicopter.

I looked at the remnants of the small wooden cross lying in the mud, near where Willie's mother and I had driven it into the ground. It was bright white then.

I thought, "What an amazing coincidence that Willie fell to earth within sixty feet of where my motorcycle was found."

Still thinking about Willie, I finished digging out the Harley and loaded it into the truck. As I drove home, different scenarios ran through my head. Suddenly, I felt queasiness in the pit of my stomach. I pulled the truck over and sat there, idling, on the side of the road.

Slowly, a revelation came to me. An explanation for everything, an explanation as bizarre as it was logical.

"No that couldn't be," I said aloud.

I looked around to make sure I was alone. I put the truck into gear, and drove on down the highway.

THE LAST DAY OF NOVEMBER
LINDA CAPPS FISHER

Maddox squinted through the slushy windshield willing the wipers to clear the glass so that she could see the ditches and avoid spending the night in one of them. The county road hadn't seen any traffic and remained a virgin when it came to snowplows. Not just this storm either, the county road department never bothered to clear this dead-end road.

This was what the meteorologists called a wintry mix. Freezing rain had turned into snow. Flakes danced in the headlights, teasing, joining the others on the gravel, the wind whipping them back up and over, drifts swooping onto the road like white sandbars. The Ford pickup hit the drifts thumping along, swerving, fishtailing. Maddox battled with the wheel, her actions and reactions, synchronized perfectly to keep her truck on the road.

Maddox tooted the horn as she passed her sister's house. Clarina's house glowed with warmth. The perfection of the fluffy snow made the old farmhouse look like a Currier and Ives Christmas card. Maddox turned into the next drive, her own house dark and empty.

Maddox vigorously stomped her feet leaving tiny balls of snow on the rug melting in the warmth of the house. Her cat rubbed against her boots, licking the icy debris. She jumped when the phone rang although she knew Clarina would call. "I was worried about you, but I didn't want to call you on the cell and distract you."

"I figured if I didn't show up soon, you would have the National Guard out looking for me." Maddox laughed, heady with relief to be home and not driving in the storm.

"You bet I would have! You are so reckless that someone has to look after you."

"The first snow of the year on the twenty-ninth of November. Does that mean twenty-nine snows this year?" Maddox hung up the phone and picked up Dixie. The cat burrowed into her coat. She set the cat down and pulled off her stocking cap. Her long dark hair swirled out with static electricity.

After a bowl of chicken noodle soup, Maddox settled into bed with a novel. She fell asleep with the light on and could hear snow pelting the window when she woke up a little after midnight to turn off the light.

Overnight, the snow piled up—close to a foot, not counting drifts. Maddox called her supervisor and told him she couldn't come to work. After the call, she went back to bed and slept another two hours. Between her job and not sleeping well at night, she was chronically tired.

After a hot shower, Maddox bundled up to go next door to Clarina's house. She layered thermal underwear, with a heavy sweatshirt and flannel lined pants. After tugging on double socks and snow boots, she was ready to go.

Her sister lived in the old home place. Clarina endured life. A good day for her was one with limited pain—a day when she felt good enough to dust her dad's lighthouse collection. Their parents had died in the same wreck that left Clarina broken and facing years of rehabilitation. She was only two years older than Maddox, but her dark hair was dull, and lack of exercise had caused her to gain fifty pounds.

Maddox decided to give Clarina a call to let her know she was coming over. She grinned as she thought it would give Clarina time to brew a pot of coffee. Maybe they could play cards. She dialed the number—the same one that had been their phone number when they lived in the house. The line was busy. She sighed. Clarina was on the internet and probably would be on it for hours.

Maddox hated the limited amount of time she could spend with her sister. She felt bad about Clarina and battled survivor's guilt. Even worse, her parents had been on the way home after taking Maddox to a friend's house to spend the night. They had finally given in to her pleading although it was freezing cold. It started to rain, just a tiny bit, and Maddox, being the youngest and incredibly cute, had gotten her way. She had always felt the wreck was her fault, and was relieved that Clarina had not once blamed her.

She shook off the depressing thoughts and stepped outside. The sun had come out, and she put on her sunglasses. No need to lock the door.

She tugged the stocking cap down on her forehead and over her ears. She picked up the snow shovel and looked at the expanse of yard between the two houses. She carefully stepped off her porch and onto her sidewalk.

Maddox evaluated the snow-covered sidewalk that connected the two houses. The snow was too heavy to shovel, and Maddox decided she would work only on the drifted areas. She could step high to go through the deep areas. The windswept ground looked easier to walk on, but icy and slick.

Carefully negotiating the path, she saw a small drift. She stepped over it, her feet shot straight forward, and she landed on her back. Her head slammed the concrete walk full force. Excruciating pain shot from the back of her head and circled to her forehead.

We all wonder how we are going to die, she thought, *and now I know*. She tried to breathe in, but it was as if her breath had been stolen from her body. The world went black. The sun went behind the clouds and snow pelted her.

When she opened her eyes, she blinked against the bright light. "Mama?"

Her mother smiled at her. "Hey, baby, you need to get up."

"Is this heaven?" Maddox asked. Her voice sounded far away and echoed in her ears.

Her mother laughed. "No, sweetie, this is the yard." Her mother was dressed in jeans, sweater, and warm boots with fur. She wasn't wearing a coat, but then her mother was famous for taking off in all kinds of weather without a coat.

"Here, let me help you. If you stay out here much longer, you'll die from hypothermia." Her mother reached out and grabbed Maddox's hands. Maddox's knees buckled when strong arms picked her up.

"Maddox, open your eyes," Clarina said.

"How did I get here?" she asked.

"You walked. Apparently you fell because you have one gigantic lump on the back of your head."

"I don't remember walking."

"I'm sure the fall addled you. I heard a noise, and you were lying in the kitchen floor. I put a blanket over you and called 911."

"How the heck will they make it? I think we better just put ice on the lump and take it from there. God, my head hurts!"

"No, they'll be here. Miracle of miracles, the snowplow came through right after you made it to the house."

Maddox tried to stand, but lost her balance. Clarina caught hold of her arm and helped her into an old armchair. After Maddox was settled, Clarina hobbled to the kitchen and came back with an ice pack.

"You're going to think I was knocked silly, but Mama was there. She pulled me up out of the snow and someone carried me. It had to be her. The wreck was my fault, if I hadn't wanted to go to stay all night..." She winced as pain enveloped her head.

Tears slipped from Clarina's eyes. "The wreck wasn't your fault— it was mine."

Maddox frowned at her. "You always did want to protect me, but I was the reason they were out in that car on a night like that."

"I never told anyone, but I'd started crying and Dad was looking in the mirror trying to cheer me up when we crashed. Mama carried me from the wreck. She wouldn't have died, but she went back to get Dad, and the car caught on fire."

They heard the siren as the ambulance made it down the road. The paramedics stomped to the door. "We got lost, but a lady down at the crossroads said we should come this way." The older white-haired man introduced himself as Steve and his partner as Brad. While Brad grabbed a snow shovel to clear the walk, Steve tended to Maddox, taking her vital signs.

The door opened and Brad stuck his head inside. "Okay, I'm ready!"

They loaded Maddox into the ambulance and the siren wailed as they started down the road. As they turned off the gravel road, Steve said, "That's where that lady was standing. She wasn't even wearing a coat. Not sure where she came from because I don't see any houses close by."

Maddox just squeezed her eyes shut. As they turned onto the blacktop, she knew where they were. It was at this corner her parents died twenty years ago today, on the last day of November.

MO-MO AND THE SPACEMAN
JIMMY CAPPS

Sam and I drove down to the old home place to bury Leroy Jackson, a boy we grew up with. These days, I lived in Columbia, Missouri, and Sam in Jefferson City, but the Lake of the Ozarks, where we were raised, and that community, close to the little cemetery where Leroy was buried, will always be home.

After the funeral, Sam and I went to have a beer at a local lakeside bar. It was early in the afternoon when we arrived at the Lost in the Woods Bar and Marina. The joint was nearly empty. As we drank our beer, Sam and I noticed several Big-Foot posters, and other Sasquatch related items decorating the bar.

We asked the bartender, whose name was Bob, what was the deal with all the Big-Foot stuff? So he told us an interesting story.

"One night, many years ago," he said, "my nephew, Jessie Lee, came barreling in here, scared and shaking, and told me a wild story. Now, Jesse Lee," Bob confided, "had been sent down here from Kansas City to stay with me for a while, for one of those, 'a little trouble at home' things. He lived in the shed behind the Marina."

Bob went on to explain, that Jessie Lee had a part-time job at the Casey's store in Versailles, twenty-five miles away. He worked there a few nights each week doing the nightly cleanup. He owned one of those little "lay-down, go-fast" Ninja motorcycles, and that is what he used to get back and forth to Versailles.

He was on his way home from Casey's the night he saw it. "He told me that on his way back from town he took the Proctor cutoff."

Bob described the Proctor cutoff as a dirt road that connected the two blacktop roads that ran into the lake area. The cutoff crossed over Proctor Creek and ran down Backbone Ridge. It was a secluded road, but it cut seven or eight miles off the trip.

"That night, Jessie Lee stopped on Backbone Ridge to have a smoke."

Sam interrupted, "Why would he stop out there in the middle of nowhere?"

"Nicotine fit, I guess. The boy smoked like a chimney." Bob

continued, "It was late September, but a warm night and a full moon was out. Jessie Lee said he could see parts of the lake stretched out below, glistening in the moonlight."

Bob yelled at a woman in the back room. "Shirley! Bring these boys another beer!"

"Not me," I said, "I'm driving.

"I'll have one," Sam volunteered.

"Well," Bob continued, "he sat there on his bike, put out his smoke, and buckled his helmet. He was going to start that Ninja when he heard something rustling the leaves, coming through the brush right at him. Even with his full-face helmet buckled up and covering his ears, he said it was loud. He assumed it was a deer. So he just sat there quietly."

Shirley, the woman in the back room, walked in. "The cooler is empty, you dumbass."

"Women," Bob said with disgust.

"Well, it stopped next to the road, about fifty feet from where Jessie Lee sat on his motorcycle. He could see a shape in the moonlight, that he couldn't quite make out, but it didn't look like a deer. Jessie noticed a foul odor and started getting a little spooked. He slowly pointed his bike at the shape and turned on the headlight...and there it stood."

Bob just stopped in the middle of his story and disappeared into the back room, while we sat there and waited in suspense. Bob returned with two cases of beer for the cooler, and a single beer sitting on top.

"Here," Bob said, as he handed Sam a can of Busch beer. "I had some cold ones in the fridge."

He put the cases of warm beer into the cooler and picked up the story from where he had left off.

"It was MO-MO, the Missouri Monster, the Ozarks version of Big Foot. Jessie claimed it to be at least seven feet tall and covered with fur, and apparently very smelly. Also, he said it was a female, because he could see its breasts."

Bob stopped momentarily, for apparent dramatic effect. "The thing is, I believed him. I heard Jessie Lee tell that MO-MO story several times. My experience is that when someone is creating a tall tale, they tend to embellish it. I can tell you this. Jessie Lee always told the same story."

"Bob," I asked, "when did this happen?"

"Well, I do recall Jessie and I watching the Cardinals and Royals in the World Series. That was about a month or so after he saw the MO-MO. The next spring, Jessie split for California. I haven't seen him since."

"That was 1985," I stated, "when the Cardinals played the Royals."

"If you say so," Bob replied. "I know it was a long time ago."

Sam and I left the lake, heading back toward Jefferson City. Somewhere, on Highway 54, near Eldon, Sam asked a question.

"Do you remember Big Ed Jackson?"

"Sure," I answered.

"Well," Sam said, "that MO-MO story, and attending Leroy Jackson's funeral, has got me to thinking about Leroy's uncle, Big Ed."

I thought about Big Ed Jackson. He had died in an institution in the nineties.

I knew him when I was a teenager, running with Leroy. He was big, maybe six-foot-four, but not fat, just big and strong. I was one of the few people Big Ed would talk to. Big Ed could not read, write and spoke badly, if at all. He had never gone to school of any kind and was bashful, or backward, if you prefer. If he heard a car coming down the road, he would run and hide in the woods. He looked fearful with his shaggy hair, full beard, and was ugly as sin.

"Well," Sam said, "this is what I am thinking. Big Ed trapped and hunted raccoons and beaver, all along Proctor Creek. Then, I am guessing that he walked up over Backbone Ridge to get from Proctor Creek, to his shack over in Buffalo Hollow.

"Do you suppose that when he caught a beaver in a trap, or shot raccoons that he carried the whole thing back up over the ridge, or that he skinned them out, and just carried the hides?"

"Unless he needed the meat," I answered, "he would have skinned them out. That would be much lighter and he could carry a lot more. Big Ed never believed in cars, he walked everywhere he went. He wouldn't even ride that old mule of Leroy's."

"Exactly," Sam said. "He would have carried the skins home, probably draped over his shoulders, skin side out. In the moonlight, those bare skins would have looked like breasts, and the rest of Ed would sure as hell pass for a Sasquatch. That idiot city kid, down here for the summer, didn't see a Sasquatch. What he saw, was Big Ed Jackson!"

"Sam," I said, "you are right. That MO-MO was nothing more than Big Ed walking home with a load of beaver pelts. But, you know, there is no way you could ever convince that kid, or Bob, or half the city slickers down here of that."

"I think it's kind of funny," Sam said, laughing.

I dropped Sam off at his home in Jefferson City and drove on toward Columbia. As I drove, I reflected on some things. Back then, during the mid-eighties, I had worked for the Missouri Department of Social Services. I was only there a few years before I moved on, but as I drove home, I mulled over one particular case—one that gnawed mightily on my conscience.

Big Ed Jackson became of interest to the Morgan County Social Services office. Some of the city immigrants that ran across Big Ed were sure that he was a dangerous man. The sheriff's office was called on several occasions. Therefore, Social Services became involved. Big Ed was brought in and was being processed for a room in the loony bin.

Because I knew Big Ed, Leroy Jackson had called me for help. Although, I did not work in the Morgan County office, Leroy convinced me to sit in on Big Ed's hearing.

Initially I tried to convince the board that Big Ed was backward, but completely sane. However, as the interviews progressed, I too became convinced that Big Ed was crazy.

He continually insisted that one night while walking home from his trap lines, on Backbone Ridge, he had seen a spaceman—a spaceman, just sitting in the dark on his rocket ship—a spaceman who had fired a beam at him and then roared off into the sky.

DRUCILLA CAME BACK
LINDA CAPPS FISHER

Drucilla's grave looked undisturbed. I guess I expected it to have a gaping hole where she had come out of the ground. I saw her today at the Landing. She was across the cobblestone street in front of Francesca's.

I dropped Gabe's hand to dash across the street. Her bright blue eyes met mine and she looked scared, or worried, or both. The trolley blocked my view for just a few seconds and Drucilla's head disappeared into the Veteran's weekend crowd.

Could I have imagined her? Or could it have just been someone who looked like Drucilla—some other woman with silky blonde hair, those high cheekbones, with an identical red silk scarf thrown over a gray wool jacket. Drucilla thought scarves were the perfect accessory. I never wore them because I always felt like they were choking me.

In front of the store, I stood on my toes while I tried to see through the crowd to spot Drucilla. There on the sidewalk lay a red scarf. I picked it up and smelled it. Drucilla's scent—a special blend of spices—lingered on the scarf. It couldn't have been her, but it *was*. I looked back across to where I had been standing, and Gabe was hugging a tall, slender girl with auburn hair. He stepped back and ran his hands along her green silk scarf. I'd seen him do the same thing with Drucilla's scarf.

Gabe and Drucilla had been an attractive couple, and I didn't blame them for falling in love. They were my two best friends and we went everywhere together.

When Drucilla disappeared, Gabe and I printed posters and plastered them at every store that would let us. Branson is such a tourist town, that some places did not want to scare the tourists over a girl they figured had left of her own free will.

Six months later, a hunter found Drucilla's bones and we found closure. It had been almost a year since we had buried her.

I jammed the scarf into my pocket and crossed the street.

The girl touched Gabe's face, smiled, and walked away.

"Hey Sara, where did you disappear to?"

"Thought I saw someone I knew," I said. "Who's she?" I nodded toward the girl's retreating back.

"Just an old friend," he said. "Are you jealous?" He gave me a boyish grin. Gabe was handsome, and he knew it. Drucilla had been good spirited about his friendly manner with women. I didn't really like it, but I didn't want to drive him away either. He might act as if he wanted me to be jealous, but I knew better.

"Nope. Sorry." I smiled at him and he pretended to be crestfallen, for just an instant, and then he picked me up and swung me around.

"Stop that!" I said, but I was giggling so hard it didn't have much impact. Some of the elderly tourists frowned at us, but others just smiled.

He finally put me down and we crossed the street to resume our window-shopping. "What do you want for Christmas?" Gabe asked.

"It's too early to think about Christmas—it isn't even Thanksgiving yet!" I said.

"How about one of those?" he asked. He stopped in front of a jewelry store and pointed to the diamond rings.

"Yeah, right," I said. Was this some kind of a test? I knew he considered me to be a friend with benefits, but he was not in love with me.

"Well," he said lightly, "maybe someday some handsome prince will sweep you off your feet and buy you one of those." His tone made me mad. I was a little cranky anyway after seeing Drucilla and wondering what that meant. I knew Drucilla was dead. Her body had been positively identified, and I had gone to her funeral.

"Hey, look what I found." I pulled out the red scarf. His face turned white.

"Where did you find that?" he asked.

"On the sidewalk," I said. I idly picked a long blonde hair off and let it drop to the ground. I crammed the scarf back into my pocket.

Gabe put his hands in his jacket pockets, and walked along deep in thought. I stepped inside a store, and while I was making my purchases, I saw the girl with the auburn hair walk past the window. When I came out of the store, Gabe was gone.

I sat on my narrow bed and watched the morning news. A photo flashed on the screen with a "Missing Woman" caption beneath it. I grabbed the remote to turn up the volume. The photo didn't do her justice, but I recognized the girl with the auburn hair.

Who was she anyway? I picked up the phone to call Gabe. "Hey, that girl you were with yesterday is missing."

"Oh, you're missing?" he said in a light, teasing tone.

"Not me, silly, that redhead you were talking to—the one you said was an old friend. They gave her name on TV, but I missed it. I just caught a glimpse of her photo."

"Now I know who you're talking about. I couldn't remember her name, but I didn't want to hurt her feelings. She'll show up."

She showed up all right. They found her body right away. When I told Gabe her name, he said he was sure it wasn't the same girl. He'd never met anyone with that name.

I would have believed him if I hadn't seen Drucilla again. It was a nice day and while I drove down 76 Country Music Boulevard, I had my windows down and playing my XM radio loud. Of course, the traffic was completely stalled, so I lost myself in the music.

I heard someone calling, "Sara! Sara!" I turned down the music and looked in the direction of the voice. Silly me, I thought. It's not as if Sara was an uncommon name.

There stood Drucilla, wearing her favorite gray jacket. She didn't have on the red scarf, because it was in my pocket. There's no way I could have heard her calling my name.

"Look up," I heard, but her mouth wasn't moving. She pointed to a flashing sign above her. Just as I looked, the star's name flashed on the sign, "Gabriel."

What was Drucilla trying to tell me? I looked at her, and she nodded. An auburn-haired woman walked up and stood next to her. They joined hands and looked at the sign. *Gabriel.*

I nodded at Drucilla. I had the message, but did I have any proof? Traffic started moving. I glanced back and they were gone. Two murdered women who had named their killer. My friend and lover, Gabe. Gabriel. Could it be? Thoughts ran through my head. Women were murdered all the time and didn't come back to tell anyone who did it.

Why were they telling me? I could just see myself going into the police station to file a report that two dead women pointed at a sign that said *Gabriel.* I think they'd just consider me to be crazy.

Turn up the radio. The thought was so loud that it sounded like a voice in my ear. It sounded like Drucilla's voice.

A Taylor Swift song was on. I had to grin. She and I totally disagreed about Taylor. She loved her, me, not so much. Somehow, I knew this was another message from Drucilla. I have to admit that I had never paid any attention to Taylor's songs, but the lyrics of "All Too Well" told me what I needed to do.

I drove straight to the police station. First, I told them about seeing Gabe with the woman who had just been murdered. Then, I pulled out Drucilla's scarf. "This is Drucilla's scarf. I recently found it. She was wearing it the night she went missing." They took my statement, and the scarf.

Gabe called later that evening, but I told him I had a headache. He sounded disappointed.

I dozed off and finally shook myself awake from disturbing dreams about detectives, clues, and Taylor Swift singing about a guy who kept her scarf. I turned on the TV just in time for the ten o'clock news. I saw Gabe in handcuffs being put into a police car.

News trickled out about Gabe. Due to recent new evidence linking him to two murders, they had served a warrant. They found a drawer full of women's scarves at Gabe's house. Trophies, they called them. Twenty-eight to be exact. He had already confessed, so I wouldn't have to go to court and explain how I came to be in possession of Drucilla's scarf.

I visited Drucilla's grave again.

"You'll never believe what he was planning on giving me for Christmas, Cilla. It was gift wrapped and had my name on it. Or maybe you knew. If he had given me that scarf, I would have probably worn it. At least once."

I heard her laugh on the breeze that ruffled my hair.

"Okay, you're laughing at me. I'm really not that dumb, you know. You never came back to point out your killer. You came back to save me, didn't you?"

The breeze picked up, and carried her laughter away. Drucilla had moved on, and I was alone in the cemetery.

THE ELEVATOR
JIMMY CAPPS

The crazy white-haired old man said his name was Peterson. By the time he introduced himself, he had rambled on so, that no one paid him any attention; still he talked.

"You can spend your whole life," he said, "and when you look back on it, most days are meaningless. The important ones," he droned on, "can be narrowed down to a few."

He was old, even older than me. Whereas I was a grandpa, he was a great-grandpa, or maybe even a double-great. The other difference, of course, was that he had gone crazy. I wasn't quite there.

He said he used to be a judge, or was it a juggler, maybe I should have paid more attention.

I did listen when he said he knew how to open the door, but wouldn't. He said he would when he damn well pleased. Yes, at first I listened, but after a while, like everyone else, I ignored him.

How long had we been stuck in this box? I couldn't tell; my Timex wasn't working. It was just looking at me blinking 12:00, off and on, like when the power goes out.

I hated these big buildings, and this thing was a monster, bigger than anything in Springfield and here we were stuck, somewhere near the middle.

Except for the old man's incessant, incoherent babbling, there was no sound in the elevator. As I sat there on the floor, I studied the other people.

There were four men, a woman, and a child, all seemingly unknown to each other, except the woman and child. The child looked to be a smaller version of the woman, maybe a daughter or a sister.

So, there we sat, on the floor, backs to the wall, the emergency lighting casting a dismal gloom. Each person, trying, in their own way to cope.

Not satisfied with my earlier explanation that the metal shell of the elevator created a dead spot, each occupant occasionally checked his or her cell phone for service.

The young man sitting next to me could have been a college

student; he was the right age. He wore a West Coast Chopper T-shirt, the kind with a swastika. His distinguishing characteristic was a silver stud stuck through his right eyebrow.

I decided to talk. After all, we might be here a long time.

"Do you ride a bike?" I asked.

"What?" Eyebrow answered with a note of incredulity, as if I had asked one of the world's stupidest questions.

"Your T-shirt, West Coast Choppers. I thought you might ride a motorcycle."

"Oh," Eyebrow said, "not hardly."

He was holding his cell phone in his hand; he flipped it open.

"Friggin' Sprint," he said.

Eyebrow just sat there looking at his cell phone as if it were an unfaithful girlfriend.

The question I wanted to ask was this: "What kind of moron would stick a metal rod through his eyebrow?"

However, that was his business, and it's not like I hadn't done stupid things in my youth, so I explained my motorcycle question.

"I ride a motorcycle, that's why I asked. My name is Jake," I said. "Jake Cobb."

"Friggin' Sprint," Eyebrow repeated, without acknowledging my introduction. He stood and moved to the farthest corner of the elevator, apparently to get as far from me as possible. He held his phone high in the air and tried again. He flipped it shut and found a new position between the little girl and the Soldier. He slid down the wall and settled onto the floor.

"Was I like that when I was young?" I wondered.

While waiting, I from lack of entertainment, and against my own personal philosophy, started labeling my fellow prisoners.

"Eyebrow" was the punk-rocker college dropout.

"Great-Grandpa" was the old white-haired man.

The soldier, of course, was "The Soldier."

And, there sitting adjacent to me was a fellow whose shoes cost more than my entire wardrobe. A few years ago, I would have labeled him a yuppie. Of course, as I thought about it, once long ago, people had probably given me a similar label. I don't think they use that term yuppie anymore, and I never liked it anyway, so I went for his watch.

It was a Rolex, though you can't be sure. Once, when I was in Singapore, I bought one for ten bucks. I could have had a really good one for thirty. So you really couldn't tell, his might have been authentic, or just a good knock-off; however, "Mr. Rolex" it was.

Completely by surprise, Mr. Rolex asked me a question.

"Do you go to Sturgis?" Mr. Rolex asked.

"No," I said. I didn't mention it, but after one visit, I made it a point to avoid Sturgis.

"My fiancée and I take our Harleys, I have a Sportster for her, and a Road King for me, to Sturgis every August."

"Do you ride to Sturgis or trailer?" I asked, even though I was pretty confident as to the upcoming answer.

"I've got a fourteen foot enclosed Featherlite."

Just as I figured, as long as I am labeling, he was one of those guys who spent too much on an overpriced status symbol, wore those sissy leather pants, and then hauled his Harley to his destination. Once there, he would cruise around town, pretending to be a big time rider. All the time, looking down his nose at riders like me, even though I have ridden across the country twelve times.

That's what I thought, but then, who was I to judge?

"I ride a Honda," I announced, and that, of course ended that conversation. Telling a Harley owner that you ride a Honda is like telling an old NASCAR fan that you like Kyle Busch.

The truth is, I did own a Harley years ago, one of those AMF pieces of junk...

I slid into the corner recently vacated by Eyebrow and slipped into a nap. It seemed like I was out for a long time, then I awoke with a thump as the elevator started moving and the bright lights came alive.

I looked around the elevator.

"Where is the old man?" I asked aloud, to no one in particular, which was good, because no one answered. I stood and turned a circle, looking around the elevator, just to make sure, even though it would be impossible to hide.

"Where is the old man?" I demanded.

"What old man?" Eyebrow asked.

Darn, I just noticed, someone else was missing too. Maybe the elevator stopped and let some people off while I was napping.

"Where's the soldier?" I asked.

"Weren't you a soldier?" Eyebrow said sarcastically. "I heard you babbling on like you were some kind of hero or something."

"Yeah, I was a soldier, we all were, but can't recall any heroes. Did this thing stop already?"

I turned to Rolex. Rolex was standing by the elevator door, as if he were the operator. He looked older.

"Where is the old man?" I asked Rolex, only Rolex wasn't wearing a Rolex. His wrist sported a simple Timex.

"Ask her," he said, indicating the woman, who was now holding a baby.

"Jesus shit," I said to myself, "where did that baby come from?" Am I losing my friggin' mind, and where is the little girl?

"What has happened?" I asked aloud.

"It is…" Rolex stated emphatically, "what it is."

"Why did you leave me?" the woman wailed at me accusingly. "Why did you go to San Francisco to live with those hippies?"

"What are you talking about?" I demanded, as the stud through my eyebrow burned furiously.

"The stud is only a metaphor," Rolex whispered in my ear.

"You should hold the baby," the woman cried, thrusting the baby in my direction. I recoiled, backing away from the woman and baby.

"Sorry, too late," I heard the old man say.

"You're back," I said as I turned to find the old man. However, all I saw was an old man looking back at me in the polished brass of the control panel.

The elevator stopped.

"This is it," I said, or was it the old man who spoke?

"It's time we got off," I heard someone else say.

"Wait," I pleaded, "is there something I need to know."

"Better figure it out quick, Jacob." That time it was the old man, it was Mr. Peterson again. He stood in front of me.

"Because this is your stop… In fact," he continued, "this stop is for all of us."

My mind raced, something strange was happening.

"Except for the woman and baby," he explained, "because, they don't exist, not anymore, except for maybe for the 1968 in your head."

I spun around to look for the woman and baby.

"Gone," he said, "just as I told you, back to '68…I suppose. Now, Jake, did you figure out that thing you need to know?"

"Yes," I said, "I believe I have."

I walked to the door, ready to see what was on the other side.

"But just out of curiosity," I asked, "which way has this elevator been going…up or down?"

"Well," Peterson said, with a note of finality in his voice, "for you Jake, we went down. All the way to the bottom."

"You mean…" I started to ask.

"No," Peterson laughed, "I couldn't resist messing with you a bit. I took you to the top."

Snake of the Month Club
Linda Capps Fisher

Annabelle shook the package she found on her front porch and peered at the faded return address. "...of the Month Club," she read. She held the package at arm's length and cocked her head to one side looking over her reading glasses, but the first word was smeared beyond recognition. She shook her head and her silver hair glistened in the early morning sunlight slanting through the withered vines and trellis slats.

Annabelle's memory had become vague, like clouds buffeted by wind, randomly blocking out the sunlight. A fuzzy recollection broke through like a sunbeam, and Annabelle remembered thrusting money at a nice young man two or three weeks ago. Thursday, that was the day, because Sadie brought lunch from the Senior Center—and she only did that on Thursdays.

Days of our Lives was on the TV, the volume so loud it made the dishes rattle. Another annoyance of growing old was muffled and indistinct sounds. It seemed like everyone mumbled nowadays. Sometimes Annabelle found herself pushing the volume on the remote control when she wanted someone to speak louder. She wasn't quite sure why that worked on the television, but not on her visitors.

On Thursday, yes, she was positive it was Thursday when the doorbell jangled, adding to the racket generated by a Cheerios commercial. She had shuffled across worn sculptured carpeting, yanked open the screen door, and demanded in her gruff voice, "Yes? What do you want?"

"Hi, I'm Craig," the young man said. His pale eyebrows shot up, wrinkling the high forehead beneath his slicked-back hair. Even with her poor eyesight, Annabelle thought he had the strangest eyes—beady, with weird shaped pupils. An ill-fitting plaid suit looked entirely too hot for the sweltering Missouri heat.

"I'm here to offer you an opportunity of a lifetime," Craig continued. The Boy, as Annabelle dubbed him, had pasty skin, much the color of the underbelly of the catfish her daddy used to catch in the old millpond.

"How much will it cost me?" Annabelle interrupted the practiced sales pitch as a heated argument blared from her TV. The show continued after a word from the sponsors. Annabelle became anxious to be rid of this person before she missed something crucial.

"Just $29.95, today only." Craig ignored the drop of moisture that dripped off the end of his nose.

Annabelle grabbed an oversized black purse from a marble table butted up to the foyer wall. She unsnapped the bag, rummaged through sales receipts, cellophane wrapped mints, a bundle of keys, and pulled out two wadded bills, a ten and a twenty. Eyes glued to the TV, she thrust the money at him. "Keep the change."

"Sign here, please." He pointed at a blank line. Annabelle's eyesight was too dim with cataracts to notice the dirt beneath his nails or the signs of fungus yellowing the tips. She squinted toward the document clutched by a catawampus clamp on a battered clipboard. She could not read the document with its teeny print.

Annabelle scrawled her name beside the big red X, barely taking her eyes off her program. She slammed the door in the face of the pesky salesman who, unfortunately, had the audacity to interrupt her stories.

Annabelle eased herself into the porch swing still holding the mystery package with the label she couldn't read. Although she sat on the low side of the uneven seat, her short legs barely scraped the floor. She ripped sticky paper off the package, throwing the curly pieces recklessly into the wind, and removed the lid. Inside, a tiny green snake flicked his tongue and slithered under the straw strewn in the bottom of the box.

"Well, look at you," Annabelle whispered to the snake. Reaching a gnarled hand into the box, she gently picked up the slithering reptile, his slick body cool against her hand. "I'll call you Jade."

The packages arrived on the fifth day of the month. Green striped garter snakes, colorful splotched ones, a king snake with golden blotches, a black snake... Soon, Annabelle's house was overrun with snakes, and although she knew she had given each one a proper name, she couldn't remember any of them. In early spring, she caught the snakes and released them in her garden, close to the zucchini hills, letting them fend for themselves.

George, her son, became suspicious that something was amiss when he noticed a snakeskin clinging to the bottom of the russet sofa. Annabelle bent to see what George was pointing at, her cotton dress riding up high in the rear. Her back kinked and George helped her straighten up, but was not to be distracted from his original concern. Of course, George always had a concern.

"How did that get there?" he asked.

"You know how these old houses are," Annabelle replied, easing into the soft folds of her chair and turning her attention back to *Wheel of Fortune*.

Annabelle didn't give a rat's behind what George thought—unless he concerned himself into thinking that she was senile and needed to be admitted to Twin Oaks Retirement Center where her sister Elizabeth lived. It was a nice enough place, but it wasn't home.

George harrumphed. "Mother, I don't think you should be living here alone."

"Maybe I could move in with you and Lucinda."

That shut him up.

Annabelle's subscription to the Snake of the Month Club expired. Annabelle sat on her porch, trying to catch a breeze, although not a bean stirred on the Catalpa tree.

On the hottest day of the year, a Toyota clattered to a stop on the serpentine street in front of Annabelle's house. All the windows were rolled down allowing the hot air to circulate. The driver stepped out and wilted onto the sidewalk. He dangled a box secured with a piece of twine, which he used for a handle.

It's that Boy, Annabelle thought.

Handing her the box, he said, "Here's your final snake. We appreciate your business." He forced a fake smile, and an evil glint in his beady little eyes promised mischief.

"The snakes are wonderful," Annabelle said, "but I have too many as it is."

"I can give you a discount as a returning customer," he said. Annabelle shook her head.

"Well, keep this one, it's free." Craig meandered down the sidewalk and disappeared from view behind Mrs. Southworth's overgrown hedge.

A rustling sound from within the package reminded Annabelle of dried seeds in a hollow gourd. She held the box close while she talked to the noisy snake inside. "You are snake #13, and that is my unlucky number. Sorry, little one, but you are not my snake."

Trudging along the cracked sidewalk, she steadied herself with a cane. She held the box through the open window of the Toyota. Looking around, she did not see the young man in the ill-fitting plaid suit.

She pulled the lid off the box and flung the rattlesnake into the car where it disappeared under the seat. Tucking the box under her arm, she hobbled back to her front porch and lowered herself to the porch swing, taking care with her arthritic hip. Annabelle slid the string back onto the empty box.

Craig ambled around the hedge, eyes shifting surreptitiously at the box in Annabelle's lap. He nodded politely. At least it could have been politely, had Annabelle not noticed the hint of a smirk, secretive and most unbecoming.

Annabelle faked the expression of a kid anticipating a birthday gift, one hand on the twine as if she were preparing to open the package. She smiled at the Boy, showing age stained teeth, and waved cheerily at him until the Toyota disappeared around the curve.

Elizabeth's Lucky Day
Linda Capps Fisher

"Today is your lucky day, Elizabeth," Sadie said. The two octogenarians shuffled along the sidewalk toward the Twin Oaks Retirement Center bus.

Elizabeth had moved to the retirement home eight months ago after Elmer died. Without Elmer, she felt incomplete and directionless. Sadie, worried that Elizabeth was going to fade away, had talked her into this excursion.

Now, Sadie struggled to hide her jealousy of Elizabeth's windfall. For the past two years, Sadie had won only small amounts at the Isle of Capri Casino. Elizabeth joined the small group for the first time today and in less than an hour hit a $20,000 jackpot on the newest slot machine, Jangle Money.

Thank goodness, Mary, the retirement center beautician, had crimped and teased Elizabeth's hair into a silver cloud this morning. "You look so lovely, dear," the photographer said as she snapped publicity shots.

Elizabeth threw her heavy black handbag over her shoulder and clutched it against her purple pantsuit. The casino recommended a check, but Elizabeth insisted on cash. She could deposit it in the bank tomorrow, but for the winnings to seem real, she had to hold the money in her hands.

Elizabeth stepped onto the bus, slapped the bag, and told Joy, the middle-aged bus driver, "I won big money!"

"I'm happy for you, honey," said Joy.

"Beginners luck," grumbled Edwin. Joy helped the old man with wispy gray hair onto the bus. His cane banged loudly against the metal steps.

"Well, I'll swan," said Ida. "I never personally knew anyone who won a jackpot."

"I won a thousand bucks once!" Edwin shouted toward Ida's good ear.

"Did you ever know anyone who won?" she asked Edwin.

"It's impossible to carry on a conversation with that woman," Edwin told Elizabeth. "She can't hear anything." Edwin's loud voice hurt Elizabeth's ears, but she nodded in agreement.

The bus pulled out of the parking lot, winding through the streets of Boonville and merged with the traffic on I-70. Elizabeth lowered her window, clicking it down a few notches, to allow a breeze. The cool wind felt good against her skin. Soon the bus veered down the exit ramp and onto Copper Road.

Elizabeth tuned out the racket of the conversation and a hush fell over her ears as the bus passed Salem Cemetery. The sod had taken hold on Elmer's grave making his final resting spot indistinguishable from the others. A tear slid down her cheek when she remembered that today would have been their golden anniversary.

"Oh Elmer, I miss you so," she whispered.

Through eyes blurred with cataracts and tears, Elizabeth saw a young man wearing a dark suit pulling the wrought iron gates shut and attaching a padlock to discourage vandals. Several graves had been desecrated lately, including Elmer's, where someone had dug up the yellow rose bush she had planted.

Elizabeth closed her eyes and leaned her head against the window and reminisced. She must have dozed because when she opened her eyes, the young man from the cemetery sat next to her, a long package loosely wrapped in white foil on his lap.

"I hear this is your lucky day," he said, his gentle voice barely audible above the argument going on between Edwin and Sadie.

"Yes, I guess it is." Elizabeth peered into the handsome face, which looked familiar through her hazy vision. She smelled Old Spice cologne, just like Elmer always wore.

"Lizzy, I brought you a memory." He opened the package and placed a long stem yellow rose in her slender white fingers, where it glowed with beauty. He brushed her face with his hand, sliding it along her smooth skin. He gently kissed her, and Lizzy closed her eyes to savor the taste of his mouth, his breath, his warmth.

Her heart sailed backward to that special day, long ago, when they had exchanged their vows. Yellow roses cascaded from Lizzy's bridal bouquet as she walked down the aisle. Through the haze of her veil, she saw him waiting for her at the altar. "You may kiss the bride," the pastor said in a strong voice. The powerful memory caused her to suck in her breath, filling her nostrils with the scent of roses.

Elizabeth opened her eyes, crinkled with a smile, her lips tingling from her husband's kiss. Elmer was gone, and her black handbag rested on the seat beside her.

Towering oaks canopied the driveway to the rambling old house loftily called a retirement center. Elizabeth glanced upward toward the crescent moon, and walked up the path, crowded with flowers, none of them yellow roses. Elizabeth's hip normally hurt from arthritis, but tonight she stepped with pain-free vigor.

Joy pulled the polished oak door open and the group straggled inside. As the news of Elizabeth's good luck traveled throughout Twin Oaks Retirement Center, staff and residents patted Elizabeth on the back and congratulated her on her winnings.

"Oh," Elizabeth said a half hour later, "I left my purse on the bus."

"I'll get it for you," Joy said. Why hadn't she noticed Elizabeth's handbag was missing? Usually, Joy checked the bus for forgotten items, but with all the excitement, she was thrown off her normal routine. In the third seat from the back, Elizabeth's handbag lay abandoned, sprawled open, the money gone.

Handing the bag to Elizabeth, Joy said, "I am so sorry, Elizabeth. I don't know who would have done such a thing."

Elizabeth shrugged and dangled her handbag carelessly, bumping it against the leg of her purple pantsuit as she ambled down the hallway to her tiny room. From the cedar chest at the foot of the bed, she removed a box. She folded back yellowed tissue paper and pulled out the lacy nightgown she had worn each anniversary.

She turned down the covers and smoothed the sheets on the bed. Elizabeth stretched out, clutching a yellow rose tightly in her wrinkled liver-spotted hands. She smiled widely in the darkness.

"Spending those few precious moments with you made today the luckiest day of my life, Elmer." Elizabeth knew it could have been a dream, but her heart told her a different story. She closed her eyes and thought she felt the bed sag beneath his weight as he settled in beside her. She drifted away to the scent of Old Spice and yellow roses.

THE KIDS IN THE BASEMENT
JIMMY CAPPS

~ PART 1 ~
THE WELFARE LADY

December 20, 1984:

Susan and Tommy Bennett waited in the Welfare Lady's office, not the inside part where the Welfare Lady was, but the outside part where people had to wait. They could see her sitting inside, smoking a cigarette. It was the worst day of their lives.

Their mother had cried like a baby, but they still took them away. Sure, they knew she was a bad mother, but she was their mother and that was what mattered.

Now, here they were, stuck in this crappy office. Susan didn't know much, but she knew things were not good. She had watched the Welfare Lady as she sat in her office all morning. The Welfare Lady's mood progressively degraded. First, she would talk on the phone, then smoke a cigarette, then back to the phones, then back to the cigarettes. Susan knew instinctively this was bad.

She held Tommy's hand tightly. "What if they take him," she worried.

The Welfare Lady was on the phone again, talking to someone else. Suddenly, she seemed happy. She had a smile on her face when she came out to talk to them. She said everything was going to be just "Jim Dandy."

Susan knew one thing for sure; things were never going to be just "Jim Dandy." Furthermore, Susan had decided that she didn't like this Welfare Lady; she was old and ugly. She liked the last one but not this one.

"I've got good news for you," the Welfare Lady said, as she stood over the children, her big phony smile stuck all over her fat face. Susan could smell her stinky perfume as it followed her out of her office.

"Your aunt is going to take care of you."

"Oh great," Susan thought with relief. "When is Aunt Rose coming to pick us up?" she asked.

Susan assumed they were going to stay with their mother's sister. That's what her mother wanted, and that's what the children wanted.

"Your Aunt Rose has called me too many times this morning. I am not very happy with her," the Welfare Lady said, giving Susan a frown, as if Susan had done something wrong.

"You children are going to stay with your Aunt Minnie, in Fulton."

"Who is Aunt Minnie?" Susan asked. She was confused; she didn't even know she had an "Aunt Minnie."

"She's your grandmother's sister, a great aunt."

"We don't know her." Susan pleaded, "We want to stay with Aunt Rose and Uncle Bill."

"Well I'm sorry dear, you can't. Your Aunt Rose lives in another state. You have to stay in Missouri until your mother's hearing."

Susan was upset. Why couldn't they go with Aunt Rose? She lived only a short drive from their rented house in Florissant, just across the state line in Alton, Illinois. Where was Fulton anyway?

"I want to go with Aunt Rose!" Susan demanded.

The Welfare Lady had dealt with this difficult child long enough. "Well you can't, she lives in Illinois."

Agnes Brown, Missouri Social Services Counselor II, had gone to great lengths to find a relative, one that lived in the state of Missouri. One who was willing to care for these children. This was good, if these children couldn't understand that, well tough. Everything she did was for their benefit, and if this bossy little girl couldn't appreciate that, well, too bad.

She forced herself back into her phony good mood.

"That is such great news!" she said as she leaned over to adjust Tommy's collar. Susan could smell cigarettes coming out of her smiley face.

"If a relative takes you, that's great news," she said as she started stuffing papers into her briefcase. "You could have been put into foster care, you know."

Susan didn't say anything about the Welfare Lady's great news, but she was relieved that, at least, the lady was not taking Tommy from her.

She still held Tommy's little hand, but did not squeeze so tightly.

They drove for nearly two hours. The Welfare Lady was impressed at how disciplined the children were. The boy slept while the girl gazed quietly out the window. She complimented them on it. She said she was used to rowdy behavior from her client's children. She asked Susan if the little boy was slow.

"No," Susan said.

Susan knew this lady had no interest in them, she was just pretending. That's what they did, these Welfare Ladies, pretended to care. Susan knew these Welfare Ladies entirely too well. The only thing that interested this one was that soon, she and Tommy would no longer be her problem.

They left the interstate and drove along a winding road.

After about thirty minutes, the Welfare Lady pulled off onto the shoulder of the road. She retrieved a Missouri state road map from her glove box.

"Shit," she said under her breath.

She had taken the wrong exit; she was on Highway 19, not Highway 54. She had jumped off the interstate too quickly. There was a town here, but it was not the right town. The sign said Hermann, she was looking for a town called Fulton, anyone could have made that mistake.

She studied the map and quickly charted a new route. She could get to Fulton by taking the back roads. There was no need to backtrack to the interstate.

This little navigational boo-boo had cost her some time, but not that much; she would just drive faster. She made plans in her head as she drove toward Fulton.

She would do a quick inspection of the house; it would pass, of course. Then she would deposit the children. On the way back to St. Louis, she could do some last minute Christmas shopping at the St. Charles Mall.

They were somewhere south of Fulton when the six-year-old boy spoke for the first time.

"What is that thing with the smoke coming out the top?" the boy asked, as he pointed out the window toward a cluster of huge buildings across a field.

"Well," the Welfare Lady thought, "maybe he isn't retarded after all."

"It's just a building," the sister answered.

"It's burning up!" the boy said.

"I think the smoke is coming out of the top, out of that big chimney," the sister suggested.

The Welfare Lady spoke. "That's steam, not smoke. It's a nuclear power plant."

"Aren't nuclear power plants dangerous?" the sister asked.

"No, of course not," the Welfare Lady answered.

~ PART 2 ~
THE AUNT'S HOUSE

The children sat in the living room, waiting. The Welfare Lady and the aunt talked and smoked cigarettes in the kitchen. Susan did not like this house, it was cold, and it had creepy, peeling off wallpaper stuck to the walls. It smelled like wet cigarettes. The house was old, ugly, and smelled bad, just like the aunt.

"I don't like it here," Tommy whispered to Susan.

"I don't either," she answered.

The Welfare Lady quickly inspected the house. The house had once been grand, but now, it had degraded severely. She thought the house was probably a health hazard; it was disorganized and cluttered. Apparently, the old woman hoarded useless junk, old people do that. However, an unwritten standard allowed some leniency for relatives. If this house had been that of foster parents, it would not have been acceptable, but this was a relative, it would do.

As the Welfare Lady inspected the house, the aunt remained in the kitchen, sitting alone. She did not bother to introduce herself to the children, or welcome them.

The children huddled at the end of a couch, wondering how long they would be here in this creepy house, but they were not told. On this subject, both the aunt and the Welfare Lady agreed; children did not need to know everything.

Susan did know some things, and she was observant and good at figuring things out. She knew that they would be with this aunt while school was dismissed for Christmas vacation.

Earlier, at the office, she had overheard the Welfare Lady talking on the phone, and Susan deduced that their mother was at a mental hospital. She heard that if their mother did not get better, the kids could not return home and would have to start a new school.

Although, Susan had figured out some things, she still didn't know about this aunt. Her first impression was bad, but maybe she was wrong about that. Maybe this aunt would be a good aunt; maybe she just looked mean.

The Welfare Lady finished talking and put her papers into her briefcase. "Come children," the aunt said, "let's see the lady off." They followed the Welfare Lady out the door. The Welfare Lady walked on to her car, started the engine, and backed out of the driveway.

She waved as she left, she was satisfied that she had done a good job. Standing on the porch, waving back to her was a made-to-order family photo, the kindly aunt, with a child's hand in each of hers.

The aunt released the children as soon as the car disappeared around the corner. She walked down from the porch to an azalea bush that grew just off the corner of her house. She squatted down, and grasped a pencil-sized branch. With a quick snap of her wrist, she broke the branch free.

"Into the house," she ordered as she walked back onto the porch.

The children entered the house as ordered.

"In this house there are rules." For emphasis, she whacked a table with the switch. "When I tell you to do something, it is to be done! Do you understand?" She stood defiantly with one hand on her hip.

Susan did not answer. A nasty snarl crossed the aunt's face. She stuck the switch into Susan's face, slightly touching her nose.

"Don't act stupid with me, do you understand, girl?"

"Yes ma'am," Susan said.

"How about you, boy?"

"Uh-huh," Tommy grunted.

Ker-whack, the sound resounded as the aunt hit the wall right above Tommy's head. "There will be no baby talk in my house, when I ask a question, I expect a 'yes' or 'no' answer. Do you understand, boy?"

"Yes ma'am!" Tommy answered.

"In this house, we all work. Follow me," she commanded.

She led the children into a big room at the back of the house. The room was cluttered with boxes, many unopened.

"This is what I do to pay the bills. It's hard work. I am an old woman; you children will help me."

Susan could figure out most things, but she had no idea what the aunt was trying to say.

"Sit down," she ordered.

Susan noticed that two small tables, workstations, were set up. These were for them, she deduced. Then the realization swept over her, they were going to be forced to work.

"Watch this," the aunt commanded. "I'm going to show you what to do."

She removed a handful of envelopes from one box, then she removed a handful of advertisements from another box.

"Tommy's only six," Susan said. "He won't be able to do it."

"Sure he can, stop your whining." She stood with a hand on her hip, giving Susan a one-squinty-evil-eyed look. It was the meanest look Susan had ever seen, and she had seen some mean ones.

"This is a simple job," the aunt said, as she passed her nasty look to Tommy, "even an idiot child should have no problem with this."

She took an envelope, and an advertisement. "Put the advertisement into the envelope, then do this." She held up a little sponge device, then dipped it into a cup of water. "This moistens the envelope." She demonstrated by rubbing the sponge across the inside lip of the envelope flap. "Then, seal the envelope and put it into this box. Any questions?"

"Not about the envelopes," Susan said, "but we are hungry, we haven't eaten all day."

"Don't lie to me girl, I know the Welfare woman fed you."

The aunt glared at the children with her nasty look again. Both began stuffing envelopes. The aunt supervised their efforts, correcting their techniques as required.

"All right," she said, "It looks like you've both got the hang of it. Do all the red boxes, those are Christmas boxes," she said, pointing at four cartons stacked in the corner of the room.

"They have to be done by tonight." She walked to the door. "Then, we will talk about supper."

~ PART 3 ~
MARY'S FAMILY

June 10, 2006:

"Mommy, Mommy!" Judy cried as she ran through the door. Her mother was busy putting dishes into the cupboard, but it was hard to miss the fact that her daughter was both out of breath and excited.

"What?" her mother answered, somewhat amused at her daughter's excitement.

"We have to move!" Judy said.

"What, move?" her mother answered. "Why would we move, we haven't even unpacked yet?"

"We have to move, because there is a ghost in this house!"

"Where, I haven't seen any ghosts. What makes you think there are ghosts in this house?"

"The kids that we met, the ones from down the street. They said there is a ghost in this house." Judy was dead serious as she waited for her mother's response, getting none she added, "We better move, before you unpack all this stuff."

Judy's mother stepped down off the chair on which she had been standing. She temporarily put her work aside.

"Come here, sweetie," she said. "Sit down and catch your breath. Now, just where is that brother of yours? This sounds like some of his doing."

"He's outside, with those kids. He thinks it's all funny."

Judy's mother walked out onto the porch. Judy could hear her call to her brother. "Buddy!" she yelled. "Get in here! Children," she said after she had collected her son, "this is an old house. It is very historic, nearly a hundred years old. In a house this old, there are always going to be some stories of ghosts. It just makes a good story; it doesn't mean it's true."

It was a beautiful home. The realtor said it was a "turn around," meaning that it had recently been restored. The house had sat empty for several years before the renovations. It was a find. When Mary heard the asking price, she was so pleased that she could hardly hide her enthusiasm.

Mary had to make the house buying decisions on her own. That was not really her choice. Her husband was in the Navy, stationed aboard the USS Nimitz, halfway around the world.

Next month, that phase of their life would end. His six-year enlistment was ending, and he was coming home.

In the Navy, he was a Nuclear Power Technician, a unique occupational field, which was also the primary source of staffing for civilian nuclear power plants. Several companies had recruited him. Together, he and Mary chose the central Missouri facility.

Mary moved the family from Bremerton, Washington, to Missouri in preparation for her husband's arrival.

Her parents, who lived in Springfield, Illinois, had a fit when they heard she was moving to Missouri. You would have thought she was moving to hell. Mary had considered their disappointment, and decided that maybe next summer she would send Buddy to stay with them for a couple of months. After that, they would be happy that the family had not moved to Illinois.

As for the house, it was perfect. First, it was close to the nuclear power plant, but not so close as to be worried about it. Also, it was close to Columbia and Jefferson City, both of which had modern shopping centers. The house itself was the best reason; it was a classic foursquare with hardwood floors throughout. In Bremerton, a house like this would have cost half-a-million dollars. Mary had underbid the asking price by forty thousand. Amazingly, the owners had accepted her bid, and she had bought it for a mere one-hundred-ten-thousand dollars.

The thought of ghosts in this wonderful house was amusing. Of course, there were ghosts. It was nearly a hundred years old, what do you expect? Every time the wind blew, or someone walked on the hardwood floors, you could hear them as this wonderful old home creaked and groaned. She was raised in an old two-story house very much like this. She was tired of living in three-bedroom, two-bath track houses. This ancient, haunted, classic home was hers, ghosts be damned.

"Children," she said, "please, let's have no more talk of ghosts."

Mary looked directly at her ten-year-old son. "Do you understand me, Buddy!"

"Okay," Buddy answered, "now can I go back outside."

"Go!" she said. "Now Judy," she said to her six-year-old daughter, "would you like to stay and help me?"

"I'd rather go outside and play," she answered.

"Okay, but if those boys start talking about ghosts again, just remember, they are boys, and you know what we say about boys, don't you?"

"Yeah, boys are stupid."

"You got that right, sister."

Mother and daughter both had a good laugh, then the daughter went outside to play, and the mother went back to unpacking.

~ PART 4 ~
AUNT MEANY

Susan and Tommy had been with Aunt Minnie for a week, and they still didn't know what was to become of them. Their sole existence consisted of stuffing envelopes. If they worked hard enough, they were fed; if not, they went to bed hungry.

The kids learned their aunt's name. She was called Minnie. However, they had a better name for her: Aunt Meany. That's what she was, mean. Susan did not like her.

She and Tommy slept amongst the clutter in the smallest upstairs bedroom. They didn't have a bed, just a sleeping bag in the corner that they shared. When the aunt left to go shopping, they were locked in the basement. The basement was not heated and it was cold.

Today, Susan had gotten into trouble with her aunt.

"Aunt Minnie," Susan asked, "when is the Welfare lady coming back?"

"She's not coming back."

"Aunt Minnie," she asked another question, "is our mother better?"

"Your mom is still in the nut house. That's where she belongs. Maybe when your daddy gets out of prison, you can go with him."

The thought of living with her dad brought conflicting emotions to Susan. It had been such a scandal when he was arrested—the minister of the church, stealing to pay off gambling debts. No wonder, her mother had gone crazy. She had been so proud to be the minister's wife, now she was an embezzler's wife.

Anyway, that was an old problem. Right now Susan was concerned about their present situation.

"We never got any Christmas, and Christmas is already over. That's not fair!" Susan said.

The aunt smiled her favorite evil smile. "Who said I had to be fair?" she snarled.

"When are we going back to school?" Susan demanded.

"You are going to school, when I send you to school."

Susan said nothing, but picked up the telephone. She started dialing numbers.

"What are you doing?"

"I'm calling 911. I may be just a kid, but I know what you are doing is against the law. I'm calling the cops!"

Susan never completed her call. For an old woman, Aunt Minnie was strong. She quickly overpowered Susan. She twisted her arm behind her back and marched her into the nearest corner.

Minnie knew how to handle rebellious children, a good thrashing with an azalea switch, then to the basement.

After beating Susan with the switch, she locked her in the basement, and then went to find Tommy. He had not done anything to warrant punishment, but she whipped him and locked him in the basement too.

Minnie figured that he needed it anyway, and it would serve a purpose. His punishment would teach that sister of his, that if she misbehaved, her brother would be punished as well.

Besides, she needed the peace and quiet. With the children locked away in the basement, she could retrieve her hidden bottle of brandy from the cabinet. She would mix up a stiff drink or two; after all, she deserved it, after working so hard supervising those awful children.

Amidst the beatings and the drinking, Minnie neglected to listen to the weather forecast. The prediction called for the coldest day of the year; the temperature was expected to drop below zero.

On a normal day, the basement was cold. On this day, it was frigid. Then it got worse. The children found a spot in the corner below a loose heating vent. It was slightly warmer than the rest of the basement, but it was still very cold.

Susan tried to climb out the basement window, which was a mistake. When she grabbed onto a pipe to climb through the window, it broke. The broken pipe sprayed water onto her.

Susan found the turn-off handle and turned off the water, but it was too late, she was soaked. Tommy, who was helping her climb the wall, was wet too.

The children banged on the door and cried for help. They could hear Aunt Meany upstairs watching *The Waltons* on TV. What they did not know, was that she was halfway through the brandy bottle and passed out in her La-Z-Boy. That was just as well; she hated *The Waltons*.

It got colder. Susan and Tommy huddled in the corner. Susan snuggled around her little brother trying to keep him warm. She covered him with an old Army coat she found stuffed into a bucket.

"I'm cold," Tommy pleaded.

"We must not go to sleep," Susan said. She did not know where she had heard that, but she knew that you could not go to sleep.

But they were so very cold. Eventually, Tommy went to sleep and Susan wrapped herself around him.

"I must keep him warm," she said aloud. Susan felt so tired, and she was so cold. Eventually, near morning, she went to sleep.

~ PART 5 ~
THE KIDS IN THE BASEMENT

The rain pounded the roof, the sound of thunder rumbled off in the distance. Mary put the children to bed and began to sort laundry. Twenty minutes later, she carried a basket of laundry to the basement. She loaded the Whirlpool and started the cycle. She picked up the book she was reading, a present from the prior owner. She had found it hidden above the ledge of the basement window. It was probably not a good pick for a stormy night, but it was the only thing she had to read in the basement, except a 1999 *Readers Digest*.

As she seated herself, she admired the job she had done with the basement. It was nicely furnished with a sofa, chair, and a table; it was a comfortable basement. As she waited for the washer to complete the first wash, she read the book, *Dead in the Water* by Jake Cobb. It was a ghost story.

After a few minutes, she decided that Jake Cobb might not be a good companion for a stormy night, so she put him away and picked up the *Readers Digest*. She thumbed through it, reading only the humor sections.

Mary scrunched up on the sofa and dozed off. She dreamed that her husband had come home from Iraq, and they were having Christmas dinner.

Mary was jolted out of her dream by a crash of thunder. Seconds later lightning lit up the night sky as thunder roared again.

"Man, that was close!" she said to herself.

Mary jogged up the stairs from the basement to the main level of the house. She walked quietly up the next set of stairs to check on her children. Both were still sleeping; apparently, they could sleep through a thunderstorm. She returned to the basement and the laundry.

She sat back on the sofa and immediately dozed off. In her dream, the family was having Christmas dinner.

Ker-bang!

This time the lightning and thunder hit at the same time. Mary was sure lightning had hit the house directly. All the lights in the house were out. Rain pelted the small windows near the ceiling of the basement.

The wind blew branches against the house. This was a real nasty little storm.

"I hope the children are not scared," Mary thought.

Just then, the lightning flashed again. Mary could see a child huddled in the corner of the basement, or was it two children?

"It must be both of them. They were frightened by the storm and came down here to be with me."

She called into the dark. "Buddy, Judy, come over here, come to my voice." The storm continued to thrash at the house. The kids did not answer.

"Kids, come here!" she called in a louder more authoritative voice. Still, she had no answer.

The lights blinked and fluttered, then the power came back on. Mary could see again. However, to her confusion, her children were not sitting in the corner as she expected.

"What's going on? It's Buddy," she thought instantly, "that little rat is up to something."

Immediately, she ran up the two flights of stairs. Buddy was in his bed, apparently asleep. Mary stepped across the hall to Judy's room; she was sleeping peacefully. She went back to Buddy's room and turned on the light. Buddy groaned but did not wake up.

"They have not been out of bed," she said to herself, then she continued her investigation:

"Is someone else in the house? Perhaps an animal, maybe I saw a dog in the corner. I bet I dreamed it up, that's what I did. I was asleep on the sofa and dreamed the whole thing? No, no, no," she corrected herself, "I saw something, something real."

Mary retrieved a flashlight from her closet, then slipped silently back down the stairs to the basement. She checked every corner and behind all of the appliances. A basket of laundry was near the corner. Was that what she had seen?

She went to the sofa, picked up the ghost story book. She walked to the window ledge and carefully placed the book high on the ledge, exactly where it was when she found it.

She rationalized the events of the evening. She must have imagined seeing something in the corner. Likely, she had just dreamed the whole

182

thing up. So much for reading a ghost story on a stormy night.

Still she did not feel comfortable. She locked the basement on her way out. Once on the main floor of the house, she searched all the rooms and closets. After ensuring nothing was on the main floor, she went to the upstairs bedrooms. Again, she searched. Finally, she was content that except for her and the children, the house was empty—no extra humans, no extra animals.

The storm was still in effect, though much diminished from its earlier wrath. Mary lay in her bed for a half-hour, unable to sleep. She got out of bed, crossed the hall to her daughter's room.

Judy lay in her twin bed sound asleep. Mary reached down and carefully scooped her up. Judy slowly woke.

"What are you doing, Mommy?" Judy asked.

"There is a storm outside, sweetie," Mary answered. "I thought it might scare you, so I'm going to put you in bed with me. So you won't be afraid."

"Mommy, I'm not scared."

"Well, you can sleep with me anyway. I like your company."

"Okay," Judy said, as she drifted back to sleep.

~ PART 6 ~
SUSAN

Susan woke suddenly. It was warm in the basement. Aunt Meany must have turned on the heater. Tommy was already gone; he must have awakened earlier and gone upstairs.

"I wish he had woken me," she thought.

At least, she noticed, the door was unlocked.

Susan resolved that her aunt was not going to get away with locking them inside the basement like that. She would call the police, just like she had tried. She knew for sure that locking children into an unheated basement was against the law.

As she crept slowly up the stairs, she made her plans. She would sneak outside, go to a neighbors house, and call. She didn't know any of the neighbors, but surely, they would help; most people did not like to see children mistreated. She wanted her mom back, and she did not want to stay with Aunt Meany. She just wanted her mom, crazy or not.

Aunt Meany was not in the house; Susan checked every room. She was not there, neither was Tommy.

She called, "Aunt Minnie."

Getting no answer, she called again, "Tommy!"

There was no one in the house. Just to be sure, she checked the house again.

"This is strange. Where did they go? Who cares? I'll call 911, then she will be in big trouble for leaving me alone." Susan found the phone inoperable. She decided to walk to a neighbor's house and ask for help. That idea failed since she was unable to open the doors.

Susan banged on the door and pushed with all of her might, but it just would not open.

"How is this possible?" she asked aloud. "That old witch has locked me in! So what, I'll just go out a window, and if it's locked shut, I'll just knock it out."

Sure enough, the windows were locked also. Aunt Meany must have known that eventually, the children would try to escape. She must have had the windows glued shut. Aunt Meany planned to work them to death!

Susan picked up a kitchen chair, and slung it against a window. The window was made of some sort of unbreakable glass, because the chair just bounced off.

"Holy smoke," she said, "I can't get out of here. I'm a prisoner!"

Susan quickly came up with an alternate plan. She bounded up the stairs to the second floor of the house. From the room where they slept, when she wasn't locked in the basement, she could see a busy street of the town. There were always cars driving back and forth. She would signal them, with a mirror, or a sign. She could get them to come let her out. Then she would find her brother.

What had old Aunt Meany done with her brother? Suddenly she felt guilty, she had been so worried about herself, wanting to get out, she had totally forgotten about Tommy; that would never happen again. She promised herself that she would find her brother, come "hell or high water," whatever that meant; it was one of her mom's expressions.

Susan planted herself at the upstairs window, mirror in hand. She waited, she waited longer, not a single car moved on the street below. Usually she could see people walking, or hear dogs barking. The town outside was dead. Nothing moved.

"Why?" Susan wondered. "What does this all mean? Where are they?"

Suddenly it came to her, something that made sense of everything. While they slept, something happened at the nuclear power plant. The whole place, humans and dogs, had been evacuated. Aunt Meany, either deliberately or accidentally had taken Tommy, but had left her.

A nuclear accident was the only thing that could account for the people, cars, and dogs all being gone. Sooner or later, they would come back. She would wait.

Susan noticed that it was dark. She felt so very tired. She would sleep on it, then think about it tomorrow. Maybe she should sleep in the basement. With nuclear radiation, and maybe the possibility of an explosion, the basement would be the safest place.

Susan woke suddenly. It was still warm in the basement. She got to her feet, she felt woozy. It was daylight.

"Well," she said, "let's try this again."

This time, as she climbed the stairs, she heard sounds coming from the living room.

"She's back!" Susan said to herself. "What should I do?"

Susan considered her options, should she try to sneak out the door and call for help? Probably, the old witch had the doors locked again and would just catch her. No, she would just stand up to her; the worst she could do was to lock her in the basement again. She needed to find out where her brother was. She would deal with her own problems after.

As she came up the stairs, Susan could see the back of Aunt Meany's head as she sat in the living room, watching TV. Susan slipped by unnoticed. She went upstairs and searched all the rooms for her brother. He was gone. Aunt Meany had taken him someplace. That explained why he was gone. She had to deal with Aunt Meany now; she needed to know what she had done with her brother!

Susan walked into the living room. Aunt Meany sat in her La-Z-Boy rocker watching TV. She ignored Susan.

"God, she looks older!" Susan noticed.

Why did she look older? Susan did not know, and did not care. She wanted to know where her brother was.

"Where is my brother?" Susan demanded.

Aunt Meany did not answer. She just continued watching TV.

Susan was angry, she had been forced to stuff envelopes, locked in the basement, left alone in the house, and her brother had been taken away. She was fed up.

Susan stepped between Minnie and the TV. "Where is Tommy?" Susan screamed into Minnie's face.

Minnie gasped for breath, and grabbed her chest. She rose from her chair, then stumbled awkwardly out the door where she fell onto the front lawn."

"Holy smoke," Susan said, "I think she's had a heart attack."

As much as Susan detested Aunt Minnie, she didn't want her to die of a heart attack, especially, since she was alone at the house with her. Susan ran into the living room to call 911.

"Oh no!" she cried. The phones still didn't work.

She ran back to the front door to check on Aunt Minnie. The door was locked again. She looked through the glass at the front lawn.

Aunt Minnie was gone.

"What?" Susan shouted, "Where are you, you old witch?"

Quickly Susan searched the house, upstairs, downstairs, and the basement. Aunt Minnie had tricked her again. She must have left while Susan was trying to call 911.

Susan tried to get out of the house again; it was the same as before. She was so tired. Susan went back to the basement and sat down.

"I ought to be hungry," she thought, but she wasn't. She thought that a bit strange as she fell back to sleep.

Later, Susan awoke with a start. It was warm in the basement. She slipped up the stairs and checked the house. Strangely, someone had removed all of Aunt Minnie's junk. Maybe she did die of a heart attack.

Susan wondered, "How long have I slept?"

Susan looked through the house, then she went to the upstairs window and stood, looking out. She stood there a long time, she felt so tired and confused. A feeling nagged at her; was there somewhere that she needed to go?

Still, she was stuck in this place, maybe there was a way out, and she just hadn't found it yet. It didn't matter anyway; the most important thing was her brother. Where was Tommy? He was only six and couldn't take care of himself. What had that old witch done with him?

"I must find him," she said. "Tommy, where are you?"

She looked in all the rooms again. He wasn't there. She was tired and would look for him later.

Later, a long time later it seemed, but how much later Susan didn't know, she awoke again.

As strange as it seemed, someone had moved more junk into the house. This was so confusing, why didn't they ever come to the basement and let her out. She was so frustrated.

"Tommy, are you here?" she yelled.

She looked in all the rooms. She stood at the window and looked out. Susan had the weird feeling that someone was watching her. Occasionally, she saw a movement out of the corner of her eye.

"There must be someone in the house, hiding from me. Come out," she yelled, "I know you are here."

Susan went back to the basement. She sat in the corner and napped.

Periodically she woke up. On each awakening, she searched the house, asking the same question.

"Tommy! Is that you?"

~ PART 7 ~
THE TURNER HOUSE

Mary drove up the street that led to her house. She had taken Judy with her to go shopping for groceries. Buddy had been a butt-hole, which was his normal mode, so Mary had left him alone at home with his precious X-box.

Now she saw him in the upstairs window, and of all things, it looked as if he was wearing one of her dresses, but the sun was reflecting off the glass. Maybe it was just a colorful shirt.

"Do you see Buddy in the window?" Mary asked her daughter. Judy didn't answer. Mary tilted the rearview mirror so that she could see her daughter. She had fallen asleep.

"Wake up, sweetie, we're home," Mary said as she shut off the motor.

As they walked up the sidewalk to the house, Judy noticed her mother kept glancing at the upstairs window. They each carried a bag of groceries into the house. Buddy did not come out to help, which irritated Mary. She yelled up the stairs at him.

"Buddy, get down here and help me!"

Just then, Buddy came through the front door, each arm wrapped around a grocery sack.

"Jezus Ke-whilli-kers," Buddy complained, "I'm carrying as much as I can."

"Where were you?"

"Outside, up the street. I saw you pull in and came as fast as I could."

"Bull crap, Buddy, I saw you, and you were wearing a..." Mary stopped in mid sentence. Buddy was wearing a white T-shirt and he had come in from outside. Apparently, what she had seen in the window, was not Buddy.

Either that or he was even sneakier than she thought. Maybe she was giving him too much credit; perhaps, one of the kids had hung a shirt from the curtain rod. That was probably the answer.

Mary put away the groceries, then sent Buddy back outside to play. She went to the upstairs room to check things out.

The curtains on the upstairs window were hanging limply. The window was slightly open, perhaps the wind had blown them around. She walked back out the front door, then down to the street in front of her house. She examined the window from that angle, the window looked normal.

Mary had not noticed, but Judy had followed her out the door, she was waiting on the porch when Mary returned.

"You saw her, didn't you, Mommy?" Judy asked.

"Saw who?"

"The girl in the window. I've seen her too, but I didn't say nothing. Buddy makes fun of me, calls me a scaredy-cat. But I ain't scared. You seen her too, didn't you, Mommy?"

"No, sweetie, I thought I saw something, but it was just a reflection off the glass."

"That's where people see her, in that window. That's why they say this is a ghostie house."

"Sweetheart, there is not a ghost in our house, that's just a story the kids tell."

"I seen her inside the house too, she looks in the rooms, but she don't see us."

"Judy, honey, we don't have any ghosts in this house. I checked this house really good before we moved in. One thing I looked for was ghosts, and there were no ghosts in this house."

"Mommy, there's another one that stays outside, but it's afraid to go into the house."

"Judy! Enough of these stories!"

Mary really liked the house and couldn't stand the thought of her husband coming home to hear ghost stories. What a bunch of cowards he would think they were!

As hard as Mary tried to convince Judy that the house was haunt free, she was not so convinced herself. The next morning she was at the realtor's office. She demanded to know the history of the house.

"Now look, Mrs. Bennett," the realtor said, "your house was built in 1910. It's an old house. People have a tendency to think old houses are haunted."

"Well can you tell me this, has anything traumatic happened there. An accident perhaps, has anybody died in my house?"

"An old house like that, probably. I'm sure some were born there too."

"How about a girl, ten to twelve years old?"

Suddenly, the realtor looked defeated. "Oh well," he said, "I guess you have heard stories from some of your neighbors."

"No," she said, "I have not talked to the neighbors. My kids have though, and now my daughter says she sees a girl in our house. Now personally, I don't believe any of this stuff, but I keep an open mind.

Now what do you know about my house?"

"I don't know anything about your house, except that you got it at a bargain price."

"Fine," Mary said.

"Are you moving out?" the realtor asked, smiling slightly.

"Of course not. Is that what you want?" She paused... "Just how many times have you sold this same house?" She slammed the door as she left.

Mary fumed as she stomped down the sidewalk, then she had another idea; there was a place where she might find some answers. It was an old hotel, converted to a museum: the Holdman Inn. It was off the main square.

Mary walked to the Holdman. She introduced herself to the caretaker, a Mrs. Betsy Michaels, a direct descendant of the original owners of the hotel.

"So you're the young lady that moved into the Turner House," Mrs. Michaels stated.

"Gee, I didn't know it had a name," Mary said.

"All the old houses have names."

"Yes then," Mary said, "that's me. I'm the one who moved in. I was wondering, do you have any history about my house?"

"Just what I know in my head. I can tell you that, if you want to know."

"I want to know."

"All right, the Turner house," she said, "was built by Doctor James Turner, about 1910. He was one of the town's most revered citizens. At that time, the Turner House was one of the finest homes in town. Exquisitely furnished and in immaculate condition.

"It was also his office, a clinic. Back then, you couldn't get to a hospital quickly, so Doc's house was the last place seen by many a dying soul. I bet the real estate people didn't tell you that, did they?"

"Not hardly," Mary answered. "Do go on."

"After the doctor died, the house passed through many hands. Over the years, it was stripped and abused. Eventually, a widow named Minerva Burns, the meanest woman in town, not one of my friends, bought it for next to nothing.

"There was a tragedy during that time, about 1984, or '85, not sure, Reagan was President. Anyway a child died in the house."

"A girl I suppose," Mary suggested.

"Yes it was. Minerva Burns went to jail over it. She was gone for nearly five years."

"Did she murder the girl?"

"Maybe, who knows? She was found responsible for the girl's death. I think she was charged with child neglect."

"Seems like five years is too short a sentence for causing the death of a child."

"Well," she said, "that wasn't the end of it."

"What do you mean?"

Mrs. Michaels continued. "Minerva did her time, but she died on the day she got out. First day back in the house, she ran out into her yard and died of a heart attack."

Mrs. Michaels went on to explain, "After that, the bank took the house and it was rented several times, but it was never occupied very long. About four years ago, it was bought and remodeled, one of those flips. Your family is the third family to move in since the remodeling."

Mary thanked her for the information.

"Ma'am," she said, as Mary prepared to leave.

"Yes?"

"Haunts, they come and go. No matter what you see on TV, haunts can't hang around too long."

"How lucky," Mary thought, as she walked home, to have found a *bona fide* ghost expert.

That night, after the kids went to bed, she sat alone in the kitchen and cried. "God, what a mess," she thought.

Her daughter Judy was convinced a ghost was in the house, and even she had to admit, she had seen some things that she could not reconcile. The question was this: was it her imagination, or was the house really haunted? Either way, it was a messed up situation.

"God," she thought, "I can sure screw things up."

How could they live in this house now? For all she knew, a child had been killed in her house.

"Too bad," she told herself, "we have to live here."

Part of her bargain price was a large down payment. She had depleted their savings, and they could not afford to move.

In two weeks, T.J. would be home; she would let him deal with the ghosts.

~ PART 8 ~
THE HOMECOMING

Mary picked up her husband at the St. Louis airport. They drove west on Interstate 70 toward the Kingdom City exit. Mary waited until both children had fallen asleep in the back of the minivan before she briefed her husband on the problems at the house.

T.J. did not believe in things he could not see. At twenty-eight years old, he had already been around the world four times and participated in two wars. A man who had just spent two years in a combat zone did not consider dead things threatening.

"Do you like the house or not?" he asked.

"Oh yeah, it's a great house."

"Then who cares if it has had some history. From the photos you sent, it looks a lot better than what we've lived in."

"It is one of the best houses in town," she said.

"Just how big is Fulton?"

"I don't know, but it has a Walmart, and two small colleges."

"Then, my dear, it's perfect."

T.J., a recent member of the Nuclear Propulsion Division, USS Nimitz, dismissed the haunting as a trivial issue.

Being a Navy wife, Mary was self-sufficient, but having her husband beside her made her feel much more secure. That life, both his and hers, had not been easy, but now, it was in the past. From now on, they would be together and that was comforting.

Mary had known her husband since high school. They had gone together during their senior year, then he left for the Navy. She was in junior college when he returned eighteen months later.

She hadn't thought twice when he asked her to leave with him. Much to her parent's dismay, she left and never looked back.

As for T.J., he had mixed feelings about leaving the Navy. He liked the job and the excitement that came with it; however, he wanted to be with his wife, and see his children as they grew. His own childhood was in dark contrast, marred with tragedy. He was raised by relatives and never really knew his parents. T.J. had known from a young age just how fragile life could be.

It was dark when they arrived at their new home. Being tired, they slept.

Excited about her father's arrival, Judy awoke at daybreak. She went into her parent's bedroom to check on them; they still slept soundly. She returned to her room and tried to go back to sleep.

Judy felt, more than heard, someone in the hall. She thought maybe they were up. She slipped out of her bed and moved quietly to the door of her bedroom. She opened the door silently.

A young girl was moving down the hall. The girl looked into each room. "Tommy, are you here?" the girl yelled.

Strangely, Judy knew that was what she was yelling, though she heard no sound. The girl passed by Judy and went into her room. She went to the window, where she stood and looked out. The girl looked from side to side. It was as if she thought someone was watching her.

She passed by Judy again and went back into the hall. "Come out," she yelled, with her silent voice, "I know you are here."

She looked in Buddy's room. "Tommy, is that you?" she asked, then moved on.

She stood at the doorway to Mary and T.J.'s room. "Tommy, is that you?" she said.

Judy watched as the girl slowly faded away.

An hour later, the rest of the family was awake and moving about the house. Mary prepared to cook breakfast.

T.J. asked Mary to delay breakfast and walk him through the house, and she gave him the grand tour. They started with the upstairs bedrooms. After the bedrooms, they toured the main living area.

"I want to see it from the outside."

Mary took him outside for the exterior examination. The outside was restored as immaculately as the interior. It was a very nice house, an excellent front porch, trees and shrubs are all trimmed.

"Let's check the basement," he said.

They went back inside and down into the basement. The basement was finished in pine paneling. It was set up as a family room.

"This is really nice," he said.

Mary thought he was spending too much time examining the basement. "Come on," she said, "I'm ready to fix breakfast."

Suddenly, T.J. jogged up the stairs

"Now that's what I call a response," Mary said as she chased T.J. back up the stairs.

However, T.J. did not go into the kitchen, he went out the front door. She went to the front door where she saw him outside in the street looking back at the house.

Before she could ask, he jogged back through the front door and went into the dining room at the far corner of the main living floor.

Mary was perplexed as her husband slowly walked back and stood in the center of the living room. His demeanor had changed; he looked as if he had seen a ghost.

"Holy smoke," she said to herself, "he's seen something and is searching the house to make sure it's not in the house."

She recalled how panicked she had been when she thought she had seen a child in the basement; maybe he had seen something in the basement too.

"T.J.," she asked, "what's the matter, have you seen something?"

Her husband did not answer, but just kept examining the house, looking in each room slowly and carefully.

"T.J.," she said. "Thomas Jefferson Bennet!" she yelled.

T.J. looked at his wife and spoke, "You know that story I've told you; when my sister and I were kids, when she died?"

"Yes," she answered.

"This is the house."

"What do you mean, 'This is the house.'"

"This is the house she died in. This is where my sister Susan died. This is Aunt Meany's house!"

194

~ PART 9 ~
STRANGER THINGS HAVE HAPPENED

Two weeks later:

Mary and Thomas sat in the kitchen table, enjoying a morning cup of coffee. It all seemed kind of funny, if not a bit weird.

"I wonder," Mary said, "if it can be explained as just pure coincidence. Of all the houses in this part of the state to pick, this is the one that I chose to buy."

"As bizarre as is seems, dear, that is the only logical answer. Stranger things have happened."

"Just name one."

"Well, I can't, but I'm sure, there has been some." T.J. Bennett's analytical mind accepted that it was an exceptionally extraordinary event, but that's all it was, a weird and odd occurrence.

"None of this means that something supernatural occurred."

Mary, who had actually seen something, had a different opinion. She was convinced that a higher power had directed her to this house.

She also believed she knew the reason they were sent to this specific house.

T.J.'s sister, Susan, had died of exposure in this house. The morning that she died, Rose Brannon, Susan's aunt, had arrived with a court order giving her temporary custody of the children. She arrived to find Susan dead and T.J. in critical condition. T.J. was hospitalized, and Aunt Minnie was hauled off to jail.

After Susan died, Mary believed her spirit haunted the house. Susan's spirit was confused and unsettled. Therefore, she was constantly searching, looking for her brother, looking for T.J.

To Mary, that made sense and matched what her daughter Judy had seen. Susan's spirit could not rest until she was sure her brother was okay. It took them, moving into this specific house, years later, to allow her that peace. Now, she had moved on to wherever it is that spirits go.

The bottom line was that the house was no longer haunted.

"And," T.J. continued, "even if some strange things occurred before I got here, it appears they stopped as soon as I arrived. Now I find that kind of suspicious, don't you?"

T.J. smiled at his wife with his little "I'm smarter than you" smile.

"What are you trying to say, smartass? You think I dreamed the whole thing up because I was afraid to be in the house by myself?"

"Well that is a possibility, isn't it? You did miss me, didn't you?"

"There is one thing I'm thankful to you for, even if you are a male chauvinist prick." She stopped short of telling him, letting him wait as she slowly drank her coffee.

"And what is that, dear?"

"Your son," the introduction of "your son" meant something uncomplimentary was to follow. "Our son," she corrected herself, "has been much better since your arrival."

"How's that?"

"Well, before you came home, and even when we lived in Bremerton, Buddy was a real jerk."

Mary noticed the kitchen door had opened slightly. Judy stepped through from outside on the patio. She had that look on her face; that look that said, she had something she just had to say.

"What is it, sweetie?" Mary asked.

"He's not good now, 'cause of Daddy," she said.

"But he is better, right sweetie?"

"Oh yeah, lots better. But it's 'cause of the old woman!"

"What old woman?" they both asked.

Mary was immediately concerned that some neighbor lady was messing around with her children.

"Come here, sweetie." T.J motioned his daughter to come to the table next to him. She complied, but obviously had something held behind her back.

"What have you got there?" Mary asked, but Judy ignored her, and turned instead toward her father.

"What old woman?" T.J. asked again.

"The old woman in the yard," Judy said. She stood in a defiant pose, one hand on her hip. Her demeanor had changed; a snarl crossed her little face.

"She helps me make him mind!"

"What old woman?" T.J. demanded.

"You know, *Daddy*," she barked. "Don't act stupid with me!"

"KER-WHACK," something hit the table, just missing his fingers.

His heart pounded, old memories rushed back. His little daughter stuck an azalea switch in his face, just inches from his nose.

"You know," she said, "Aunt Meany!"

WHEN THE SNOW FALLS IN SILENCE
LINDA CAPPS FISHER

The mountain village known as Silence was snowbound about once a year. After the storm, dirty snow water dripped from the edges of the buildings and washed away the icicles. Each time, a young woman would be missing, but no bodies were ever found. Sheldon Howell, editor of the weekly paper, called the incidents the Snowman Crimes.

"Sign says you need a waitress." A woman held the hand-lettered construction paper sign in her hands. Her fingernails were chewed off leaving the tips barren.

She glanced around with green eyes that dwarfed her thin face. The converted log cabin café was filled with an optimistic number of tables covered with red and white checked cloths.

Fran knew the stranger was down on her luck by the condition of her shoes—scuffed toes and heels worn down on the outside edges. Skinny arms and legs stuck out from her potato shaped body. *Good god, the girl was pregnant.*

Fran couldn't remember the last time she'd seen someone with blonde hair that shone like a morning sun on a clear day. Only someone as young as this girl could look so good with a stocking cap pulled down to the top of her eyebrows.

"Do you have any experience?" Fran asked sticking a pad in her pocket and a yellow #2 pencil sideways into her ponytail. She shifted three plates on her arm and picked up a cup of coffee. Fran was the working owner of the Coffee Shack and had the flat feet and varicose veins to prove it.

"Yes, Ma'am, I do," the girl said.

Fran placed a plate in front of the editor, an unshaven man hunched over a laptop. Like windshield wipers, his shaggy hair snaked across thick glasses. He shoved up the sleeves of a Denver Broncos sweatshirt exposing thick forearms covered with tattoos. Sheldon glanced up from his laptop, scowling at the intrusion.

Fran waddled onto the next table and said over her shoulder, "Then grab a pad and get their orders." Fran nodded toward a cluster of tables where local retirees congregated each morning.

The girl removed a tattered red coat that looked like a homeless shelter castoff. She approached a man dressed in bibbed overalls and a flannel shirt. His faded blue eyes crinkled at the corners when he smiled at her. "Honey, you look like you need breakfast more than me," Clint Webber said.

"Dad, don't be harassing the young lady," said the big guy sitting across the table from the elderly gentleman.

"I ain't senile yet, Dan. You don't need to be tellin' me how to behave."

She smiled at Clint, not taking offense at his personal remark. "I just can't eat this early in the day."

Dan studied the menu although Fran had not changed a single item on it for more than two years. "I'll take a No. 6," he said.

Fran carried a carafe of coffee to the table. "Fellas, this is my new waitress…" Her voice trailed off as she realized she didn't know her new employee's name.

"Latisha," the girl said, concentrating on her pad, determined to keep the orders straight.

"Y'all be kind to her 'cause I can't seem to keep help around here."

That evening, Fran locked the front door and flipped the sign to "Closed." She insisted Latisha eat a hot roast beef sandwich with big scoops of mashed potatoes smothered with brown gravy.

Latisha walked up a steep incline to her rented studio apartment on the backside of a white two-story house. Paint peeled off in nickel-sized pieces, exposing the original coat of Copenhagen blue.

Latisha eased herself into a wicker chair and sighed as she sank her feet in a warm solution of Epson Salts. Her back ached, but she was relieved to have a job and a place to stay.

The days were swallowed up with a bland sameness while Latisha waited for the arrival of her baby. The morning coffee club doted on her, encouraging Latisha to take her morning break at their table. She sat quietly and drank her glass of milk while she listened to the old men's spirited conversations.

Dr. Dan joined the group each morning before going to the animal clinic. He lacked his dad's charm, but his strong chiseled features softened when he smiled. His obsidian eyes promised secrets to be shared if he chose.

Latisha was uneasy with the editor and plopped down Howell's order each morning without speaking. Sometimes she felt Sheldon's gray eyes track her movements around the room, but when she looked his way, he was staring at the computer screen. Promptly at ten o'clock each morning, he folded up his laptop and left a dollar tip.

No one asked, but everyone assumed, no father would be present when the baby was born, which had to be soon. For Christmas, Dan gave Latisha a kitten to keep her company until the birth. She spent her evenings knitting baby clothes and watching the kitten unravel the ball of yarn.

On New Year's Day, a storm blew in without warning. Snow fell in clumps from ashen skies and drifted into dirty mounds. "It's just as well this ugly snow didn't fall at Christmas," said Fran.

The scraping of the snowplow could be heard until dark. For hours, the plow groaned forward and *beep-beep-beeped* backward with little effect on the accumulation. The people in the small mountain town knew that sometimes you just had to hunker down and outlast the snow.

Some folks handle stress and isolation better than others do. Old timers sipped coffee and ate Fran's homemade apple pie. Sam Page, an old man with a snow-white beard, licked the cinnamon off his fork, and said, "Wonder who'll go missin' this time."

"Shush," said Fran, "I don't want Latisha to hear your stories. She's due any day and you don't need to upset her."

"Better hope she doesn't have the baby until after the roads open, or Dr. Dan'll have to deliver it," Sam said talking with his mouth full of pie.

The customers left for the night, and while the two women washed tables with oversized dishcloths, Fran said, "Stay with me tonight. You're in no shape to trek up the hill to your place. Mine's closer."

"Oh, I'll be okay," Latisha said, but after taking a look out the plate glass windows at the swirling snow, she agreed to stay with Fran. "I worry about the kitten, but I always put out plenty of food and water for her."

"She'll be okay. You know them cats have nine lives."

The wind howled around the corners and rattled the windows of Fran's tiny house. Fran was glad for company on the snowbound night when the people of Silence were trapped with themselves. She turned back the downy comforter in the pink bedroom for Latisha. And they went to bed.

Around midnight, Fran heard screams. She bolted out of bed, flung open Latisha's bedroom door, and flipped on the light. Latisha lay bent in agony on the bed, sweat dripping from her forehead.

"The baby," she said. "The baby is coming."

"I'll call Dan. He can deliver that baby as well as anyone."

Fran picked up the phone and punched in the numbers. Putting the receiver to her ear, she heard the silence of an out-of-order phone.

"The phones are out. I'll go get him."

"Don't leave me!"

"It won't take ten minutes. He can do a much better job than I can."

Fran knew Latisha was worried only about having the baby alone. She knew nothing about the women who disappeared and were soon forgotten by everyone but the editor.

Fran locked the door and thrust the key in her pocket. The wind whipped her heavy coat around her large body. She trudged through deep snow. Her toes were numbed by the cold powder overflowing into her boots. The night should have been hushed by the snow, but instead screamed of danger and reeked with fear.

She pounded on Dan's door and shouted his name, just to have her voice blown away with the wind. Finally, Dan opened the door and stood there fully dressed. "Fran, what are you doing out on a night like this?"

"The baby is coming."

"Let me get my bag and we'll head to Latisha's place."

"She's at my house." Fran felt less vulnerable following Dan's big frame. They stomped their feet on the welcome mat but left puddles on the hardwood floor.

Fran threw her hands over her mouth to stifle her scream when she saw the empty bed. Latisha's clothes were folded neatly in a chair, but her boots and coat were gone. "Oh, my God. She's missing."

"We'll find her," Dan said. "She can't be far. I have an idea where to look. Lock your doors and if you have a gun, get it out. Don't let anyone in except me."

Dan flipped on his flashlight and followed the footsteps in the snow. They led in the direction he expected. Snow pinged Dan's face as he doggedly trailed faint footsteps quickly being erased by drifting snow. At the end of a familiar walkway, he swung open a wrought iron gate, his feet sliding on the slick concrete steps. Dan took out a key, silently turned the lock, and pushed the door open.

He heard muffled cries and groans. Latisha was lying on the bed with her knees bent. A picture of Jesus hung at an angle on the wall, like it was about to fall off the hook. The pregnant girl thrashed with pain from the birth.

She wore one of Fran's nightgowns, which fit loosely over her huge abdomen. Beneath her, a plastic sheet lay on a rough blanket covered with fuzz. Dan's father leaned forward in a chair, a knife clutched in his right hand and Latisha's tabby kitten in the other.

"What are you doing?" Dan asked in a matter-of-fact tone.

"I had to save her from the Snowman," he said. "I went to her house but she wasn't there, so I went to Fran's."

"She's having her baby."

"I know. If she hurries up and has the baby, it won't disappear too."

Latisha's eyes opened wide with fear.

"I hate for her to be the one," Dan said softly. Clint scooted closer to her.

Dan moved to his dad's side, looking down at Latisha who shut her eyes as a contraction racked her body. "She really is beautiful, isn't she? I think she's the best yet."

"The Snowman had already been to her house. Her door was busted down when I got there," Clint said. "I found her at Fran's."

"At least we can save the baby."

"Yes. That's the best we can do. You know the Snowman has to satisfy his hunger and better a stranger than one of our own."

The next morning when the retirees gathered at the Coffee Shack all the talk was about the disappearance of the new waitress.

"Maybe her boyfriend came and got her," said Clint.

"How the hell would he get here?" asked Dan.

"It's a mystery," said old Mr. Page as he lit his pipe.

"Hey, you can't smoke in here," said Fran. "I have a hard enough time breathin' without second-hand smoke."

The keys clicked on Sheldon Howell's laptop as he typed. Thank goodness, there was finally some news. He finished the story and pushed the delete button, just like he had after writing the other Snowman Crime stories. He closed his laptop and left a dollar tip.

"I'm ready to order now," Dan said. "Unlike the rest of you, I have work to do."

"I'm coming," said Fran. "I can't keep any help around here. Seems they always disappear."

"Just make sure the next one is not pregnant," said Clint.

"Don't worry," said Fran, checking the bassinette to see how little Latisha was doing. "It's a bitch to find good daycare these days."

Dirty water dripped from the edge of the roof and splattered onto the construction paper "Help Wanted" sign.

GOTTES WILLE
LINDA CAPPS FISHER

Martha strolled along the shady lane toward the simple white church. She shivered, but knew it wasn't the blustery weather that caused the coldness within her soul. The October wind whipped her long black hair into her eyes, and she impatiently stuffed it back into the bun. That's when she realized her prayer kapp was missing.

Mamm would have scolded her. "Where is your kapp? Why are you so careless, Martha Elizabeth?"

Martha lived far from Mamm now. Papa and Mamm had moved to Ohio to find husbands for her younger sisters. It was already too late for Martha.

She kicked walnut, oak, and maple leaves into the wind, where they swirled like a small tornado. A smile tugged the corners of Martha's mouth, giving her plain face a Mona Lisa look. Her mother never suspected that sometimes Martha left her prayer kapp on the ground while she and Bobby McGowin lay in the leaves, looking up at the sky, playing "What If."

"What if...you weren't Amish?" Bobby asked.

"What if...you were?" Martha countered. Her hazel eyes locked with his green ones.

The object of the "What If" game wasn't to answer the unanswerable, but rather to open their minds to new possibilities. Martha and Bobby fell in love when they were eight years old. The blond boy and dark-haired girl carefully guarded their secret. They met beneath the Indian trail tree in a secluded glen.

When they were sixteen, Bobby kissed Martha in a different way. She was surprised and angry.

"Who have you been kissing?"

"No one," Bobby said, his face beet red.

Martha knew he lied, but she loved him too much to press for an answer. She kissed him back, her mouth hard with anger. They fell back onto the ground, tussling and rolling on the orange autumn leaves.

Bobby's breath came in gasps, but he pushed Martha away. "I love you too much to hurt you," he said.

That began what Martha remembered as the year of Bobby. He gave her his class ring in the spring. Martha wore it on a string hidden beneath her plain dress close to her heart. Her every waking moment was filled with thoughts of Bobby and his muscular body pressed tightly against hers.

After Bobby started college, Martha waited for him in the glen on weekends. One September day, she heard leaves crunching on the path and her heart sailed with joy. She ran to Bobby and threw her arms around him, placed her ear to his beating heart.

"I'm so busy in school," he said. Bobby, the boy she loved, had turned into a man, and Martha wrestled with her desire to please him and her commitment to the life her ancestors had chosen. Long after Bobby left, Martha huddled in the leaves like a wounded animal.

In late October, Martha walked up the trail toward Bobby's house. Her feet crushed brittle autumn leaves, sounding like a herd of whitetail deer. At the end of the trail, she quietly watched as Bobby drove up in his red Mustang. He opened the door for a scantily dressed girl. Bobby pulled her into his arms, and held her close as they kissed. Martha's world went silent except for the blood rushing in her ears.

Walking hand-in-hand, the girl stretched one arm in front of her, slender white fingers splayed, as she admired a glittering diamond ring.

"I can hardly wait to show your parents," the girl said in a shrill voice. That was when they saw Martha.

"Who is that weird girl?" she asked.

"Just an Amish girl, who isn't quite right," Bobby replied. "It's okay. She's harmless."

"I don't like the way she's looking at us. Maybe you should call the sheriff."

The couple disappeared into the house, but not before Martha saw Bobby fondling the girl's behind through her skin-tight blue jeans. Martha vomited—her stomach contents splattering the leaves at her feet.

Before Thanksgiving, Martha married Jakob, a widower almost as old as her father. He was a plain man, a good man, who didn't question the early arrival of their son. Elijah was a perfect baby with beautiful green eyes.

When Elijah died in his sleep a few days after birth, the Bishop said, "It's *Gottes Wille* that the baby died." He really thought Martha Elizabeth was too simple-minded to care for her baby. She spent hours rocking in a chair, her eyes seeing something no one else saw, her lips turned up in a mysterious smile.

Martha paused in front of the church as she remembered the day she saw Bobby with that woman. Her name was Tiffany and after he finished college, Bobby married her at a fancy ceremony at the country club. Martha didn't see anything holy about that matrimony.

Martha walked past the church and through the open gate of the cemetery. Normally, the final resting place was neat, but today windblown leaves huddled against the headstones like homemade patchwork quilts of glorious autumn hues.

Martha brushed the leaves from baby Elijah's headstone. Where do the leaves go, year after year? Eight autumns had come and gone since Papa made the tiny coffin for his firstborn grandchild.

Martha pulled Bobby's ring from her apron pocket, the frayed string still attached. The day she saw Bobby with Tiffany, Martha hid the ring beneath the Indian trail tree and thought she had buried her dreams of Bobby.

Because of Elijah, she couldn't forget Bobby. From the moment the baby first moved inside her, he was a reminder of her foolishness and humiliation.

She dug a small hole, and buried the ring near Elijah's headstone. On the freshly turned dirt, she placed orange leaves the color of Mamm's pumpkin bread. She remained on her knees, her head bowed to pray. The earthy smell of the leaves reminded her of the secret glen.

"Here's your kapp. It was beneath 'our' tree," Bobby said with love and sadness in his eyes.

Martha placed the bonnet firmly on her head, tying the ribbon. She turned her back to Bobby and cast her eyes downward in imitated prayer. Her mind was racing and God didn't enter into her thoughts.

"Was Elijah my son?" Bobby placed a hand on her shoulder.

She looked up as if he had intruded upon her fervent prayers. "He is with his Father," she said, deceptively gesturing toward Jakob's grave.

Bobby gently patted Elijah's gravestone. "I'm drawn to this grave and come here often, you know."

"I have no words for you. Go away." She pretended not to watch, but with a sideways glance, she saw the stoop in Bobby's shoulders as he walked away.

"Why did you have to remind me so much of him, Baby Elijah?" She spoke the words softly, but she knew that Elijah heard her. "You would have been alive to comfort me." Her words held sorrow and regret for the powerful love that made her steal the baby's breath away and close those green eyes.

His baby voice joined the whispers of the wind, "What if...I hadn't died?"

"We cannot change *Gottes Wille*," she said. Her lips turned slightly upward as she and Baby Elijah shared their secret.

THE NIGHT BOATS
JIMMY CAPPS

The old man had lived along the banks of the river for as long as he could remember; then when it became a lake, he just moved up the hill a bit. His house was what some derisively called a tarpaper shack, but to him it was home.

The old man's land was an eighty-acre spoon shaped peninsula that stuck out into the lake. The property was isolated from the mainland by a steep rocky hillside. However, the eighty acres gave him ample hunting ground and grazing for his mule.

His home sat at the end of the peninsula, and afforded him a three-sided view of the lake. Today, like most evenings, he sat on his porch. In his hand, he held an ancient brass telescope. Occasionally, he looked out across the lake. Every few minutes he would reach down to pet his companion, Rusty, a red hound who lay at his feet. Often he talked to Rusty, asking his opinion on things.

"What do you think, Rusty, are we going to get some rain?"

The old man wanted rain; he needed rain. Since no roads connected the peninsula to a highway, to go to town, he had to row his boat across the lake to his brother's house. Once there, he could ride with his brother to the town of Versailles.

They usually went to town the first Saturday of each month. He didn't have any money, and there was no sense going to town. The rain, though, could make a difference, because his potatoes, tomatoes, and corn sure needed some rain.

The peninsula was once part of his family's homestead. Back then, the homestead was a large productive farm that straddled the river. It comprised several hundred acres of prime bottomland; however, when the lake came in, it covered the good land, leaving hilltops on both sides of the lake.

His brother Zach loved farming, so he took the Morgan County side, which was better for farming. The old man took the Camden County side, which was better for fishing and trapping, his specialties.

A second benefit of the peninsula was that it kept people out, and the old man had little use for people.

He picked up his telescope again. "By golly, Rusty," he commented, "I think there may be a big fish on my eastern trotline."

In the evenings, from his porch, the old man often did a visual check on his trotlines, because fish provided the bulk of his food. He liked fish and could eat it every meal, and often did. His goal now was to catch a really big fish, and just in case he had one on his line, he needed to take his boat out to check it.

Just a few weeks ago, when he and Zach had gone to Versailles, he had met a man that lived twelve miles down the lake at the Rocky Point fish camp. That man said he would pay top dollar, up to seventy-five cents a pound, for any fish that weighed over fifty pounds.

That Rocky Point man confided that he would take those big fish to Jefferson City. He would go on television during the Ozark Jubilee show and claim that he caught them himself. That way, he could advertise his fish camp. The bottom line was that a big fish meant cash money, something the old man needed.

"We best get down to the boat and see," he said to Rusty. Before leaving, he went into the house and retrieved a kerosene lantern.

"Hey Rusty!" he said, as they walked down the short path to his boat. "Did I tell you, I saw Zach yesterday? He is feeling poorly. Tomorrow we got to go there and help him butcher a hog. I sure could use some pork and lard.

"Oh yeah, I forgot to tell you, Zach, he got him a letter from his boy, Bill. He is doing good up there in Kansas City making those Chevrolets. Him and his wife has got three kids now."

When Bill had last visited the old man, three years ago, he said this peninsula, someday, was going to be worth a lot of money.

"Much better than Dad's land," he said. "There'll come a time that land like yours, that touches the water, is going to be very desirable."

He went on to talk about how the land down by Bagnell Dam was being developed, so that rich folks could build cabins on the lake.

The old man was quick to point out the foolishness of this, because why would any city person want to live down here in this hard land.

"They don't want to live down here," his nephew explained. "They just want to come down on the weekends, in the summer, to fish a little and water ski."

The old man knew what he was talking about; he had seen those idiots being dragged behind a boat on those skinny boards. He just could not see how something so stupid could be any fun.

"I just hope them fools never make it to this end of the lake!" he said to his dog Rusty. Apparently, Rusty, not having any frame of reference as to what the old man was saying, did not respond.

The old man, was still thinking of his nephew's conversation when again he addressed Rusty. "That's total foolishness, city slickers building cabins on this lake. Hell Rusty, they'll never make it through the first winter."

Rusty gave a low *"ruff, ruff"* response, indicating that at last, he was paying attention.

"I do like this lake," the old man said. He could not imagine living anywhere else, but he sure did miss the river.

"Oh, the river," his mind meandered back.

He had worked on the river as it saw its last days. When he was a young man, he rode tie rafts from Cole Camp Creek to the railhead in Bagnell. His daddy had taught his boys how to bring the tie rafts down the twisting river. Nowadays, he and Zach were some of the last survivors of that era, and they too would not be long for this world.

"Oh hell," he mumbled to himself, "a body can't live forever!"

He stopped momentarily at the lake's edge. He pointed out across the lake toward Proctor Cove. "I used to have a trotline, just over where the cemetery was," he said to Rusty. He thought about Proctor, the old town that he had grown up in, now forty feet underwater.

He pushed his long, skinny, metal rowboat out into the lake. The sun had gone down, and it was already getting hard to see. He put his back to the oars and sent his old rowboat gliding across the water. A few minutes later, he reached the end of his trotline. He picked up the Clorox jug that was attached to the end of the line.

While sitting on his porch earlier, he had seen it being violently jerked around and pulled under the water. However, now it felt as if there was nothing on it. Then, slowly, the entire trotline started to move to the side.

"Oh, there he is, Rusty old boy."

The old man wanted to land the fish as soon as possible, to negate its opportunity to escape. If he rushed the fish, he knew it could be lost as well.

So, in this endeavor, patience was a virtue. He held the line in his hand, keeping a light but constant pressure on the fish. By doing this, he could eventually tire the fish out.

As he held the fish, the sun slowly went down. Not long after, the full moon came out. Its reflection cast a beam of light across the warm surface of the water. The frogs started their croaking and the night birds called. It was a beautiful night.

Still, the old man held to the fish.

"Rusty," he said, "this could be a hundred pound fish." He rubbed Rusty's head with his free hand. Rusty, licked the old man's hand back in apparent agreement.

The old man, with his free hand, retrieved his pipe and tobacco from a bucket in his boat. He filled the pipe and lit it. He did the same with his kerosene lantern.

He smoked his pipe while maintaining pressure on the fish, waiting for it to tire. Rusty sat contentedly at his feet.

Then something new happened. Inexplicably, the frogs and night birds of the lake went silent. Then, a thin layer of fog slowly materialized from upriver. At first, the fog was just a wisp. Then it stretched down-river, moving ever so slowly like a giant gray snake slithering silently down the lake.

In the distance, the old man heard a familiar, but long missing sound—the *thump, thump, thump,* of a single-cylinder steam engine.

He immediately thought about the movie. Last spring, he and Zach had driven Zach's old pickup into Versailles to sell their winter's worth of furs. The fur buyer, James Stone, had talked them into seeing a movie. Neither the old man, nor Zach, had seen a movie since the movies started talking, so they just decided to go watch one.

He had seen movies before, some forty years ago, when they were silent, but these movies today, they were much better. The pictures were colored and the people talked.

The movie was called the *African Queen*, and it was about a man and a woman on a boat. One thing was confusing, and he should have asked James Stone, but didn't want to reveal his ignorance. It was this, the woman kept calling the man "Charlie," but James Stone said his name was Humphrey. All that aside, the boat was the interesting part. It was almost a dead ringer to some of the old boats that ran the river when he was a kid, and damned if that wasn't the sound he was hearing now.

The old man also had an idea of what the sound meant. He personally had never seen it, but he knew many an honest man who had testified to what was coming.

He put away his pipe, and sat silently in his boat. Rusty whimpered, and snuggled up beside him.

If it was what he thought it was, the old man had no desire to deal with it, and normally, he would have headed full speed for the bank; however, he could not leave the fish.

He just hoped they were not looking for him.

Seconds later, he could distinguish the laughter of men and women.

"Yes," the old man whispered to Rusty, "this here is what I was afraid it was."

The old timers had talked about these things. Old dead river men ran the river at night extracting their kind. As far as he knew, around these parts, Zach and him were the only ones that still lived, just waiting their turn.

Where these things came from, and where they went, those old timers did not know. They said they came from somewhere upriver and disappeared somewhere downriver.

The old man knew that modern folk could never comprehend such a thing; it was too illogical. Tie rafts had not floated these waters since the 1920s, but the old man knew, sometimes logic just didn't cut it.

The Night Boats were coming. They were rumored to be a half-mile of tie-rafts, and miscellaneous old riverboats. From Osceola to

Osage City, these events, that happened only occasionally, were witnessed by few and spoke of by even fewer. Tonight, it seemed, the old river men were coming to retrieve one of their own.

The old man waited, silent in his boat, watching as it came, drifting out of the fog. Then he saw it, a huge tie raft, a quarter-mile long, being tugged along by an old steam powered riverboat. *Thump, thump, thump,* its old steam powered engine quietly said.

The boat pilot seemed to be scrutinizing the banks for any sign of life. If detected, he stood ready to guide the raft back into the fog.

The old man and his boat seemed to be of little concern to them, as the raft, only a few feet away, slid slowly past him.

As the raft passed by, the old man observed the party. There were some wild things going on. A makeshift platform of planks strewn atop the raft was lit by torchlight. Catfish frying on an open fire, fiddle playing, and dancing. Yes indeed, this was quite a party.

The main attraction seemed to be a poker game. The old man could see an empty chair: did this mean the guest of honor was yet to be found? Could it be for him? He didn't think so, as he still held the fish, which was certainly a living thing, as was Rusty; therefore, he too must be alive.

He continued his observation of the party.

Gathered around the poker game were more than twenty men. Dozens more ambled along the raft: drinking, laughing, and cussing. Mixed among the men were a generous supply of young hillbilly girls, green as grass and as dumb as turnips.

Their voices carried to him, close, but yet like a thousand feet away.

"You'ns quit that grabbin' at my titties," one of the girls squealed in delight.

A drunken partygoer fell into the lake. The old man heard him call out, "Hey gall-dang-it, throw me a rope, a'fore I git drownded again. Hee, hee." He was pulled back aboard and quickly found one of the girls. Pulling the side of his overalls open, he bellowed out, "Help me here Sadie, I thank they is a fish in my britches."

Without hesitation, the girl plunged her arm through the side panel of his overalls. She quickly searched, then screamed out, "You shore do, but don't fret none, it's just a minner!"

The party erupted in laughter.

Still unnoticed, the old man watched as the procession slowly passed by. Then at the end of the raft, he saw him. It was his brother. Zach was walking from the back of the raft toward the front, walking with an unfamiliar spring to his step.

"Zach!" the old man yelled. "Zach!" he yelled again.

Zach just smiled and kept walking right past the old man. He kept walking forward on the raft, heading toward the poker game.

Then, just as it came, the raft, the party, the laughter, and his brother Zach, all disappeared downriver. The raft was gone, dragging its tail of fog behind it.

Again, the night returned to normal. The night birds and frogs resumed their songs.

The old man still held to the trotline. And he continued to do so, for another forty-five minutes, then, at last, a seventy-pound catfish came to the surface and rolled onto its side. The old man reached down with his dip net. He spoke to his dog Rusty. "Rusty, he seems to be ready."

The old man dipped the fish, and lifted it into his boat. After securing it to a long length of parachute cord, he dumped it back into the water. He hung the kerosene lantern from his long handled gaff, then suspended it out over the bow.

He started rowing the boat, and after a bit, the fish swam contentedly alongside the boat.

"Well, Rusty," he said, "let's get this fish down the lake to Rocky Point. We can be there by daylight."

Rusty barked, *"Ruff, ruff, ruff."*

"I know," the old man said.

"Ruff, ruff, ruff," Rusty barked again.

"I know, I know, 'what about Zach.' I heard you the first time, no sense repeating yourself. And, about Zach," he said, as he patted Rusty's head. "We will see to him tomorrow," he said. "He ain't going nowhere."

THE AMETHYST PROMISE RING
LINDA CAPPS FISHER

Sixteen-year-old Amanda walked around the sagging sofa, the scarred coffee table, and gravitated toward a group of cardboard boxes. Mattie Fowler's accumulated bric-a-brac and prized possessions were scattered throughout the yard in front of her white farmhouse. The house was rundown, and one of the green shutters hung haphazardly by one corner.

Amanda was bored. She came to this sale with her aunt and uncle who lived in the boonies. Her parents were so into family that they sent her to spend a week with her relatives each summer. Aunt Anna and Uncle Ed were good people, but they were country folks and loved going to auctions and thought picking through dead people's belongings was great fun.

"What ya gonna bid now," the auctioneer sang out, holding up a framed arrowhead collection. Everyone knew that Mattie was a strange one and had spent a lot of her time digging in the dirt for Native American treasures. How much odder can you get than to hang yourself in the barn when you know no one checks on you, and it could be weeks before your body would be found?

Mattie had been Aunt Anna's friend and they had grown up together. "Mattie always was a sad one and never got over her boyfriend dying in Vietnam," Aunt Anna explained to Amanda. "She insisted on riding the train to be with his family in Warrensburg for the funeral and wouldn't let anyone go with her. It just broke her spirit."

The hot Missouri sun beat down on Amanda's head, and she wished now that she had worn that silly old straw hat Aunt Anna offered her this morning. Thinking it looked entirely too fuddy-duddy, she had refused. Now her head was so hot she felt like she could spontaneously combust.

An oak tree shaded one end of the long folding table. For a lack of anything else to do, Amanda went to poke through the boxes on that end. Digging around in a box, Amanda found some hand-crocheted doilies. Looking at the intricate lacy designs, she moved them to the side. Most of these boxes were full of junk and this box was no exception. Other than the half dozen doilies, the box contained a dozen or so stained tea towels, a few plastic trinkets, and a tiny wooden box. Amanda opened the box and found a blackened silver ring with a deep purple amethyst stone nestled in a gaudy setting.

Amanda jumped when a voice behind her said, "Did you find something?"

"Aunt Anna, you scared me. Yes, I did find something. Amethyst is my birthstone." Amanda slipped the ring onto one of her long slender fingers. It fit perfectly.

"If you want it, I'll bid on this box. I'd like to have some of Mattie's doilies."

On the way home, Amanda was squeezed between her aunt and uncle in Uncle Ed's battered up Ford pickup truck. Amanda slipped the ring onto her finger and Aunt Anna promised to use her silver polish to make the ring shine like new.

After Aunt Anna's fried chicken dinner, Amanda pulled back the double wedding ring quilt and fluffed up the feather pillows in the spare bedroom. She settled in for the night admiring the amethyst ring as it glowed in the moonlight that slanted through sheer curtains blowing in the summer breeze. The steady droning of cicadas and tree frogs lulled Amanda to sleep.

"Mattie, this is a promise ring," Stephen said. The two young people sat on the front porch swing while Mattie's parents slept peacefully in the upstairs bedroom at the back of the house.

"I will always love you Stephen, and I'll miss you so much while you're in Vietnam."

"I'll miss you too, Mattie. When I get home, we'll get married. You'll be out of school by then." Moonlight made the hollows under Stephen's brown eyes more pronounced. Mattie knew he was worried, and she had a bad feeling.

She placed her hand on his cheek and kissed him tenderly. The moonlight glinted off the amethyst ring, and the ring soaked up the power of the night.

Amanda woke up, and brushed tears from her cheeks with a corner of the quilt. What had she been dreaming? All she could remember from the hazy dream was an old woman holding an American flag neatly tucked into a triangle. Beside her sat a girl, not much older than Amanda, wearing a blue dress. The girl had buried her face in her hands, and her body shook with sobs. The amethyst ring on one of her slender fingers glinted in the sunlight and glowed as if it soaked up power from the sun to compensate for unfulfilled promises.

Old Foxfire, the rooster, crowed enthusiastically as dawn broke in the eastern sky. Amanda pushed back the curtain and saw the golden orb of the sun streaked with red, orange, and amethyst.

"Something feels different this morning," she said aloud. As Amanda shook off the dream, she remembered that today she would take the Amtrak home. That probably explained the subtle memory of a train from her dreams.

The train chugged into the station on schedule and Amanda hugged her aunt and uncle before she boarded. The doors clacked shut, and with loud warning whistles, the train headed east toward Kansas City.

The train's rocking motion lulled Amanda to sleep. After her restless night, she slept soundly through several stops. When she awakened from her dreamless nap, she stretched and looked around her.

A young woman sat on the window seat across the aisle from her. The passenger wore a blue mini-dress with white pumps and carried a white clutch purse. She opened her handbag and drew out a lacy handkerchief to dab her eyes. The girl had a quaint look about her that reminded Amanda of the way her mother looked in pictures from the sixties.

The train stopped and the young lady stood and stepped in line behind an overweight woman wearing red shorts. Amanda noticed the girl wore an amethyst ring in a silver setting, identical to hers. Amanda checked her hand to make sure her ring was still there. When she looked up, the girl had already moved forward. Amanda stood to get another glimpse of her, but saw only the lady in red shorts nearing the door. No one stood behind her.

Amanda jumped up and briskly made her way down the aisle, but the girl was not in any of the seats in that car. Amanda looked out the window at the group of people standing on a concrete slab surrounded by luggage. She saw a lot of people dressed in T-shirts and shorts, but no one wore a blue dress. Thinking the girl may have gone to the dining car, Amanda searched the rest of the train. Not long after she returned to her seat, she reached her stop.

Back at home in her own canopy bed, Amanda found her sleep tormented with dreams of love, war, and grief. She began to think of the ring as a circle of memories tugging her toward the past and trying to suck her into them.

The girl on the train was in the dream, and Amanda began to feel burdened with her sorrow. After several more restless nights, she reluctantly placed the ring back in the wooden box and tucked it away in a drawer. She never wore it again, but couldn't bring herself to get rid of it.

Ten years later, Amanda decided she needed to clean up the clutter in her life with a yard sale. Her husband, Brad, had left her for some young thing he met at the office. She sat behind a cigar box with some change just as the sun came up in the east slashing the sky with garnet, opal, and amethyst.

A young couple, holding hands, walked up her driveway. With the young man's square-set shoulders, Amanda thought he was probably from the nearby airbase. The couple separated to look at the different tables. The man held his hands behind his back while he glanced at items. Amanda could just imagine his mother harping at him through his formative years with the admonishment, "Look, but don't touch!"

His training made him hesitate when his eye fell on the ring. Finally, he reached out and picked it up.

"It is so beautiful," he said, his voice quiet, yet rich with emotion.

"Yes it is," Amanda agreed.

"How much is it?"

"Stevie, what did you find?" The girl with shiny brown hair smiled at the young man. Her eyes lit up when she saw the ring. "That's my birthstone."

Stevie shot an eyebrow up in a questioning look. Amanda realized she was staring at a young girl who looked hauntingly familiar. "Ten dollars," she said, her voice coming out in a croak.

The man handed her a ten-dollar bill, and the young couple walked away hand in hand. At the end of the driveway, the girl teasingly asked him, "Are *you* going to wear that ring?"

Amanda opened her mouth to yell, "Come back," but no sound came out. From the dredges of her memory, she recognized the girl from the train. A tear dripped down her cheek as she realized she didn't have the power to change anything.

The couple walked away, arms around each other, watching the sun glint off the ring. "No," he said. "This is a promise ring. Then, when I get back from Afghanistan, we'll get married. I'll miss you so much, Mattie."

The ring began to soak up the power of the sun to set in motion another circle of unfulfilled promises and broken dreams.

Working on Shorty's House

Jimmy Capps

~ Part 1 ~
Driving to Shorty's

My name's Jesse Driscoll. I was riding with my brothers, William and Abel; we always called them "Willing and Abel," a family joke. They sat in the front, while I took it easy in the backseat.

Abel had a Ford F150 crew cab. Behind it, we towed a rented cherry picker, the big kind, with a man bucket. The Driscoll Brothers Construction Co. was on the move.

"The old town is about dead," William observed.

"The people are still here," Abel said, "but Walmarts has killed off all the businesses."

As I sat there in the backseat, I thought about the town. A few years ago, Elisabeth and I moved back. For years, we had lived wherever the company sent us: Chicago, Memphis, LA, and Orlando, to name a few. Now that I was back in this hoe-dunk place, I liked it.

"Hey," I said, "I like living in Palmer. I even like Walmart." It always bugged me when the locals pronounced it as "Walmarts" instead of "Walmart."

"That's progress for you," Will noted, "Wally World taking over."

Calling it "Wally World" was even worse.

The boys had come to town to rent the cherry picker for a job on Shorty Nelson's old place. The house was located thirty miles away, way down at the end of the "Point."

Falcon Point Development is not what it used to be, but I like to go there now and again, to get back to my roots, I guess.

So I hitched a ride.

I decided to keep my opinions about Walmart to myself

I consider the Point my home, although I haven't lived there since I went off to college, way back when. But that's where I came from.

When I was a kid, we lived in the upper end of the Point.

My grandpa owned land in the upper Point, even before Shorty Nelson bought the lower end in 1955. The folks always lived there until they died off, now only Abel is left.

Abel lives on the old place, where we were raised. My other brother, William, doesn't live in the Point full time, but he owns a cabin there. Most of the time he lives in the city.

The rest of us, the girls and me, we moved to the cities. That's the way it goes.

Abel turned left from the highway onto the notorious Falcon Point Road. The easy part of the ride, the asphalt part was over; the rest of the road, the part going into the lower Point was gravel, rocks, and mud. The hell of it is that it was paved once, now only a few lonely chunks of asphalt hang on.

"Watch out for that chughole!" I shouted to Abel.

He hit it anyway. All kinds of crap that he had stashed on the dashboard pitched up into the air. A Louis L'Amour book flew off and landed in William's lap.

William thumbed through the book, then threw it back on the dashboard.

"I like Louis L'Amour," Abel said, "his stories are straight forward and to the point."

"Well," I said, "Louis is good; however, I prefer a story that's twisted, so you don't know what's coming."

I didn't want to criticize his taste, and I've read Louis L'Amour, and liked him. However, there seems to be a pattern. The bad guys tear up the place and endanger a beautiful young woman. The good guy overcomes adversity, defeats the bad guys, and rides off with the gal. Come to think of it, I guess there's nothing wrong with that.

"Stephen King's pretty good," Will volunteered, then added a disclaimer. "Well the movies are anyway, I haven't actually read one of his books."

"Screw Stephen King!" I said, with distaste. "Hell, I can figure out what's going to happen by the second chapter."

"Well I like Louis L'Amour," Abel restated.

"If you want to read something really twisted," I said, "try a Jake Cobb story. Now, there's a real lunatic."

Apparently, neither of them cared for my taste. Lately I've found that talking to Will and Abel is like talking to a brick wall.

But I do like my stories twisted. I suppose I look at life from a different viewpoint than most. Being told you're terminal will do that for you.

Since the cancer, I try to see my brothers as often as I can.

I can tell you one thing for sure; death is going to catch us all, sooner or later. Me, somehow, it missed, so far that is. Nobody can quite figure it. I was as good as gone, but here I am, better than ever.

Remission, the doctors said. Well, what do they know? Most doctors are full of crap anyway, no smarter than a good car mechanic.

God just gave me a second chance, that's what it was. Why I don't know, but I'm grateful for it. Enough of that, I don't like to dwell on the morbid.

Speak of morbid, this Falcon Point Development is a dismal place. It's amazing how I can have fond memories of such a miserable place. When I was a kid, back when Shorty ran the place, it was a high-class operation, but not now. Now, it's a dump.

This time of year, in the winter, it really sucks. The roads are either muddy or frozen and anyone with the means to leave has. The funny thing is, in the summer, it's nice. The sun shines and the leaves are green, but not now, now the trees are just like the people; they are alive but look dead.

~ PART 2 ~
THE SHOOTING

As I remember, it was about this time of year, during the dismal season, that Shorty killed his wife.

She was a young woman, about thirty years younger. I suppose she married him for the money. Shorty was a rich man, back in the day. That was in the early sixties, the same winter Kennedy was killed.

222

I never knew exactly how they hooked up; rumor had it, he used some political pull to get her paroled out of Tipton.

However, my folks knew Shorty well, and I do know exactly how they separated. I've heard that story more than a few times.

"That friggin' cherry picker needs to be tied down again," Will shouted. "It's drifting around like a spazo back there."

Abel slowed to a stop, shifted in his seat and looked into the rearview mirror. I thought he was looking right at me. The problem is I have no idea how to tie down a cherry picker.

"Hey," I said, "don't look at me. I've got my best suit on." Which wasn't true, but I didn't want to admit that I couldn't do something as simple as tie down a cherry picker.

"I got it," Will shouted as he jumped out of the truck and proceeded to take care of the problem.

Will's all right. I mean, he is my brother, and he's tried to reform, though it doesn't come natural. Damned if he's not the fisherman of the family. He could catch crappie out of the back of a cement truck, but I like hanging with Abel, he's probably the best of us. He keeps the old place looking nice.

Shorty's young wife, she was a looker. When it came to looks, she was way above Shorty's league. I can't recall her name, so I'll just call her "Missy."

Well one night, Missy came in late from partying. Shorty had waited at home; he didn't have much choice, he was sick, with emphysema, I believe. Regardless, when she came home, she was drunk and in a mean mood.

Shorty was sick and damn mean himself. He was also pissed off. That, folks, is a diabolical combination.

I lit a cigarette, I noticed Abel sniff the air.

I caught his hint and quickly got rid of the cigarette. Now you would think I would have given the damn things up after all that took place, but the way I figure it, "what the hell!"

Will jumped back into the truck, and we were rolling again.

"So who are these people that bought the old Nelson house? Are they local?"

"Name's Butterfield. Man, wife, and a kid," Abel answered, "and no, not local. Kansas City people, moving to the country, living their dream."

"Same story, different people," I said, "probably won't make it through the winter."

"Are they in the house yet?" Will asked.

"In and out. The wife, she's been staying with some friends further up in the Point, but she might stop by to 'supervise.'"

"Kind of a nuisance is she?"

"She's not really a problem. It's just that I talked to the husband about what needs to be done, and I got a list, but you know how it is, she thinks she is protecting her investment. She stops by sometimes, but not always."

"Do they know the history of the house?" Will asked.

"Not hardly," Abel answered. "Nobody that lives down here knows the history, none but me. Everyone that lived here back then, they have long since moved."

So, as I was explaining. Shorty's pretty young Missy came home about three in the morning, drunk and smelling like the prize hooker at a bachelor party.

Shorty had been awake all night, sitting there in his nine-hundred-dollar La-Z-Boy Rocker/Recliner, sick, coughing up his rotten lung, spitting into a bucket. He was madder than a hornet.

"Did I ever tell you about those little girls on the school bus, back when we were in high school?" Will asked. "The ones that lived in Shorty's house?"

"No," Abel answered. "What are you talking about?"

He had me too. I didn't know what "little girls on the school bus" had to do with the history of Shorty Nelson's house.

So, Will went on to tell what he overheard on the school bus one day in 1968. It kind of led you to believe that Shorty Nelson's house might be haunted.

Then Abel told a related story, from years later. Something that happened to a guy he knew. When you put all the pieces together, it led you to conclude that the house really was haunted.

I suppose they argued, but Missy, she wasn't one to be bullied. Once she figured she had taken enough crap from Shorty to last a lifetime, she pulled a gun down from the rack above the fireplace.

She jacked around with it trying to get it to work. It was an oddball gun, at least to her. It was a Savage-24 "Over-and-Under" shotgun rifle combination, 22 on the top, 410 on the bottom, a really nice gun, but somewhat complicated.

~ PART 3 ~
WORKING ON SHORTY'S HOUSE

We arrived at the house. The boys unhitched the cherry picker and set it up. William worked on the top, operating the cherry picker, while Abel worked inside.

They were doing something with a triple insulated pipe for a wood-burning fireplace, one of those complicated construction things. Will on the high side of the house, hanging out there in that bucket, looked dangerous to me.

I did everyone a favor and stayed out of the way. I needed a smoke anyway, so I dug a fresh pack of Kool's from my pocket and lit up.

Well, Missy continued to fumble with the safety of the Over-and-Under. She had downed an inordinate number of Margaritas and her brain was numb from the tequila; it will do that for you. Therefore, she couldn't decipher the operation of the firearm.

Despite, or perhaps, because of her intoxication, one idea was clearly fixed in Missy's numb brain. That was, once she mastered the gun, she was going to blow Shorty's ass to hell.

However, it was Shorty's lucky day. Despite Missy's efforts, that of pointing the gun at Shorty and pulling the trigger, it refused to fire.

It was Missy's unlucky day, as Shorty had a Smith and Wesson 38, Chiefs Special, five-shot revolver, stashed in the nightstand next to his recliner, right beside the bucket of spit.

I walked around and scouted the place out, I guess it was cold outside, but cold doesn't bother me much, so I enjoyed the walk. For such an ugly area, it was sure pretty around Shorty's house. I liked Shorty's old house. It's funny how we, the old timers, still called it Shorty's house. Nowadays, nobody even knows who Shorty was.

This old house is over fifty years old; nevertheless, it is still a beautiful home. Once, it was certainly the grandest house on the west-end of the lake, probably all the way down to Hurricane Deck. It is still in good shape. Apparently, the house had been well maintained.

Abel had an explanation for its condition. He had discussed it when we talked about the haunting. He thought it was in such good shape, because people wouldn't live there long.

After checking out the dock, I walked back up to the house and checked out the patio. It fronted the sunny side of the house and overlooked the driveway and lake.

The patio was furnished with a high-end wrought iron table and chairs. I found a chair and settled in. There was a book on the table.

I lit a Kool and picked up the book. It was a Louis L'Amour Western and must have been left there recently, because it hadn't been rained on. It was different from the one Abel had in the truck, different name that is, same story.

Now Shorty, he was a veteran of WW II, by God, and he knew how to use a pistol. He did not hesitate; he shot Missy right above the eyes, dead center in the forehead, blew Missy's brains all over the wall and part of the ceiling...

And that was the end of that.

I don't know how long I had been sitting there on the patio, but I must have drifted off. That's when I heard William cussing up on the roof.

"GOD-DAMMIT, I mean, GOD-DERNIT, Abel, don't jerk this fuh...

FRIGGIN' thing around when I got my fangers in the crack."

"Don't be such a pussy," Abel yelled from inside the house.

Behind me, I heard a voice.

"The boys seem to be having a little trouble."

Gee, I jumped, as the voice caught me by surprise. I spun around in my chair and there she stood.

"Hey," she said, "I didn't mean to scare you. I guess you were napping when I walked up. I thought you were awake. Sorry."

"Oh yeah, I'm awake...NOW." I didn't admit to being scared.

"Who are you?" she asked, in a matter of fact manner. She was a tall woman. Well, tall by my standards, maybe 5'10, thirty, tops. Not that I noticed, but she had long dark hair, a buckskin jacket, silver and jade jewelry, and a fancy straw fedora.

"Jesse Driscoll," I said, "at your service."

I stood, like a real gentleman, smiled and offered my hand. She ignored my hand as she took the book from the table. My last pack of Kools still lay on the table.

"Do you have any Winstons?" she asked, as she thumbed through the book.

"Sorry," I said, and sat back down.

"Camille," she said, "call me Camille."

Camille was very attractive, tanned, perfect teeth. I couldn't tell her eyes, with the sunglasses and all.

Something else had materialized as I napped. A car was parked in the driveway, a fully restored 1957 Chevrolet Bel Air—the two-door hardtop version, the one collectors go crazy over. Jesus, what does something like that cost nowadays?

"I'm here with my brothers, the guys working on the house," I said. "I don't work much anymore, semi-retired, and all. Nice car."

"It's my husband's. Personally, I don't like old Chevys. I prefer a Cadillac, a new Cadillac."

"I drive an Olds," I said.

She took off her sunglasses, snapped them into a case, and put them into a bag that hung from her shoulder. I could see her ice-cold blue eyes with their perfect decorations. She was something.

~ PART 4 ~
JIMBOB AND SAM

Then, there was the other story, the other bit of information.

A family moved in, maybe twenty years after the shooting. They probably never knew about the shooting. I suspect, most of them that moved in never knew about the shooting.

Well, the father was a hotshot land developer, one of the newer kind, the get-rich-quick kind. Not like old Shorty who really tried to build something. All this guy had in common with Shorty was that they lived in the same house.

I'll call him Sam, Old Sam.

"Well an Olds is not a Caddy, but it's close," she said. "How about one of those Kools?"

"Sure," I said, and handed her one of my cigarettes. She dug a gold plated Zippo out of her fancy leather shoulder bag and lit the Kool. As she put away her Zippo, I caught a glimpse of a pack of Winstons in her bag.

"Gotta go check on the work." She looked toward the house, but she just stood there smoking the Kool. She thumbed through the Louis L'Amour book.

Then for no apparent reason, she started explaining. "This is the first house I've ever owned. My husband had other houses, his first wife got those. But this house, this house is mine. It's the first house that was ever mine. I'm kind of protective of it. You understand, don't you?"

"Sure," I said. She tossed the book back on the table, turned and walked toward the front door.

"Gee what an uptight bitch," I said under my breath.

Well Sam had a teenage daughter, and she had a boyfriend. Let's call the boyfriend JimBob. One night, as he had done on prior occasions, JimBob sneaked into the house to visit his girl. Old Sam was wise to this trick, and was waiting for JimBob when, late at night, he came slipping into the house.

Unexpectedly, she came back, I wondered if she had heard my comment.

"You know," she said, "I can check on the work later. It's you, I'm curious about. What are you doing here?"

"I'm just riding along with my brothers, that's all. I liked your patio, so I thought I would just sit out here in the fresh air." Gee, she had me on the defensive. I felt like I had just stepped into a job interview.

She took a seat in the opposing patio chair, then propped her boots on the table. Tony Lama half boots: round toe, walking heel, more than just common "country girl" footwear.

"Hey," I said, "I'm just a simple hillbilly, who likes to get back to his roots now and again."

She smiled. She was truly a beautiful woman.

Old Sam put a pistol to JimBob's head and marched him to the basement. He did this quietly, so as not to wake anyone else in the house, the other occupants being his wife and daughter.

Once in the basement, Sam opened his safe and proceeded to throw twenty-dollar bills onto the floor.

"Where do you live?" she asked.

"Right now, I live in Palmer."

"But, not always?" It was a rhetorical question, but I answered anyway.

"No, not always."

"Those brothers of yours, working on my house, they are hillbillies, but you're not."

I really did not need to explain myself to this woman, but she was very attractive and interested in me. That was odd. I guess I liked the attention, and it was her house, so I spilled my guts.

"I was raised near here; I am from this part of the country."

"What do you do now? What does semi-retired mean?"

"It means, I used to be somebody, but I'm not anymore," I said.

She stared at me, apparently not willing to acknowledge such a stupid answer. So I gave a better explanation.

"Sometimes I show properties, not big properties, like this, just small lots, up in town. That's what I was doing when my brothers came by and I decided to ride along."

"You don't belong here," she said. "You're out of place. You should not come here again."

At that, she stood and went into the house

"Gee what an uptight bitch," I said again, this time aloud.

Now, JimBob, he was no genius. But even a fool like JimBob soon realized that Old Sam's bizarre behavior had an ulterior motive. Sam planned to kill him and lay it off as a home intruder killing. However, Sam had the drop on him and JimBob was trapped. Until, unexpectedly, a tall young woman walked into the basement.

JimBob seized upon Sam's apparent terror in seeing the woman and escaped through a window.

Within months, two things happened; Sam moved his family back to the city from whence they came, and JimBob found another girlfriend.

I sat alone on the patio and thought about that smartass woman. Then I thought about the history of the house, trying to figure things out. It gave me a headache, thinking about all those things. Finally, I came to some conclusions, and then I closed my eyes, just for a second.

Suddenly, she was back on the patio.

She was sitting in the chair across from me. How long had she been there? I must have dozed off.

"Give me another smoke there, partner." She smiled sweetly. Her nasty demeanor from earlier had vanished.

"You got your own; smoke your damn Winstons," I smiled back at her.

"It's the principle," she said. "If you want my company, you have to pay something."

I gave her my last Kool, then reached into my pocket and found a fresh pack. I lit up while she sat there smiling at me.

"Well," she said, "have you figured it out yet?"

"Figured out what?" I said.

"For starters, what we have in common."

The truth is, I had figured out some things. As a result, chills ran up and down my spine. I was a little spooked, but I wasn't going to show it. I put on my best poker face.

"We have nothing in common, because you, dear, are not real. And I am."

She laughed and stamped her high-class boots on the floor in apparent delight. "Of course I'm real. Maybe it's you, mister, 'back to you roots, phony hillbilly,' maybe it's *you* that's not real."

She kind of got to me there, hit a nerve I guess. I was a little shaken, as the possibilities started to sink in, but I just smiled at her.

The strangest things cross your mind in times of stress. What crossed my mind was that Bruce Willis movie where the little boy talked to dead people. Just for a second, I considered that possibility, but I knew better, this experience had a simple, medical explanation.

I had seen many hallucinations while undergoing treatment; none as good looking as this woman, I have to concede that. Still, they were nothing new to me, and they were nothing to be concerned about.

"I've dealt with your kind before," I said.

"Really?" she said. She crossed her legs; they were nice. A perfectly shaped tanned calf appeared between her Levis and the Tony Lama's.

She leaned forward across the patio table that separated us. Her face was close to mine. She inhaled a long drag from the cigarette I had given her.

"I don't think so," she said as she removed her hat. Smoke curled from a hole in the center of her forehead, more smoke came from somewhere behind her head.

She stood and stepped around to my side of the table. She squatted until her face matched mine again. She laughed, then turned slowly on the heels of her boots, showing me the back of her head.

A section the size of a lemon was missing, smoke drifted out of the cavity.

She turned back to me and smiled.

~ PART 5 ~
THE GIRLS ON THE BUS

Then there was the thing that had set us all to thinking it was haunted in the first place; it was the little girls on the school bus.

Their family had moved into the house during the summer and had decided to stay the winter. Does this sound familiar?

It was the nicest house they had ever lived in. The father thought it would be good for the children to get out of the city.

"You still haven't figured it out," she said.

She picked up her hat and slipped it back on her head. "How does this look?" she said, as she turned around for my approval.

"Still got some of the hole in the back of your head showing," I said.

She pulled a silver brush from her purse, removed her hat, and brushed her hair back. She put on her hat, then casually tapped the brush against the table, dislodging small bits of brain matter.

She turned around again.

"That's better," I said.

"Look," she said, "sooner or later, you will figure it out. When you do, try to remember this. This is as good as it will ever get for me. If I move on, it will be to some place far worse. You, however, can go somewhere nice, but that's your choice."

She put her sunglasses back on. "So," she said, "I got a deal for you."

"Sorry sweetheart, I don't make deals," I said. "Besides, I do have it figured out."

She smiled at me as if I was an idiot. "Tell me then."

"You are a figment of my imagination," I said, as confidently as I could muster.

"Apparently," she said, "you don't know diddle squat."

"You are a delusion," I insisted, "brought on by chemotherapy and drug treatments, and a little brain damage, that kind of thing. If I just ignore you, you will go away."

"Denying reality doesn't change it," she said.

"Trouble is," I said, "you're not real."

"All right," she said, "I'm bored. Here's the deal, a one-time offer."

"You're not real," I said

"You stay out of Falcon Point, and I'll stay out of Palmer."

"You're not real," I said, and closed my eyes. "Not real, not real, not real," I repeated aloud.

The school bus picked up the little girls every morning. They were cute little girls, one a couple of years older than the other.

"I'm scared," the little one said.

"You're just being a baby," the older one answered.

"But she is really scary. She is really scary, and you don't ever see her," the little one cried.

"It's like Mommy said, it's just your imagination."

"No it ain't, there is, there really, really is a woman in our house."

"Well," her sister said, "even if there is you need to pretend there ain't."

~ PART 6 ~
DRIVING HOME

I opened my eyes; she was gone. The Chevy was also gone.

Obviously, this was not the wife Abel thought might come by to supervise. I knew exactly who she was supposed to be. My imagination had cast her as Shorty's wife, long dead, good old Missy or Camille, whatever her name was…that's who. However, as I told her, I had a nasty habit of hallucinating. But I had to admit, she was different from my other "imaginaries."

Just then, Abel came walking out of the house. It looked as if he had finished; he carried his tool pouch. My head was spinning.

"I hope you boys are done, because I'm ready to go," I said.

"Have you got everything?" Will shouted to Abel from across the yard.

"I'm good," Abel said, "let's get this thing back to town, it's costing me twenty bucks an hour."

I smoked one last cigarette as the boys hooked the cherry picker to the truck. They loaded their tools and we left for Palmer.

I sat in the backseat of the crew cab on the way home. Abel and William talked. My mind was too preoccupied to join in.

Something nagged at me. I knew that I had missed something. Something important. Maybe beautiful Camille "with the hole in her head" was right; perhaps, I had not figured it out yet.

The main question bugging me was this: Is it possible that Camille was the ghost of Shorty's long dead wife? If so, that meant that some sort of life after death existed, and at least that was comforting.

Or, more likely, was Camille just a figment of my imagination? Perhaps a substitute for Elisabeth. Maybe I just needed some female companionship. However, that did not explain the bullet hole in her head. Unless my imagination put a bullet hole in gorgeous Camille's head to compensate for the guilt I had felt about Elisabeth.

Each explanation had problems.

Maybe if I told the whole thing to Abel, he could figure it out. Would he think I was crazy? Hell, I didn't care. I probably am crazy.

As we hit the blacktop, Will dropped off into a nap. Abel drove along; he looked contented. Perhaps I shouldn't burden him with my problems.

Maybe I should do as the little girl on the bus had suggested, "even if there is, pretend there ain't." After all, I had beaten cancer by ignoring it.

You know, the doctors and Elisabeth made a big deal of that, my non-acceptance of the sickness. I was in denial, they said. Eventually, Elisabeth and I separated over it.

Come to think of it, that's what Miss Camille "with the hole in her head" said. She said it in different words, but it was the same message.

I guess I did need to talk it out, and Abel was always a good listener. So, while Abel drove, and William napped, I started talking.

I laid it out in logical order, just like Louie L'Amour.

And that helped. It eased my mind, I guess, because as we rounded the corner coming into town, it came to me.

"Hey, I got it!" I shouted, as I slapped Abel on the shoulder. Abel turned his head, but like a good driver, he kept his eyes on the road ahead.

"Yeah," I mumbled, less enthusiastically, "I got it."

"William," Abel shouted, "wake up!"

"Yeah that's me," I said, "the king of denial."

"Wake up, William," Abel shouted again. "We're passing by Jesse now."

Abel geared the truck down and tipped his hat at the cemetery. That was just like Abel, to acknowledge a brother. He was always the best of us.

ABOUT THE AUTHORS

Jimmy Capps was born, lived, and died............. but hasn't quite died yet.

Linda Capps Fisher prefers writing short stories because they fit her attention span. Someday, she hopes to finish her longer works in progress.

www.ingramcontent.com/pod-product-compliance
Lightning Source LLC
Chambersburg PA
CBHW051429170626
46809CB00006B/2383